Strictly
BUSINESS

ALSO BY RUTH CARDELLO

CORISI BILLIONAIRES

The Broken One
The Wild One
The Secret One

THE LOST CORISIS

He Said Always
He Said Never
He Said Together

THE WESTERLYS

In the Heir
Up for Heir
Royal Heir
Hollywood Heir
Runaway Heir

LONE STAR BURN

Taken, Not Spurred
Tycoon Takedown
Taken Home
Taking Charge

THE LEGACY COLLECTION

Maid for the Billionaire
For Love or Legacy
Bedding the Billionaire

Saving the Sheikh
Rise of the Billionaire
Breaching the Billionaire: Alethea's Redemption
Recipe for Love (holiday novella)
A Corisi Christmas (holiday novella)

THE ANDRADES

Come Away with Me
Home to Me
Maximum Risk
Somewhere along the Way
Loving Gigi

THE BARRINGTONS

Always Mine
Stolen Kisses
Trade It All
A Billionaire for Lexi
Let It Burn
More Than Love
Forever Now

TRILLIONAIRES

Taken by a Trillionaire
Virgin for the Trillionaire

BACHELOR TOWER SERIES

Insatiable Bachelor
Impossible Bachelor
Undeniable Bachelor

Strictly
BUSINESS

RUTH
CARDELLO

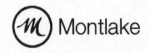 Montlake

Published by Montlake, Seattle

www.apub.com

Amazon, the Amazon logo, and Montlake are trademarks of Amazon.com, Inc., or its affiliates.

ISBN-13: 9781542038225
ISBN-10: 1542038227

Cover design by Eileen Carey

Printed in the United States of America

This book is dedicated to my little Amelia.
Grammy loves you.

DON'T MISS A THING!

www.ruthcardello.com

Sign up for Ruth's newsletter:
Yes, let's stay in touch!
https://forms.aweber.com/form/00/819443400.htm

Join Ruth's private fan group:
www.facebook.com/groups/ruthiesroadies

Follow Ruth on Goodreads:
www.goodreads.com/author/show/4820876.Ruth_Cardello

CHAPTER ONE

JESSE

The flustered-looking brunette whose briefcase had just popped open and dumped papers at her feet was the reason I was still in jeans. I blamed her for the fact that I was wearing work boots for the second day in a row. When I'd offered to pretend to be my twin brother, Scott, I'd imagined investing only a few hours into the charade.

I should've already been back in my office in Brookline, fielding calls from news stations regarding the most recent and most impressive contract Rehoboth Heating and Cooling had ever landed. When my older brother, Thane, and I had taken over our family's company, we'd decided to reach beyond the traditional local and government contracts my father had courted. Instead of investing in machinery to increase production, we'd used our trust funds to aggressively recruit the top minds in related fields. It was a gamble that was finally paying off.

A privately owned company, Bellerwood, had just contracted us to design and install our alternative to traditional thermal control systems in the multibillion-dollar space station they were racing to get into orbit. The deal would add a string of zeros to my family's net worth.

Yet there I was, standing on a porch with peeling paint, wondering why the hell I'd agreed to stay on another day. When Crystal Holmes, a rep from Steadman Oil, rescheduled the meeting she'd arranged with Scott, I'd seen it for what it was—a classic power play. No different than all the times I'd made business associates wait while I finished a phone call. If things were ratcheting up, I couldn't let Scott handle it on his own.

I had expected Ms. Holmes to be a seasoned negotiator. Instead she was beautiful and teetering on high heels as if they were new to her. Her skirt hiked up deliciously each time she bent in an attempt to gather what the wind had other plans for. I was attracted—any man would have been—but it wasn't something I'd act upon. Wide eyed and innocent was far from my type.

Embracing my role, I hooked a thumb in a front pocket of my jeans and leaned a hip against the railing of my brother's farmhouse porch. I could have helped her, but the first rule of engagement was to never give up a position of advantage. In life, regardless of one's situation, the strongest and the most prepared were the ones who thrived. Scott didn't see that yet, but he'd learn.

Saving his farm was lesson one. Steadman Oil had already offered more for the land than it was worth. They'd already sent lawyers to town hall to dig up anything they could use against Scott. Ms. Holmes was a distraction, a dirty little trick even I was above resorting to. It was surprising that Scott's naive belief that things worked out for people who tried their best and played by the rules hadn't already cost him everything.

After resecuring her papers in her briefcase, the woman ran a hand over the curls that were coming free from the loose bun at the nape of her neck. She had a rocking body: ample breasts that strained to pop open the top of her shirt and legs that went on forever. Scott would have been putty in her hands. When it came to being identical, our similarities were only skin deep. I was far harder to sway.

Normally nothing would have lured me from the office, but Thane understood that I couldn't sit back and watch Steadman Oil outmaneuver Scott. Call it pride. Rehoboths didn't lose, and if someone came for one of us, we faced them down together. Loyalty was the foundation of our family—for the men at least. My mother hadn't held to that philosophy. She'd had no issue with walking away.

Scott wasn't a Rehoboth. Separated at birth, we'd been adopted by different couples—neither of whom had known that there were two of us until recently. I still wouldn't have known of Scott's existence had an old college friend not sent me an online article of Scott holding up a fucking duck with a prosthetic leg he'd designed for it. My friend Isaac had sent me the article as a joke—the ultimate doppelgänger doing something so far removed from what I would do that it was hilarious. To Isaac.

Me? I was mildly amused at first. It was interesting to see someone with so many shared features. That was it.

Until I couldn't stop going back to that photo of Scott. He looked too much like me for it to be a coincidence. An uncomfortable conversation with my father led to a DNA test with Scott, and voilà . . . I had another brother. A twin. One who was about to lose his farm.

"Scott Millville?" Ms. Holmes asked in a breathless voice.

"That's me," I lied.

She squared her shoulders. "My name is Crystal Holmes. We have an appointment."

"Had," I said. "Yesterday. I was here. You were . . . ?"

She walked toward me. "Unavoidably detained. I did text you asking if it would be okay if I came today."

"I don't recall responding that it would be." I looked her over again—so humble, so tentative. I didn't believe it for a second. Just how stupid did they think my twin was?

She held my gaze and smiled. "And yet here I am."

I pushed off the railing and slowly made my way down the steps. Although she was doing her best to appear nonthreatening, we both knew she wasn't. How far would she take the game? Stopping less than a foot from her, I looked her up and down slowly, then nodded toward her and her briefcase. "You have nothing I'm interested in."

The flush of red that spread up her neck was a tell that my comment had stung. Her smile wavered but held. "I'm sorry you feel that way."

She looked away and bit her bottom lip. God, she had the act down. What would her next play be? When she raised her eyes to mine again, they were dark and troubled. "Please. It's a new offer, a better one. You should at least hear it before turning it down."

"I could not have been clearer about not wanting to sell."

Her shaky smile thinned her lips. "Yes, but Steadman Oil is now prepared to revert the land as well as your subsoil gas and oil rights back to you after a term."

Interesting and unusual. "And the farm?"

"The house could remain, but the fields would be unusable for an agreed-upon amount of time."

"So I could have it all back after you destroy the land."

"Site cleanup is part of every project Steadman Oil does. It's a very generous offer, Mr. Millville. Much more than you could sell the property for. And the farm gets to stay in your family."

"What makes you think it won't regardless?" She switched her briefcase from one hand to another, not yet smooth enough to conceal when a question was difficult for her. Was it deliberate, or was she truly so inept? It was mildly entertaining to test her act. I bent closer and lowered my voice. "Or that I want a family?"

"I didn't mean to . . ." Her mouth opened and closed a few times like she was a fish out of water. "I'm sure the farm is important to your parents."

"My parents are traveling the country in an RV and enjoying their retirement. That's why it's my name on the deed." I had no idea how Scott's parents felt about the farm, but that was irrelevant to the outcome. My goal was simply to keep Ms. Holmes off balance long enough for her to make a mistake and reveal something I could use.

She cleared her throat. "Yes, which is the reason I'm here to speak with you."

I leaned closer, close enough that her eyes widened and the air sizzled. "So let me get this straight . . . Steadman Oil is prepared to lease my property, then return subsoil rights as well as the property free and clear at the end of the lease? Along with returning the land to the state it currently is in?"

"It's all in the proposal."

"I'm sure it is." I straightened. "Unfortunately, I have chores to do. The animals won't feed themselves."

"Oh." She looked down at her attire, then back at me. "Could you use some help? My hotel is about a ten-minute drive. I could change and return."

I should have said no. Until just then, I'd had no intention of going anywhere near the barn. The most reasonable course of action would have been to set up another meeting with Ms. Holmes somewhere later that day away from the farm. "I don't have all day to wait around."

"I'd hurry." She glanced down at her phone. "I could be back in thirty minutes. Then maybe we could sit down and look over the terms." Her eyes filled with hope, and we stood there saying nothing for long enough that it got awkward.

"Maybe." It wouldn't hurt to read over the new offer. I should at least know what I was refusing for Scott. I frowned. She'd almost gotten me to say one of the most dangerous words in a negotiation—*yes*. One concession often led to another. I growled, "Was there something else you needed?"

She shook her head and took a step back. "No. No. Sorry. I'll be right back." With that, she turned and fled to her car.

I folded my arms across my chest and stood there, more than a little aroused, watching her drive away. Sending in a hot woman to muddle the male brain during negotiations was a tactic as old as time itself. What was irritating was that I hadn't been immune to the ploy.

After she'd gone, I called Scott. He answered on the first ring and asked, "How are the animals?"

I shrugged even though he couldn't see me. "Fine, I guess. Just as you said he would, one of your employees—LJ—came by last night while I was out. I left him a note to skip this morning so I wouldn't have to deal with him. This plan only works if no one knows about our switch . . . but I should probably feed the animals."

"I'm coming back."

"No. The rep from the oil company has already been here and is returning shortly. I'll have what I need soon, and then you can return."

"What do you think the rep will give you?"

"Information."

"Do I want to know what's going on at my farm?"

"Nothing illegal. I bend the law; I don't break it."

He made a pained sound. "I don't like this."

"Do you have a better plan?" I didn't wait for him to answer. "Before you say you do, let me assure you that you don't. Waiting and hoping isn't a plan."

"I'm glad I don't have to pretend to be you, because you're an asshole."

"Maybe, but I'll also be the reason you won't lose." I looked over at the barn, which could use a coat of paint . . . some nails . . . a lot of things. "Although she said this offer is even better. It's a term lease. If the amount is high enough, are you sure you want to turn it down? Eventually it will all revert back to you, *and* you'll have cash in hand."

"I'm not selling or leasing the land—no matter what they offer."

"That's all I need to know."

"You do need to feed the animals, though. All of them. Do you have a pen and piece of paper? I'll walk you through what to do."

"No, but how complicated could it be?"

He sighed audibly. "I'll stay on the phone while you feed."

"That won't work. The rep is returning to help. I need to look like I know what I'm doing."

"Hold on—your plan is to have the oil rep do barn chores with you? And you don't think that will give away that you're not me?"

"She's beautiful but doesn't appear all that bright."

"How beautiful?"

I took a moment to savor a memory of those long legs. "Temptingly so."

"Don't sign anything."

Who did he think he was talking to? I'd never agreed to a bad deal in my life. "Stop worrying. I've got everything under control."

CHAPTER TWO

CRYSTAL

As I sped toward my hotel, I tried to calm my nerves. More than anything else, I didn't want to disappoint my uncle again. Telling him that I'd missed my first meeting with Scott Millville had been tough enough.

Not that my uncle's response had been harsh. Once I'd told him my reason, he was understanding, but we both knew I'd let him down. My phone buzzed with a message. I ignored it. Whatever anyone wanted could wait until I wasn't driving.

A moment later, my phone rang. I answered, even though I wasn't keen on doing that while driving, either, not even with Bluetooth, but I needed to know that it wasn't an emergency. "Hello?"

"Have you met the farmer yet?" Ellie, my best friend slash roommate, asked.

I let out a relieved breath. "I did. He wasn't too happy to see me, but I believe I've smoothed that over."

"I'm so sorry about yesterday."

"Don't be. You would've done the same for me."

"I would, but it was bad timing. So did he read over the offer? What did he say?"

"We didn't get that far. I'm heading back to my hotel to change into jeans. He said he'd consider looking it over if I help him with some barn chores."

"That's . . . odd."

"Agreed, but it's better than the flat-out no he started with."

"I suppose." After a pause, she said, "This is my fault. I should have waited for the tow truck by myself. I need to stop watching movies where a scenario like that leads to women ending up in a cage under some guy's floorboards."

"You definitely need to stop watching those. But seriously, I'm glad I could help. That's what friends are for, right?"

"Right. So was the farmer as yummy as he looked in the photo you showed me?"

My skin flushed as I remembered him standing on the porch, all muscle and broody eyes. If asked, I would have said I valued intelligence and humor over the package they came in, but he was a man I'd bet any woman would have been drawn to. I might have briefly indulged in a fantasy that involved him tossing me over his shoulder and carrying me to his bed . . . or the stairs . . . or wherever he wanted.

Ellie chuckled and asked, "Not willing to say? That hot?"

I smiled. "Actually, yes."

"I wish I'd gone with you."

"Too late." Wanting to keep things light, I joked, "I saw him first. He's all mine."

She chuckled. "Does he have a brother?"

"Sorry, no. Guess you'll just have to find your own gorgeous farmer."

She countered in a serious tone, "Be careful. I don't want to see you get hurt."

"There's no chance of that. All that will come from seeing him again is the ability to tell my uncle that he read over the proposal and is at least considering it."

"I still don't understand why your uncle didn't deliver the proposal himself. Why ask you? You don't even work for him."

"I asked him the same thing. He said his team had come on too strong and put Mr. Millville's guard up. He wanted to defuse the situation, and I'm as nonthreatening as they come." That particular description of myself hadn't sounded as bad when my uncle said it as when it came out of my mouth. What was I? Tapioca pudding?

"Your uncle didn't ask you to sleep with him, did he?"

"N-noooo," I sputtered. "Why would you even suggest that?"

"I saw the way you were dressed when you left this morning."

"Hey, you're the one who didn't want to come clothing shopping with me. According to the store clerk, this is business appropriate."

"For what kind of business?" Ellie was brilliant, even by my standards. She'd gotten her first college degree by fifteen, but tact wasn't her strong point. Sometimes it made for uncomfortable conversations, but her heart was always in the right place.

I glanced down and nearly swerved into the wrong lane when I saw way more cleavage than I'd expected. I'd purchased a smaller shirt because my size wasn't on the rack and the only other option was two sizes too big. The shirt was tight but not revealing when modestly fastened. Somehow, though, the top button had come undone, and the shirt had shifted upward, gaping above my breasts. "Tell me I didn't leave the house with half my bra showing."

She made a noncommittal sound.

"You should have said something."

"I didn't want to diminish your confidence. You were already nervous."

With good reason. Why did I think I could do this? I choked on an embarrassed laugh while dragging my shirt together with one hand and resecuring it. What a show I must have given the farmer—chasing papers all over the driveway with my shirt half-open. "This deal is important to my uncle. When I told him I wasn't sure I was the right person to handle this, do you know what he said? He said I was because he *trusts* me. I can't screw this up."

"Crystal, I know you think you owe him everything, but you don't. You would have been okay even if he hadn't come into your life."

I parked outside my hotel and turned the car engine off. "You don't know that. You didn't see me after my parents died. I was . . . lost." Hands clutching the steering wheel, I fought to keep my thoughts from going back to the night that was easily the worst of my life.

Lost didn't fully describe how I'd been right after my parents' deaths. Shattered. Yes. Broken into shards of my old self, with no hope of being put back together.

My family was small, just my parents and me. No living grandparents. No cousins I knew of. We'd been very close and all we'd ever needed. Losing them had gutted me.

I hated the drunk driver who caused the accident that cost both my parents their lives, hated myself for deciding to double my course load to speed my college degree along in the year before their accident. Regretted every weekend I'd chosen to stay at campus and study rather than go home to see my family.

As I planned my parents' funeral, I faced the cold reality that I was alone. All my academic achievements, everything I'd thought mattered, no longer held value. I stood over their caskets wishing I'd been in that car with them.

That was how my uncle found me. He put an arm around my shoulders and told me everything would be okay. I'd always known my father had a wealthy brother, but I had no memories of him. He should have felt like a stranger to me. He didn't.

He'd been a life raft appearing beside a sinking ship.

Family.

He helped me through the overwhelming task of sorting through my parents' bills and legal papers. I didn't know what I would have done without his help. He guided me through selling my parents' home and encouraged me to stay enrolled in college. I wouldn't describe my uncle as a warm person, but for some time after my parents died, he was my lifeline. In the beginning I would have stretches of time when things seemed fine, but then I'd falter, my grades would slide, and I'd begin to feel like everything was falling apart.

I didn't tell him, but he knew. His response? He'd send someone to collect me, fly me off to wherever he was on the globe, and we'd spend a few days together before he had someone fly me back to college. That was it. No lectures. No motivational speeches. He gave me something I treasured more than anything else—his time.

After a while, I regained my footing. Even when I no longer required interventions, I would still ask him to fly me to him, and he always did. He never married, never had children of his own, and I liked to think he needed me as much as I needed him.

When I completed my postgrad work in chemistry, he offered me a job. I smiled as I remembered his reaction when I told him that I wanted to be a flavorist. He was surprised that a PhD in chemistry was required to make processed food taste the way it did. After I'd explained the history and complexity of "natural and artificial flavors," he nodded once and confirmed that there was no need for anything to taste good at an oil company.

It wasn't a joke.

Nor a slam.

My uncle was a pragmatist. He was straightforward and action oriented. I didn't doubt that he loved me, but also I didn't feel for a second that he was disappointed that I'd chosen a career that wouldn't be useful to him. He focused on what was, rather than wasting time on considering what anything should be.

Sending me to meet Scott Millville was a strategy that must have had the potential of working, or my uncle wouldn't have suggested it. All I had to do was believe in myself as much as he did.

With a jolt, I realized that my mind had wandered and that I'd stopped listening to Ellie. I checked the time on the dashboard of my car. "Ellie," I interrupted her, "I have to run inside and change. I'll call you later."

"Okay, but think about what I said."

I grimaced and promised I would, then ended the call. High heels and all, I sprinted with my briefcase into the hotel. Once inside my room, I stripped and hunted through my overnight bag for the jeans I'd brought to drive home in. I almost hadn't secured a hotel room, but I hadn't known for sure if I'd be able to meet Scott that day, and I was determined not to leave until I did.

I stepped into a pair of jeans, then caught my reflection in a mirror after I pulled a T-shirt over my head. Scott's voice echoed in my thoughts. *"You have nothing I'm interested in."*

I tucked my shirt into my jeans and looked myself over with a critical eye. No, I wasn't model material. Average height. Average weight. Not too much stood out about me. Except my ample chest, but that often felt more like a curse than a gift. Small-breasted women had no idea how lucky they were. Few shirts were made for my shape. Most were either too tight on the top or too loose around the waist.

In general, I was comfortable with how I looked, but Scott's comment had stung. I had nothing he was interested in? Nothing? I turned to look at my jean-clad ass. Okay, so it wasn't the tight little kind you'd see in a magazine, but it wasn't that bad.

I sighed. *I should be relieved he's not attracted. Imagine how complicated that would be.*

CHAPTER THREE

JESSE

I stood at the entrance of the barn and shuddered. The stench was gag worthy. Urine. Manure. The air was so thick with the essence of both I could nearly taste it. I finally understood why my father hadn't allowed us to have pets growing up . . . they were disgusting.

A donkey brayed from the far end of the aisle. A rooster crowed. Heads of all sizes and shapes of barn animals poked out from stalls, and all those eyes focused on me. When I thought it couldn't get worse, a flock of chickens surrounded me, and that was when I learned that some shit the size of an egg.

Careful not to step on them or their droppings, I made my way to the feed room. As I looked over the various unlabeled bins, I conceded that I probably should have listened more closely when Scott rattled off the instructions. I made an audible sound of disgust.

From behind me an amused male voice said, "It's not all that bad."

I recognized the voice as someone who had called me the night before: LJ. "Why are you here?"

"Scott called me." My head snapped around at that, and he exclaimed, "Holy shit, you two really are identical."

I held his gaze and my silence as I weighed my options for the best way to deal with this complication. LJ was almost twice my age and a good foot shorter. I'd never been big on physical intimidation, but if that was what it took for him to keep his mouth shut, I'd go there.

LJ continued, "If you weren't pale and prettied up in new clothes, I wouldn't have realized you aren't him."

Pale? "Thanks?"

"And your expression is a giveaway. Scott smiles more."

I rolled my shoulders back and stood taller. It wasn't ideal that LJ knew about me, but I'd always been able to think on my feet. Maybe if I spoke really slowly, he could follow along. "In a few minutes a woman will arrive who needs to believe I'm Scott. You want to be helpful? Don't speak while she's here."

"You mean the beautiful woman from the oil company? Scott said you sounded sweet on her."

Oh my fucking Lord. "Just start feeding the animals." *I can claim there is an emergency somewhere else on the farm and take Crystal there.*

"I'm here to supervise, not work."

"You're lucky I'm not actually Scott, because you'd already be fired."

He laughed. "I'm a volunteer."

I shook my head. *No.* "Hold on. You feed all these animals and clean up after them—for *nothing*?"

He shrugged. "I enjoy it." He scooped up a chicken and cradled it to his chest like one would hold a small dog. When he spoke again, he addressed the chicken rather than me. "Rento, don't mind him; he's still young enough to not understand that the best things in life tend to get your hands dirty."

"Okay, I've heard enough. You need to go. Now. I'll have Scott text you when I leave later. Then you can return and cuddle the shit out of all the animals you want. But you are not going to stay and screw this up."

LJ didn't spare me a look. Instead he spoke to the chicken again: "If I didn't care so much about Scott, I'd let this jackass fail." Across the barn, the donkey brayed again as if in protest. LJ called out, "Sorry, Winnie, you're right—I shouldn't insult you like that." He put the chicken down and looked me in the eye. "There's a label maker in the grain room. I'll put directions on everything. I'll stick around to put the animals out, but I'm sure you can figure out how to clean a stall. There's a wheelbarrow over there next to the shovels and picks. There's a manure pile out back. Just add it to that."

Not going to happen. "I'll pay you a hundred dollars to clean up after I leave."

LJ shook his head.

"Two hundred."

He laughed. "Wow, you are nothing like Scott."

I took that as a compliment. "Three hundred."

He rubbed a hand over his chin. "Why are you helping him?"

"He's my brother." My explanation rang true because it was.

LJ nodded. "Scott said you're rich."

"Scott shares too much." LJ was probably holding out for more because he knew I could pay it. "Name your price."

"I don't have one." He looked around and breathed in as if he were standing in a field of flowers and not a filthy barn. "I understand why Scott agreed to have you come here. I didn't when Scott first told me, but now I do."

I didn't know what he was referring to, but nor did I care to. "Well, now that we've cleared that up . . ."

"I'd better get going on those labels." He walked past me into the feed room and pulled a label machine off the shelf. After he printed the first and attached it to a plastic tub, he said, "Don't rush back to wherever you came from. And don't give up. Scott and this farm . . . you'll think they couldn't possibly save you, but they will."

Why had Scott shared our plan with a man who was obviously mentally unstable? I spoke slowly again, as one would to a child. "I'm here to help *him.*"

He returned his attention to the labeling machine and printed another sticker out. "I thought the same thing when I first met Scott." The sound of a car pulling into the driveway caught my attention. LJ picked up a marker and wrote a phone number on a dry-erase board on the wall. "That's my number. Text me if you need me. I'll be working in the background. Now, go distract your friend for a few minutes. I need a little time to finish here."

I hesitated at the door. "You do realize that for a lot less effort you could do all of this yourself? I'm willing to take the rep for a walk around the property instead."

He turned to meet my gaze. "Why did you ask her to feed the animals with you?"

It was a valid question. "Easiest way to shake someone up is to get them on unfamiliar territory."

"Exactly." With that, he turned away again and continued labeling buckets.

Confused, I shook my head again and made my way out of the barn to meet Crystal. The sooner I determined if she knew anything worthwhile, the sooner I could return to the city, where things actually made sense.

I don't know what I expected when I stepped out onto the driveway. The woman exiting her car temporarily stole my ability to think clearly. I'd never found jeans and T-shirts all that sexy, but the way she filled hers out was sinful. I took a deep breath and reminded myself that every seemingly tentative step she took was deliberate.

But—*damn.*

She stopped when she reached me and smiled. "I'm ready to work."

"I'm not . . ." I stopped there and cleared my throat. "Ready."

She cocked her head to one side in question.

Nothing. I had nothing. Irritation with myself flooded in. I wasn't the kind of man who let anything rattle him. On a regular basis I fielded tough questions from heads of state as well as reporters without breaking stride. I had a healthy social life and more options for female companionship than I had time for. There was nothing special about this woman.

Yet I couldn't look away.

Or form a coherent sentence when she looked at me like there was nothing standing between the two of us being together, like we weren't both circling each other, hoping to find a weakness to exploit. I turned my irritation on her and demanded, "How long have you worked for Steadman Oil?"

Her eyebrows rose in response to my tone, and she looked away. "Not long."

I bet. "A year? A month? This week?"

Her cheeks flushed red. "Does it matter?" Her voice was deliciously breathless, and when she raised her eyes to mine again, I temporarily forgot why we were there. What farm? What twin? I tried to imagine what Thane would say if I told him that for just a moment, winning hadn't felt important.

He wouldn't have believed me.

I stood there, tempted to lean down and taste those slightly parted lips of hers. It did matter if Steadman Oil had hired her for the sole purpose of being a distraction. She might've been a paid actress or a stripper for all I knew. She didn't send off the vibe of being either, but better men than me had been fooled by beautiful women.

My father for one.

I leaned in and growled, "It does. Before I waste any more time with you, why did they choose you to deliver the proposal? What are your qualifications?"

"My qualifications?" Her chest rose as she drew in a deep breath. When her tongue darted across her lower lip, I nearly groaned aloud. "I'm trustworthy."

I took a moment to weigh it against what I'd expected her to say. Unable to resist, I raised my hand to touch her face but stopped just before making contact. "I highly doubt that."

She blinked a few times quickly. "You don't know anything about me."

"True." The air between us sizzled. "But I know why you're here, and that's enough."

It took her a moment to respond. "I'm here because my uncle asked me to be."

Her uncle? That rocked me back onto my heels. "Your uncle?"

"Art Steadman."

"This just got more interesting. Why would a man like Steadman send his niece into a situation that has the potential of turning ugly?"

Her eyes widened. "He wouldn't."

"Oh, but he did." I straightened and looked her over. She was either a pawn or a really good liar. I couldn't decide which.

She took a step back. "I'm here to show you the newest proposal. That's it."

I didn't believe her, but unless she turned tail and ran, I would have time to get the truth out of her. I was strategizing how I'd do just that when her attention was drawn away from me.

"Oh, poor guy, what's wrong with his leg?" She crouched down as a quacking duck approached her.

Thankfully, I knew. "He lost his foot to a fishing line."

"That's so sad." She reached out to touch the duck, and he nuzzled his head under her hand. "Aww, he's friendly. What's his name?"

Now that was beyond what I'd bothered to retain. "Duck."

Her eyes flew to mine. "You named him *Duck*?"

"I like to keep things simple."

Her attention returned to her new feathered friend. "Now I remember—I read a story about him. You made his prosthetic leg with a 3D printer." She paused. "I thought his name was Alphonse."

It might be. So she hadn't come to the meeting unprepared. She'd just admitted that she'd looked into Scott. Good, she was beginning to show her hand. "Officially, but his nickname is Duck." I pocketed my hands and frowned. Considering why she was there, I shouldn't have been uncomfortable lying to her, but I was. "Like me. My name is Scott, but my friends call me Jesse." I had no justification for that last part, other than wanting to hear her say my name.

She nodded while petting Alphonse. "If we become friends, I'll remember that."

I bit back a smile. She had layers to her and more grit than I'd expected. I didn't want to like anything about her, but it was a struggle to come up with the opposite.

When Alphonse quacked loudly up at Crystal, she laughed, then asked, "What does he want?"

"Food, most likely. I haven't gotten around to feeding them yet today."

"I thought farmers were up with the sun."

I shrugged. They probably were. "Ready to head into the barn?"

She straightened and wiped her hands on her jeans. "Absolutely. A deal is a deal. Although I should warn you: I'm a city girl. I'll have no idea what to do, but I'm good at following directions."

My mind instantly headed to the gutter with that one, and I had to assure my cock she wasn't referring to the X-rated scenario I'd just imagined. I forced my feet into motion. As we walked, Alphonse followed us.

Crystal paused to watch him move. "I love the leg you made for him."

I stopped as well. "But?"

She bent to give it a closer look. "Have you considered silicone? Using it might allow him to have a more natural gait." If any woman had a more perfect ass, I'd never seen it.

I forced my attention from her to Alphonse, who was quacking and hobbling around us. There was a stiffness to the material Scott had used that did seem to hinder his range of motion. An easy fix. Scott might not know that advances in 3D printers made the use of other materials possible. "I'll try to remember to mention that."

She straightened and joined me. "To whom?"

"To the person who made the first leg for him."

She gave me a long look. "I thought you had."

I gave myself a mental kick. For someone who was considered sharp in the business world, I was already getting sloppy around her. "With a friend's help. I don't have my own machine."

She nodded. "I could help you come up with a prototype for a new one if you'd like. Utilizing a combination of materials, we could design a socket as well. Maybe take a second look at the interface for comfort. I've never made anything like that, but I have friends who enjoy figuring out how things work."

It was my turn to stop and give her a hard look. "What did you do before you started working for your uncle?"

She shifted uncomfortably. "I'm not employed by Steadman Oil." She raised both hands in plea. "Technically I never said I was."

I cocked an eyebrow.

Her shoulders rose and fell. "Okay, I'm sorry I misled you. I'm here as a favor for my uncle, but as his niece, not as an employee. Does that make a difference?"

"Lies always matter." Mine, although necessary, would as well. They were piling up, creating a wall between us and any possibility of acting on the attraction we had for each other.

She let out a shaky breath. "You're right. I'm sorry."

Her apology hung in the air. I felt her guilt as if it were my own. No way could she be as sweet as she appeared, but I felt compelled to say something to make her feel better anyway. My tone was harsher than I meant it to be when I said, "Don't be. When it comes to family, we all do what we have to."

Her smile was quick and captivating. "Thanks for understanding."

We stood there, simply staring into each other's eyes again. The world and all our lies faded away. For a moment it was just her, that beautiful smile of hers, and the temptation of her lips. She swayed forward. I bent my head until my mouth hovered over hers.

"All set, Scott," LJ called from the door of the barn.

Crystal jumped back, and I raised my head. "Who's that?" she asked.

"LJ. He's a volunteer." *And a slap of reality.* "He wanted to finish up something before we headed in."

"A volunteer?"

I parroted something Scott had once told me about his farm. "I run an unofficial rescue. Every animal here is a little broken but special in its own way. I take in the animals others consider throwaways."

"Oh, wow." The dreamy tone returned to her voice before her expression became pained. "I had no idea."

My jaw tightened. I didn't like that the adoration in her gaze had nothing to do with anything I'd ever done. It made no sense to me that her opinion should matter to me one way or another. She was nothing to me. Less than nothing: she was an adversary. Without responding, I strode away, into the barn, and left her to follow.

Once inside, the first thing I noticed was that each animal stall was now clearly labeled with the animal's name and a number. I walked into the feed room and noted that LJ had also labeled each tub with a corresponding number and note.

Crystal joined me in the small room. We didn't speak at first. As the silence dragged on, she looked around. Finally, she said, "Everything is so organized."

"I wouldn't know what to do if it wasn't." That, at least, was true. Things were strained, but they were better that way.

"I'm sure." She placed a hand on one tub. "Do you mind if I start with Alphonse? Seems simple enough. Fresh water and a scoop of feed in the black bowls just outside the barn door. I can do that. Is there a spigot?"

Rather than addressing a question I didn't have an answer to, I asked, "If you're not employed by your uncle, what do you do?"

"I'm a flavorist." As if she guessed what I would ask next, she said, "It's my job to make processed food taste like it's not . . . while looking for ways to make it better for you."

"So you work for a food company?"

"Several. I co-own an independent lab. We're usually contracted for specific projects. Ever wonder how a food can have thirty percent less sodium but claim to taste the same? We're the ones figuring out how to make that happen. Once we determine a certain solution, it can often be applied to a variety of foods."

A flavorist? Why had her uncle chosen her as the one to deliver the proposal? I gave her another once-over and conceded that he'd chosen correctly if what he'd wanted was to distract Scott. Still, that seemed like a job a man would assign to a woman he didn't care about. He'd sent his niece. It didn't speak highly of Steadman's character.

Why? Why her? The question nagged at me. "So you studied chemistry."

"Enough to have a PhD in it."

I'd underestimated her. That was never a good thing to realize about an opponent. "Where did you go to school?"

"UMass Amherst." She shifted from one foot to the other. "Is this an interview?"

I held her gaze. "In a sense. I like to know exactly who I'm dealing with."

Her lips pursed as she appeared to choose her words carefully. "I'm not that complicated. I spend all my time in a lab coat, mixing aromas and chemicals while cracking jokes only other chemists would laugh at. Not very exciting."

She sounded sincere and definitely looked more at home in casual attire. Could she be telling the truth? If so, how did she fit into her uncle's plan? I didn't believe for a second that all he wanted her to do was hand Scott the offer and leave.

I glanced around until I saw a sink. "You can fill the water bucket here."

"Of course." She started to do just that, then paused. "I'm beginning to understand why this place is so important to you. I hope the deal you work out with my uncle allows you to help more animals."

There it was—the circle-back pitch. Disappointing but expected.

I looked her in the eye and said, "I don't see that happening."

She turned the water on and seemed to want to say more but didn't. Alphonse quacked up at her impatiently. She laughed, turned the water off, and headed out of the room with his water and feed. He followed behind noisily.

I walked to the bin closest to me and read the instructions on it. Molly the miniature cow had anxiety issues. *Stay inside the stall with her. Pet her and talk to her until her grain is gone. Pen is outside on the left. Fill her hayrack outside and put her there. She will eat the hay if you put the donkey with her.*

What the hell? Whatever.

I filled a bucket with the amount listed and sought out the damn cow's stall. There was a hook for the bucket on the far wall, which meant I had to go inside. I did, careful to avoid her dung. When she moved to eat, I stepped away. She stopped and looked at me.

"No."

Now, I liked cows as much as the next person—on my plate. I had no desire to touch or leave smelling like one.

But she made no move toward her food, instead just gave me a sad look. I shook my head. "Eat, then I'll put you outside. Go on. You don't need anyone with you to do that." She didn't move, and my frustration grew. I leaned closer and muttered, "I'm not Scott. This little act might work with him, but I don't actually care if you eat—so have at it."

She lowered her head and gave me the most pathetic look. I groaned. "Oh, for God's sake." I stepped closer and put my hand on her back tentatively. Did cows kick? I had no idea. "There. Happy?"

She made a little sound and turned to the bucket and began to eat. When I lifted my hand, she stopped. I replaced my hand, and she dug back into her feed. Of course Scott would have an emotionally needy cow. Knowing him, he'd probably paid for her. I sighed and ran my hand back and forth over her back. "How does a cow even get anxiety?

What the hell do you have to be stressed about?" She shifted closer to me, leaning against my leg. I kept talking only because it seemed to comfort her. "You want stress? Try being my father's son. You know what he would have said to me if I had told him I needed someone with me so I could eat? Yeah, me neither. You know why? Because I would never have said that to him. No one would. He devours weak people like that for breakfast."

Molly continued munching, so I continued talking. "Your problem is you think you can't do this alone, but it's all in your head. You can. All you have to do is focus and believe you can reach your goals, and you will. Don't settle for this version of you. Trust me: work this through, and you'll feel better about yourself."

CHAPTER FOUR

CRYSTAL

When I returned to the feed room, Scott was already gone. I headed into the aisle, and his voice drew me over to a stall. At first I couldn't make out what he was saying; once I could, my hand went to my heart, and I gasped.

My impression of Scott Millville had been all wrong. He might have come across as impatient and tough, but that was all an act. As I watched him reassure a small bovine that it could find confidence, my heart melted. He was so patient—so tenderhearted.

As if sensing my arrival, he turned, and our gazes met. He'd already made it clear he wasn't interested in me, but for a moment it sure didn't feel that way. The cow beside him nudged his hand. Without looking away from me, he gave her back a rub, and she returned her attention to her food. I glanced down at the sign on the front of her stall. **MOLLY.** I looked back at the cow, hoping he hadn't already seen how I felt in my eyes. "She's small. Is she full grown?"

He gave her another pat. "Miniature."

I stuffed my hands in the front pockets of my jeans. "Have you had her long?"

"No." A moment passed in which neither of us spoke, and then he said, "She doesn't eat unless someone is with her. Anxiety."

Heart thudding wildly in my chest, I put his talk with the cow into context and had to blink back the kind of tears a woman gave in to when she saw a fireman save a kitten. I'd never wanted a man more nor felt more ridiculous for it. I was there for a reason and one I was struggling to feel good about. "Well, she sure is a lucky cow."

"That's one point we are in full agreement on."

Molly finished her grain and turned in her stall to face the exit. I looked around, saw a halter hanging beside the door, and held it out to Scott. Rather than accepting it, he asked, "Would you like to put it on her?"

"Sure." I slipped into the stall. "Just slide it over her head?"

He gave me a look I wasn't sure how to interpret.

Silly question, I guess. Of course that's how to do it. I moved closer. "Hi, Molly. I'm going to put this on you. You don't bite, do you?" Molly stood there, chewing on something in her mouth. I posed my next question to Scott. "Cows are docile, right?"

He shrugged.

I flexed my shoulders. "I'll admit that I'm nervous about doing this if you admit that you might be enjoying my discomfort a little too much."

A smile shone in his eyes before it stretched his lips. "I admit nothing."

Playful. Sexy. I shifted closer. "You might want people to believe you're a tough guy, but you're not fooling anyone. Evidence of what a good man you are is all around you."

He frowned, and for a moment I thought my comment had irritated him. He leaned closer and in a low, tense voice said, "It depends on your definition of *good*."

I swallowed hard. The intensity of the moment was too much to sustain. I looked away and held out the halter in front of Molly. She slid her head into it. I secured it and felt a burst of pride. "I did it."

Our eyes met again. "You did."

Molly nuzzled my hand. "I think she likes me."

"Then you should definitely lead her to her pen. I'll get her hay and the donkey. They do better together."

I gave the side of Molly's face a rub that she leaned into. "She really is the sweetest thing." I located a rope and attached it to the halter. "Come on, Molly. You want to go outside?" I'd had a dog when I was a child, but that felt like a lifetime ago. Still, I told myself leading a cow couldn't be much different. A perfect angel, she walked at my side and practically guided me to her paddock.

I had just released her when Scott appeared with a donkey and a wagon full of hay. I opened the gate for him and took the rope he handed me. "Hold on to her for a minute. I need to put the hay out. Don't let her free until I remove the wagon, because she has limited vision."

"Oh, poor baby." I ran a hand down her thickly furred neck. "From age? An accident?"

Scott didn't respond, but there was a chance he hadn't heard me since he was filling a rack with hay. When he had the wagon outside the paddock again, I reached to release the donkey, and he said, "Put her next to Molly. They take care of each other."

"A Seeing Eye cow and an emotional-support donkey?"

His eyebrows rose, and I would have sworn he almost smiled. "It's that kind of farm."

"Special." I waited until I'd joined him outside the gate to say, "I had no idea. I'm sure my uncle doesn't either."

His eyes narrowed. "You say that like it would make a difference."

I wanted to say it would, but I couldn't speak for my uncle. I wasn't naive enough to believe he'd become as successful as he was without making some decisions that might haunt him. Still, I had to believe he would make sure whatever deal he offered would ensure that all the creatures Scott had would still be well cared for somewhere as nice as they currently were.

With a good amount of disgust in his tone, Scott said, "Well, at least you didn't lie." He looked me over again. Everywhere his gaze touched, my skin warmed. "Tell me something about your uncle."

I shifted from one foot to the other. I was beginning to think the reason Scott had asked me to help him was so he could pump me for information about my uncle. I was certain I didn't know anything I couldn't share, but I also felt I should be careful. "He loves me."

Scott's eyes narrowed again. "And?"

"And I love him too. He's the only family I have."

"Ah."

My hands went to my hips. "Ah?"

He shrugged. "That explains why you're okay with him strong-arming this farm away from me and destroying the land."

I gasped. "That's not what's happening at all."

"Isn't it?"

I looked away. My uncle wasn't a criminal. Making an offer wasn't the same as strong-arming someone.

Scott stepped closer and tipped my chin up with his hand. When my eyes met his, his were flashing with a fire I hadn't expected. "Don't waste a moment feeling bad about something that won't happen anyway."

It was hard to breathe, hard to think about anything past how much I wanted him to kiss me. His grip tightened on my chin, and my lips parted. Desire flooded through me.

A male voice called out from the barn. "Take your time; I'll finish feeding the animals. At the rate you're going, they'll starve."

Scott dropped his hand.

I let out a shaky breath and stepped back. "We should probably go help him."

After a moment, Scott said, "We'll clean the barn; then I'll look over the paperwork you brought."

That was better than the *maybe* he'd given me earlier.

And somehow worse.

"Thank you."

He turned and strode off toward the barn. I sprinted after him.

Cleaning stalls should have been a miserable chore, but it gave me time to watch him in action. His back muscles rippled beneath his shirt as he shoveled. His biceps bulged each time he emptied the wheelbarrow. And oh Lord, when he walked down the aisle with bags of shavings on his shoulders, I leaned against the shovel and enjoyed how my body hummed with anticipation.

Sure, I knew sex between us wasn't possible, but it was incredible to realize I was capable of being that attracted to someone. I tried to remember the faces of any of the men I'd dated and couldn't. Not a single damn one of them.

He caught me watching him, and the angry look he gave me was oddly hot. All I could picture was that emotion fueling the passion between us.

I did feel bad about what he'd said about my uncle's intentions, but considering that Scott was adamant that he wouldn't even lease his land . . . what did it matter? My job had never been to convince Scott, just to make sure he read the proposal, and he'd already said he would do that.

I didn't get out of the lab often—surely no one could fault me for allowing myself to enjoy a view I might not get again soon . . . or ever. Why had no one ever told me how *sexy* farmers were? That kind of information might have swayed my studies to agriculture. Or husbandry. Or anything a man like Scott was into.

He shot me a look on his way by and raised an eyebrow. "Unless you plan to spit shine it, that stall is done."

I straightened and wrinkled my nose. "Okay, so I'm not as fast as you are, but in my defense, you've been doing this your whole life—it's my first time."

There was no sympathy in his eyes as he nodded toward the five or so stalls on each side of the aisle. "I've done eight. This is your . . ."

Second, but I didn't need to admit it; he knew. My hands came to my hips. "I wasn't aware we were in competition."

He rested an elbow on the top of a rake. "In life you're either winning . . . or you're not."

Cocking my head to one side, I spoke my thoughts before I filtered them. "You're an interesting mix of nice and . . ."

"And?"

"Not?" I added lamely.

He didn't appear offended. "Nice is overrated."

My chin rose. "I don't agree. I'd say that at the end of the day a person's character is what matters most."

"I love that you can say that with a straight face." His expression was so jaded I had a difficult time reconciling this side of him with the side that took in broken animals. "Let's pretend for a moment that you actually believe that. You know what happens to someone who follows the rules and plays nice? They get pushed around, taken advantage of, and if no one steps in to wake them up . . . they lose everything."

"Is that what happened to you?" It would explain a lot.

"Never."

He said it like a warning, and my eyes widened. I had tried to learn a little about Scott before coming to meet him. Nothing I'd found had hinted at a reason for the anger I felt bubbling in him. In fact, even when refusing previous offers from my uncle's people, he'd been pleasant enough. At least that was what my uncle had said. Was he reaching the end of his patience?

Understandable, but perhaps a reason I should get the offer in his hands sooner rather than later. I asked, "Are there any more chores, or are we done?"

He gave me a long look. "We're done."

"I'll go get the papers from my car, then." When he didn't respond, I turned and hurried out of the barn.

I paused at my car. Even though I wasn't one to normally give in to fantasy, I let myself imagine what he would say if I told him the only proposal I was interested in was the one that would get me into his arms. *Oh yes.*

I groaned. Or *oh no.* One, he'd probably think I was looking for a marriage proposal. Two, I couldn't imagine facing my uncle and having to tell him, *The land proposal? Yeah, I decided that wasn't as important as having sex with a complete stranger.*

Sex with a stranger. Could I actually do it? I wasn't a risk-taker. I tended to order the same food when I went out to eat, drove the same way to and from work each day, jogged on a treadmill instead of outside, because I found comfort in the predictable.

I was just as careful with my social life. I'd had sex five and a half times in my life with the same man, and it had been equally unimpressive each time. The half? We'd given up and decided to watch a movie together instead.

Scott excited me more with a look than a naked Eugene ever had. If we'd met under different circumstances, maybe . . .

Who was I kidding? I wouldn't have had the nerve to act on how he made me feel regardless of how I'd met him. I smacked my hand to my forehead.

And why was I feeling guilty?

Sure, Scott was a gorgeous, animal-rescuing man, but the fate of his farm wasn't my responsibility. I wasn't trying to sway him one way or another. He and my uncle were both adults and perfectly capable of making their own decisions. My only role was that of a glorified courier.

Alphonse would have a home wherever Scott ended up. If Scott accepted my uncle's offer, he'd have enough money to build an amazing barn somewhere else with an even larger area for Molly. If he wanted, he would be able to afford to take in more animals. I had nothing to feel bad about.

And if he refused the offer? My uncle could find another property. In all the world, there had to be better plots of land. What could possibly be so special about Scott's?

I was overthinking the situation.

Plenty of things that felt good were a bad idea, and I normally had no problem saying no to them. I didn't eat an entire pie in one sitting. I never fell asleep in the sun. I was too smart to allow myself to engage in unhealthy situations.

Scott was definitely not a possibility. The quicker I put some distance between the two of us, the better.

Taking a deep breath of resolve, I opened the front passenger-side door of my car. No briefcase. I leaned inside. Nothing. It was then I remembered taking it with me into my hotel. I checked the trunk just in case, but I already knew where it was—beside the bed at my hotel—dammit.

Breathe.

Consider your options.

I weighed driving back to my hotel without telling Scott and hoping he didn't notice a thirty-minute-or-so absence. *No, he might see me leaving.*

I considered walking back into the barn and trying to make a joke out of my mistake. He didn't come across as someone who would find humor in that.

There was the option of texting my uncle and having him send me a digital copy of the offer. I closed my eyes and leaned back against the rear of the car. No, I didn't want to do that either.

Oh my God, how could I have been so careless? My uncle asked me to do one thing . . . one thing . . . and this is how I repay him for all the kindness he has shown me.

I hugged my arms around my waist and struggled to keep my breathing even. *This is not the time for a panic attack. Not here. Not now.*

Just breathe.

In.

Out.

In.

"Is there a problem?" Scott asked from beside me.

My eyes flew open, and I jumped to the side in surprise, stumbling as I did. He caught me by one of my arms to steady me. When I regained my footing, I simply stood there looking up at him, wishing his other hand were on me as well.

He bent closer, so close I thought he might kiss me, and said, "Are you okay?"

Breathe. Don't do anything stupid like reach out and touch those beautiful lips of his. "I'm fine."

"I should have thanked you for today."

You could now. I bit my bottom lip to keep myself from saying that. "That's okay. I was happy to help."

His eyes darkened, and his hand tightened on my arm. I didn't complain. It was actually sexy in a way I wouldn't have expected. "You sound so damn sincere."

"Because I am."

"No, what you are is a bad idea." His breath was a warm caress. "A very bad idea. I'm just not sure I care."

He feels the same pull I do. A little devil in me brought his earlier claim to my lips. "I thought I had nothing you were interested in."

The heat in his gaze supported his next words. "I lied." He searched my face. "But that doesn't mean I'm foolish enough to let you sway my decision."

"I wouldn't want to."

His other hand came up, and he buried it in the hair on the back of my head. "Then this is how it'll go. I'll read the proposal, turn it down, and then you decide if you want to stay or go."

Desire shot through me, and I shuddered beneath his touch. It was a struggle to not simply launch myself into his arms and skip to the *stay* part. "I would agree to that plan except for one minor issue."

"So no." His hands fell away. "Good."

"Good?"

"I needed to know."

My head was spinning. "Needed to know?"

"How far you'd go."

"What?" Disappointment welled within me. For a moment I had been so certain he was as attracted to me as I was to him . . . but he wasn't. He'd been testing me. Anger welled in me. "That was such a dick move. What if I'd said yes? What if, after a lifetime of mediocre sex, I had chosen you and tonight to try for something better? I would have failed in your eyes? You know what? Fuck you." I turned away from him and strode toward the front of the car.

"Hold on. What?" He was beside me just as I slid into the driver's seat.

"You heard me." I grabbed the car door and slammed it shut, then rolled down the window an inch. "Now, back up so I don't drive over your feet."

"Crystal—"

"I'd give you the papers now, but I forgot them. I'll drop them off on your porch tomorrow morning. Read them. Don't read them. I don't care." I turned on the engine and revved it. He stepped back only when the car began to move.

Dirt flew from beneath my tires as I floored the gas. I was angry with him but angrier with myself.

Because I would have stayed.

CHAPTER FIVE

JESSE

I was still in the driveway processing what she'd said when LJ walked up beside me. "I like her."

"That was her goal," I replied.

LJ scratched the back of his neck. "I can understand why you wanted to spend some time with her, but did it help?"

"Not one damn bit." The experience had left me with more questions than answers. "She believed I was Scott, though."

LJ chuckled. "She must not know a thing about farms."

"Clueless about them, but smarter than I thought. She has a PhD in chemistry."

After a sharply indrawn breath, LJ said, "That's not good."

I glanced at him. "Why?"

He shook his head. "I was hoping she was just a pretty face. If I were you, I would keep her as far from the farm as possible."

"She's dropping off paperwork tomorrow morning."

"Meet her somewhere else."

"Why? What is here that Steadman would want a chemist to see?"

LJ shrugged as if he didn't have an answer to that. "Just keep her out of the house." After a pause, he asked, "Are you staying until tomorrow?"

"Looks that way."

"I'll need help feeding tonight. I'm not as young as I used to be."

I looked him over, then raised and lowered one shoulder. Despite the smell, I felt good after a couple of hours of manual labor. Although I hit the gym on a regular basis, I had definitely used muscles I hadn't in a long time. I was tired, but a good tired. "That's fine."

He nodded. "And tomorrow morning. We feed at eight a.m. Keeping to a schedule is better for the animals."

"Whatever. I'll be up anyway."

"Besides, you're so good with Molly."

"Shut the fuck up."

LJ let out a muffled laugh. "I shouldn't laugh at you, but you remind me so much of how I was when I first met Scott."

I doubted that, but I was curious. "Don't tell me that you also asked yourself how long it would take to wash off the stench of manure."

He smiled. "I asked myself more than that. I had a serious heart attack a few years ago. My doctor warned me if I didn't lower my stress level, I was destined for another, and there was no guarantee I'd survive that one."

"Don't feel like you have to tell me the whole story."

He laughed. "God, you're an ass. Not that I wouldn't have said essentially the same thing back then. I remember thinking most conversations were a waste of time. I also didn't see the point of coming out to the country. My son bought me a little cabin just down the street, though, and convinced me to stay in it for a week. He suggested I take up fishing. I didn't do anything back then unless there was profit in it, but he was adamant, and I promised to try it just to shut him up."

"Fascinating." *Not.*

Unbothered by my lack of enthusiasm, LJ continued, "My blood pressure was sky high when I first arrived, and I spent more time on the phone than baiting hooks. When Scott and his parents invited me over for dinner, I didn't expect to enjoy myself. What could I, the founder of G-Force TechMods, have in common with farmers? Well, I discovered, not a lot, and yet more than I imagined."

GFTM was one of the largest tech companies in the Northeast. *What the fuck?* My head snapped around. No. Impossible. "You're *Leo Jarcisco?*"

He smiled. "The one and only."

"I wasn't aware that you'd stepped down as CEO."

"I haven't."

"Then what the hell are you doing here?"

"Lowering my blood pressure the natural way while learning how to be a better person."

I shook my head. "No, seriously."

LJ sighed and glanced over his shoulder at the farmhouse. "You don't believe me because you think there is nothing here worth learning. I get that. I felt the same way. Look at this place. The Millvilles are one step ahead of foreclosure. They have fields they don't use, a barn full of animals they won't eat, and no drive to make the changes that would improve their situation. They could do so much better. That's what I thought, too, in the beginning. I even offered to help them."

"With?" As he spoke, I tried to piece together how he fit into the bigger picture. One tech mogul. One oil company. Both circling my brother's farm. What was I missing?

"Financial advice. Business ideas. They seemed like good people who just required a nudge in the right direction. Scott said the only help he needed was in the barn. I thought he was joking. I lived in a penthouse. All of my exercise came from a gym. I not only had no idea how to care for animals; I had no desire to learn. He talked me into helping out one day, then the next, and before I knew it, I was sleeping better, waking easier, feeling younger. I discovered I could get as much done working remotely as I'd ever done in my office. I'll admit, I've also grown attached to Scott's motley herd. I thought the Millvilles needed me, but really I needed them. As a token of my appreciation, I bought Jill and Ryan a motor home and sent them off to see the country."

I mulled over what he'd said, then arched an eyebrow. "No, seriously."

He laughed. "I like you, Jesse. You say it like you see it."

Not always, not while figuring a situation out. I definitely had questions for Scott.

I wasn't buying LJ's story. Was there a chance he was also after the land? It didn't make sense that he would be, but not much about Scott's farm did make sense. "So everyone who comes here leaves happier and healthier?"

"Happier? Not everyone. Scott has had some disappointments, but he doesn't let that close him off. I find that inspiring. Since coming here, I've let go of a lot of anger I didn't realize was weighing me down. I'm more optimistic thanks to your brother and his parents."

"That's the story you're going with?"

"It's one you could claim as your own as well, but you have to want the change."

Okay, I've heard enough. "There's nothing I want that I don't already have."

"I don't believe that." He gave my back a slap that took me by surprise. "And neither does the woman who tore out of here."

I tensed and snapped, "She'll be back. We have unfinished business."

"Yes, you do." He started to walk away, then stopped and turned back. "I'd stay, but I have a call scheduled with Trudeau. I'll be back at six, though."

"I'll be here."

When he left, I headed into the house to shower and change. Although why I should bother, considering I planned to end the day back in the barn, was beyond me. How many times a day did a farmer shower? I could justify at least three.

A short time later, I settled onto a couch with my laptop and a cheap beer I'd found in Scott's fridge. I expected to find it difficult to focus but whipped through my emails in record time. LJ might have had a point as far as the benefits of fresh air. I couldn't remember a time, outside of a few sailing trips in college, when I'd spent as much time outdoors.

Not that my thoughts didn't wander . . . I had more questions than I had answers. That had never stopped me before, though. I was confident that when I did solve the puzzle, it would also be one I could handle.

My greatest distraction?

"What if, after a lifetime of mediocre sex, I had chosen you and tonight to try for something better? I would have failed in your eyes? You know what? Fuck you."

She'd only said it to mess with my mind.

It was working.

I sent a text to Scott explaining that I needed one more day at the farm but that with LJ's help, all the animals would be well cared for. I didn't want him running back and outing me before I saw Crystal one last time.

A lifetime of mediocre sex?

"What if I'd chosen you and tonight to try for something better?"

I could definitely do better than mediocre.

My cock swelled in my fresh jeans. I considered myself a good judge of character, but when it came to Crystal, I couldn't differentiate between what I knew and what I felt. I had a larger problem than wanting to fuck her.

I wanted to believe her.

My phone buzzed with a call from Thane. I answered with a sigh. "I'm staying another night."

"Do you need anything?" Thane took pride in being a good older brother. He didn't yet consider Scott family, but since he was essentially babysitting him while I was at the farm, that would hopefully change.

"No. I have everything under control. How is Scott?"

"He's—Scott. How much he looks like you is still a little unsettling, but I'm getting used to it."

"Don't let anyone meet him."

"Oh, don't worry; I don't intend to. I gave him the remote to your automated apartment. He's been playing with it like a child. You'd think he'd never seen hidden TV screens or voice-activated lighting. You'll probably want to reboot your system when you get back. My guess is he'll have changed all of your settings."

"That bad?"

"I never thought I would have to explain how a bidet works to a grown man, but I did it for you and the sake of your bathroom floor."

I smiled. "I appreciate that."

"He made his own account on your toilet because apparently even twins have different analprints."

"Oh my God, I'm sorry. I owe you big."

"You do. We had a lengthy discussion on how your toilet not only identifies users but what kind of data it accumulates and how. For your shower I simply directed him to an online manual. I wish I'd done that for the toilet."

I gave in to a chuckle. "Sounds like you're already getting the hang of having a second little brother."

"I'm working on it. How are you holding up?"

"It's definitely different here. He doesn't have any house staff. Nothing. No housekeeper, no cook. I've been washing my own dishes."

"The horror." He was giving me shit, but I didn't care. He would have been just as bothered.

"I know, right? I'm reasonably certain my laundry will stay dirty until I figure out how to use the washing machine . . . if there is one here. He might wash his clothing in a creek or something."

It was Thane's turn to laugh. "After having spent time with him, I can imagine that."

Changing gears, I asked, "What do you know about Leo Jarcisco?"

"Besides that he started and still runs a very successful tech company?"

"Yes. He works here, feeding and caring for the animals, for free."

"You're joking."

"I am not. I'm still trying to wrap my head around it. He has to have an ulterior motive, but I don't know what it could be."

"*The* Leo Jarcisco?"

"I know. It's insane, but I googled him, and that's him."

"Or his secret twin. I hear it's trendy to have one now."

I groaned. "Don't even start. Thank you for being absolutely no help."

Not sounding bothered by my accusation, Thane said, "So what's holding you there until tomorrow?"

"I haven't seen the proposal yet. It's being delivered in the morning."

"Didn't you meet the oil rep yesterday?"

"No. She came by today instead."

"Without the proposal?"

"She forgot to bring it."

"No."

"Yes."

"Sounds like Steadman is losing interest in the farm."

"I don't believe so."

"Then he should fire her."

"He can't. She's his niece, and she doesn't work for him."

"You're right . . . it does sound strange over there."

"More than you know. See if you can get Scott to open up more about his farm. There's something he's not telling us."

"Will do. While I'm playing sleuth, want to tell me what's really going on with the oil rep?"

"Nothing. Her name is Crystal. She's beautiful. Funny. Intelligent. If we had met in any other way—"

"Don't sign anything."

"Oh my God, Scott said the same thing. Have I ever impulsively signed anything?"

"No, but—"

"But nothing. I'm here for one reason and one reason only—to make sure Scott doesn't lose his farm."

"Which all sounds good, but—"

"But what? What makes you think I can't handle this?"

After a pause, Thane said, "Something in your voice when you described her."

"You're imagining things. Sure, I find her attractive, but that's it. She's no different than any other woman I've met. In fact, I'll probably forget her name the moment I return to Brookline. There is absolutely nothing special about her."

"Oh boy. Call me tomorrow when you're reading the proposal. We'll go over it together. And make sure you don't have a pen anywhere around you."

"Goodbye, Thane."

"I'm serious. Call me tomorrow."

"Fine. Now, forget about me and go do something worthwhile . . . like making sure Scott stays hidden and out of trouble."

"He's fine. Worry about wrapping up your side so you can get your ass back to work."

"My guess is I'll be on my way home by midday tomorrow."

"Sure."

"I will be."

"I'll believe that when I see it."

"Do you really think I'd want to spend another minute here that I don't have to?"

"So you won't be calling me tomorrow to tell me you need another day there?"

"Absolutely not."

"A hundred dollars says you will."

"You're on."

That will be the easiest hundred dollars I've ever made.

CHAPTER SIX

CRYSTAL

I paced my small hotel room, alternating between berating myself and reassuring myself that all I'd damaged so far was my pride. After showering and changing, I sat on the corner of my bed and let out a long sigh. *I should have told him I'd drop everything off tonight; then I could go home and wallow in a gallon of black raspberry ice cream with Ellie.*

Ellie. I need to tell her I won't be coming back tonight. I sent her a quick text.

She responded with a string of emojis, which I believe was meant to inquire if I was going to have sex that night.

The eggplant was a penis—that much I knew. I didn't understand the peace sign. Was she asking if I was at peace with his penis? Fireworks had to be an orgasm. I rolled my eyes. Ellie was on a kick to be cooler, but if texting was reduced down to a string of vegetables and vague symbols, I would return to simply calling people. I decided to FaceTime her.

As soon as her image appeared on my screen, she asked, "So?"

"I'm not entirely sure what you asked, but no."

She made a pained face. "It's probably for the best. Imagine how complicated that would have been."

"Oh, I know." *I've imagined it. In detail.*

"How did your meeting go?"

I flopped back onto the bed. "You don't want to know, and I wish I could forget."

"I'm sorry. He wouldn't read over the papers?"

"That wasn't the problem."

"What was?"

I closed my eyes and covered them with my arm. "He was soooooooooo good looking. By that, I mean I would have eaten tacos off his stomach."

"You don't like tacos."

"Exactly."

"But you're not into one-night stands, so you said no."

"Worse."

"He didn't ask you to stay."

"Worse."

She gasped. "He's a creep and tried to force you?"

"Okay, not as bad as that."

"I need a hint."

I lowered my arm, sat up, and looked her in the eye. "He asked me to stay as a test, not because he wanted me to. He wanted to see how far I would go to get him to read over the papers."

"I don't like him."

"Me either. He's an ass. In fact, I told him to fuck off."

"I can't picture you doing that."

"It happened."

She pursed her lips. "What will you tell your uncle?"

"Nothing yet. I'm delivering the papers tomorrow morning. I told Scott he can read them or not; I don't care. But hopefully he'll at least look them over so this trip wasn't a complete waste."

She nodded without speaking for a moment, then asked, "What do you plan on wearing tomorrow?"

"Oh, crap. I didn't bring another outfit." I looked down at my black leggings. I wasn't about to wear the skirt and revealing shirt again. I definitely wasn't putting my dirty jeans back on until they were washed. "I guess it doesn't matter."

"Oh, it matters. You can't leave him thinking he won. You need to go shopping again. Find something that will make him wish his head hadn't been so far up his own ass today."

I burst out laughing. "And then what?"

"Then walk away. Head held high. Leave him wanting more."

"Hello, Ellie? You know who you're talking to, right? I'm not that kind of woman."

"You were this morning."

I did smile at that before I remembered how feeling that way had led to disappointment. "You might have thought that, but he didn't."

"He doesn't matter. You do. Don't let anyone else choose your next outfit for you. Don't dress for him; dress for yourself. Pick something that makes you feel good about yourself. My mother always says beauty is ninety percent confidence. I'm not sure if she says that because she doesn't think I'm beautiful, but believing it has helped me. Remember that award ceremony I went to? The one where I had to wear a gown? I pretended I was gorgeous, and I had a great time."

"You are gorgeous." Ellie didn't have classically beautiful features, but when she smiled, she lit up a room.

"So are you. Get an outfit that makes you feel that way, and you'll knock his socks off."

"His socks are better off staying where they are."

"You know you want to leave him drooling."

My cheeks flushed. "Do you really think I could?"

"I don't *think*—I know."

I stood and walked over to the mirror. "I haven't had my eyebrows done in a while."

"Get them done."

I looked down at my hands. "And I could use a manicure."

"They always make me feel better. Get a pedicure as well. Ooooh, the one with a foot massage if you can find one. I love those."

"That does always make me feel better. You know what? I'm going to do it. For me, not for him. I'm going to do some things tonight to make *myself* feel better. Thanks, Ellie."

"Anytime."

I let out a slow breath. "Ellie, I would have stayed if he'd wanted me to. I've never done that before, but it didn't feel wrong. What does that mean?"

"It means I may have to learn to like him."

I shook my head. "I'm just dropping off the papers on his porch. I might not even see him."

"You will."

"This is crazy, right? I don't want to live on a farm. I liked his place, but I can't imagine wanting to take care of all of those animals every day. He and I have next to nothing in common. If I was ever with him, it would only be for the sex. Is that even worth it?"

"Um, yes? Hell yes? You need to be with someone who doesn't make you want to watch a TV show over having sex."

"That *would* be nice."

"You and I have the same problem—we spend too much time in our heads. My mother has been through countless men. She lives life on her own terms and is one of the happiest people I know. When things stop being fun, she simply moves on."

"I'm not sure either of us should be taking dating advice from your mother."

"I'll tell you what she doesn't settle for—boring sex. She might not be doing better than us, but she's certainly not doing worse."

I couldn't argue that point. Ellie's mother might move through men like a hot knife through butter, but Ellie claimed she was happy. I couldn't even look at my exes without feeling bad about myself . . . so who was I to judge? "He doesn't want to have sex with me."

"I bet he does."

"Sex for the sake of sex . . . won't that leave me feeling empty?"

"Not if he knows what he's doing."

I choked on a laugh. "Have you been sleeping with someone and not telling me?"

"His name is Jonathan, and it's recent, but it has been a game changer for me."

"I can't believe you didn't say anything."

She made a face. "He's twenty-one."

"That's not so bad. You're only twenty-six."

"He's still in college."

"Oh."

"Yeah. I met his friends. They don't have jobs. Some still live with their parents. I felt a million years older than them."

All of Ellie's talk about wanting to be cooler and act younger made sense now. "Does he know what you do for a living?"

"I told him I'm a pharmacist."

"Oh boy."

"I know. I couldn't tell him about our lab. He already thinks I'm smarter than he is. And I am, but he is on his college's wrestling team and is head-to-toe muscle. When we're together, it's all sex. We don't have to talk. I kind of prefer not to. It's so good I don't want to ruin it by focusing on why it shouldn't be. I know it can't last, but I don't care. We work hard, Crystal. It's okay to cut loose now and then."

"Wow. So all those times you headed off to the gym and came back smiling . . ."

"I was with Jonathan, but in my defense, I *was* exercising."

I chuckled, then sobered. "Ellie, don't ever feel like you can't share things with me. I wouldn't judge you."

"I know. It was more about me than you. I'm sharing now because I want you to see that it doesn't have to be a 'forever' thing to be good. Jonathan is good, really, really good. And extremely temporary."

Smiling, I collected my purse from the table. "I'm happy for you, Ellie, and thanks. You always know what to say to make me feel better."

She laughed. "That's not what you usually claim."

"Okay, so you're often blunt, but I like that about you as well. We all need a friend we can depend on to tell us what they really think."

"Same. Sorry I didn't tell you about Jonathan."

"I understand. I'm just happy that you're happy."

"Me too. Now go out there and get some for yourself."

CHAPTER SEVEN

JESSE

I woke early the next morning. LJ and I fed the animals and cleaned the barn in a fraction of the time it had taken the day before. There was a rhythm to it that, once I understood it, made the process flow.

I would have finished even sooner if Molly hadn't kept walking away from her hay every time I did, despite having Winnie with her. There was an area on her neck that must have been bothering her, because she calmed only while I scratched it. I told LJ he needed to check the area out for a bug bite or something. He didn't seem concerned at all. I sent a text to Scott about it. His response?

LOL

Not helpful. If I had been sticking around longer, I would have had the vet out. The poor thing had enough issues without adding *itchy* to the list.

Freshly showered, I took my laptop onto the porch to get some work done in the fresh air. It wasn't solely so I wouldn't miss Crystal, but I had to admit she had been on my mind.

No matter how many times I went over our interactions, I kept coming to the same conclusion . . . implying that I'd only asked her to stay as part of a test really had been a dick move. It wasn't something I'd planned.

Had it even been a test? Or a suggestion that had popped out of my mouth in the heat of the moment?

One she'd turned down . . . causing my pride to kick in. Like a child.

Don't want to be with me? Well, I didn't want to be with you first.

Not my best.

I sat there with my unopened laptop, frustrated with the fact that I couldn't get Crystal out of my thoughts, as well as that Thane hadn't been able to find out more from Scott. Information was power, and I didn't like the feeling that Scott was hiding something.

Curiosity had driven me to do a quick search of his house the night before. Not proud of it. Would do it again under the same circumstances. If Scott was into something illegal, I was willing to guide him out of that trouble as well. Family stayed when everyone else walked away. Not all family, but the men in mine were solid.

Outside of a disturbing number of superhero comics in Scott's room, there were few surprises. I discovered his mother had a toy drawer. I would take that knowledge with me to my grave and would never again look through an older couple's things. Never. A man only made that mistake once.

I'd almost given up then, but when I tried the door to the basement and discovered it was locked, I did a search for a key that would fit it. I didn't find one, but I was pretty much done looking in drawers.

I stood and nearly dropped my laptop when Crystal's car pulled up the driveway. Heart racing, I put my computer on a small table and tried to look like I wasn't excited to see her.

She exited her car, clutching a large manila envelope to her chest. I didn't know how she'd done it, but she looked even better than she had the day before. This time she was in a pair of white cutoff shorts and a black-and-white halter top that was modest but in the most delicious way. All legs and breasts, hair loose and flying in the wind behind her.

If she was looking for an apology, I was willing to give her one, with my tongue, all night long. Fuck, she was dangerous.

I moved to the top of the steps. She walked to the bottom. Her cheeks were flushed, and she looked a little embarrassed, but she met my gaze. "I brought the proposal."

"I can see that." Brilliant comeback? No, but it was the best I could do while so much of my blood was heading to my cock.

She began to walk up the stairs, then stopped.

I began to walk down, then did the same.

I cleared my throat. "About yesterday."

Her chin rose. "Yes?"

"What I said—"

"Doesn't matter."

"I shouldn't have—"

"Honestly, I've already forgotten about it."

I moved down a step. "I haven't." I descended another step. "I was an ass."

She took a moment to digest that. "You were, but there's no need to relive it." She held out the folder as I continued to approach. I didn't reach for it. She waved the envelope between us. When I still made no move to accept it, she said, "Will you take the damn papers so I can leave?"

That right there was the problem I was fighting with myself regarding how to handle. The rational, sensible response would have been to take the papers and let her leave. LJ seemed to think it was dangerous to even have her at the farm. I hadn't learned enough from her to justify further association. There was only one reason to delay her departure, and I avoided complicated hookups. No married women, women with children, friends of anyone I'd been with. I kept things simple. No promises. No drama.

The issue was—I wasn't feeling sensible. Having her near me was sending my senses into a heavenly overload. The anticipation of her touch had my body revving. "Not yet."

"You promised to read them."

"And I will. Later." Sure, it was blunt, but a man had to be when the clock was running down. If she left, there was a good chance I'd never see her again, and I wasn't ready for that to happen.

She tossed the envelope down on one of the steps. "If you think what I said yesterday had anything to do with whatever you decide to say to my uncle, you're wrong. My part in this is done now. The rest is between you and him."

"Good." I moved closer while her parting remarks from the day before echoed in my thoughts—as did the reason for them. "Then you should definitely not rush off." It was a shame I couldn't tell her the truth. Whatever happened between us had zero chance of leading anywhere. Everything she knew about me was a lie. If all she was looking for was a little fun, that didn't matter. I just needed to be clear. "Spend the day with me."

She searched my face. "Why would I do that?"

There were times when words were not the most effective way to express oneself. I dipped my head and gently brushed my lips over hers. She froze, then relaxed into the kiss. Sweet, hot, inviting without being bold. That kiss was one I knew I wouldn't soon forget. I raised my head and smiled down at her. "Because it's what we both want."

"Is this another test?" She brought a hand to her lips and swayed a little. I steadied her by putting my hands on her hips.

"I wish it were. No, this is me trying to convince you to stay because I spent most of last night imagining how good we'd be together."

Her eyes rounded. "You did?"

"Oh yes." I wanted for there to be no confusion. "I want to spend the day in your company and tonight in your arms."

"Oh." She blinked a few times quickly. "You just put it out there."

"Things are less complicated that way." A slow grin spread across my face. "Interested?"

"I don't normally do anything like this."

"There's nothing about this that's normal for me either."

For a moment time suspended. Would she stay or go? I had no idea. With nearly any other woman I would have said it didn't matter, but I held my breath and waited. I wanted her to stay, more than I'd wanted anything I could remember. I saw the decision in her eyes even before her hands crept up to rest on my shoulders. It made me think this attraction was as unique and strong for her as it was for me. The playful smile that curved her lips was nearly my undoing. "I might need one more kiss before I decide."

"Gladly." This time I swooped down and laid claim to her lips with all the passion building within me. Her mouth opened beneath mine, and I deepened the kiss. My hands tightened on her hips, shifting her forward so she was fully against my growing excitement.

Touch for touch, she met my passion with her own. I pulled her closer. She melted against me and made a sound that sent fire shooting through me.

There was nothing beyond her and how good she tasted. I kissed my way down her neck and loved how she arched back to allow me better access. Had I swung her up into my arms and carried her inside, we might have had sex right then. Instead, I hesitated, and LJ's warning came back to me: *Keep her out of the house.* When I lifted my head, we were both breathing heavily. Despite how certain my body was that it knew her, there were still too many unanswered questions. "Let's get out of here."

In a husky tone that would send any man to his knees, she said, "Where would we go?"

I wanted to say right inside to Scott's bed, but that wasn't an option. "How much of Rhode Island have you seen?"

"This area."

"Would you like to see Newport?"

She looked away, chewed her bottom lip, then met my gaze. "Yes."

Normally I would have led the way to one of my own vehicles, but Scott's collection consisted of an old, beat-up truck with questionable brakes and a tractor. "Want to drive?"

Her eyebrows shot up, but she nodded. "Sure."

I sprinted into the house with the envelope. I pulled a few condoms out of my luggage and stuffed them in my wallet—always better to be prepared than not. A few minutes later I was seated in the passenger seat of her hybrid, giving her directions to the Brick Market Place.

"Less than an hour away," she said when the ETA came up on her GPS.

"Everything in Rhode Island is."

She nodded and started down the driveway. Not driving allowed me the luxury of studying her profile as she drove. I didn't like that she looked nervous. I wanted to be with her, but caring about her moods would lead to feeling guilty that I was lying to her. It was a slippery slope to start down. My loyalty needed to remain with Scott.

We meant nothing to each other, and therefore nothing we did would mean anything. We were two adults satisfying a need; that was all. The only way this would work was if we both walked away from it regret-free.

What if she wasn't the kind who could?

When we had sex, would she call out Scott's name? How would I handle that? I was surprised how much I hated the possibility. Names shouldn't matter because this was a casual hookup. No promises. No drama.

Her reason to be at the farm was over. Mine soon would be as well. There was no reason our paths should cross again after this day.

Unless one of us wants them to.

"I'm not that fucking stupid," I muttered.

She glanced at me. "What did you say?"

"Nothing." Indecisiveness was the death of action. What I needed to do was stop second-guessing myself. She was an adult. No one was forcing her to spend time with me. For all I knew, this might be part of a plan to soften me up before I read the proposal. I had nothing to feel guilty about.

She flexed her hands on the steering wheel when she stopped for a red light. "This wasn't how I planned for today to go."

"No?" That piqued my curiosity. "What *was* your plan?"

She shot me a quick side glance. "It was silly."

"Tell me." As I spoke, I placed my hand on her bare thigh and loved how her cheeks flushed when I did. Soft. Smooth. I began to mentally chart the path my mouth would take later.

Another quick look. "I was still upset with you about yesterday."

Up and down, slow and sure, I caressed her thigh. "Understandable."

When my hand grazed the edge of her shorts, her eyelids lowered, and she let out a shaky breath. "I chose this outfit hoping—"

"Yes?" I slid my fingers beneath the hem of her shorts. Her nipples hardened beneath her top, and that was all the permission I required to slide my hand down the inside of her thigh to the very edge of her underwear. "What were you hoping for?"

Her legs parted ever so slightly. A man didn't need more of an invitation than that. I stroked a finger across the material of her underwear, back and forth, then slid beneath to dip into her wet slit.

She gasped but kept her hands on the wheel and her eyes on the road. I dipped a finger in deeper until I grazed her nub and circled it gently at first, watching and experimenting with pressure and speed. When a man got it just right, a woman's expression would change—*yes, there it is.*

Cock straining against the front of my jeans, I demanded, "For this?" I settled into a rhythm that had her eyelids lowering and her breathing turning ragged and audible.

She shook her head and shifted her position to allow me even better access. I drove one finger inside her while continuing to work her clit with my thumb. Hot. Wet. Nice and tight. I mentally thanked every woman who had been vocal enough with what she liked to train my hand to adapt and please. No two women were the same, but when patience and skill were applied, there were common pleasure points. My fingers were long, thick, and knowledgeable. I swirled. I thrust. I experimented until I found just the spot that had her begging me not to stop.

Taking advantage of the pause she made at a stop sign on an otherwise empty road, I increased my speed and leaned over to growl into her ear. "You're close, aren't you? Let it happen. Right here."

She put the car in park and closed her eyes. I thrust a second finger inside her, in and out the best I could in the confines of her loose shorts. Her sex clenched around my fingers, and she threw her head back as an orgasm rocked through her body. I felt the shudder that followed it and slowly withdrew my hand from her shorts.

"Wow." She shot me a huge smile.

I released my seat belt so I could lean in to kiss her neck. "Exactly what I was thinking."

Her expression became more self-conscious, and she lowered her voice. "I should feel embarrassed, but I don't. We hardly know each other. How is it possible that this feels right?"

It did. It felt so right that it also felt wrong. I wasn't the man she thought I was. It wasn't just my name that she had wrong. She had an entire impression of who I was that wasn't based on anything I'd ever done. A car came up behind us and honked a horn. Crystal jumped and fumbled to put the car back in drive. I waved for the other car to go around. It did. "There's something freeing about temporary. Tomorrow you'll go back to your regular life, and so will I. Today will just be a gift we gave each other."

"A gift."

"A nice memory."

"Because we won't have a reason to see each other after today." She didn't sound like the idea was upsetting to her. It was more like she was weighing it out and deciding if it was what she wanted to do.

"Exactly."

Crystal started driving again. "Temporary can be good."

My stomach was tied in knots. I resecured my seat belt and said, "It sure can be."

She nodded. "I like the idea of seeing my time with you as a gift. You're actually good for me. I was beginning to believe there was something wrong with me."

"Wrong?"

She shot me a glance. "How honest do you want to be?"

I was beginning to wish I could completely come clean, but I wasn't about to admit that. "You can tell me anything."

"I've always found it difficult to . . ."

"To?"

"Orgasm with someone else there. I can do it on my own, but even when sex was good, it wasn't that good."

What the fuck? "If sex didn't end with you having as much pleasure as your partner did, it wasn't *good*."

"I have a problem turning off my thoughts during sex. I can't relax and let go."

"Who told you that?" I growled deep in my chest.

"The last guy I was with."

"He was a fucking idiot."

Without missing a beat, she said, "His IQ is genius level, and he has made substantial contributions to slowing the deterioration time of foods."

"Some of the smartest people I know are some of the most clueless when it comes to life skills."

Her smile started tentatively but then shone. "I'll concede that he was not great in bed. We were compatible in so many other ways, though, that I kept thinking it would get better."

"But it didn't."

Her nose wrinkled, and her smile faded. "Eventually we just started snuggling and watching TV instead."

No wonder she was thirsty for something good.

She continued, "They say ninety percent of attraction is in a person's head. On paper we were a perfect match. I don't understand. Like us. We have nothing in common. I had never stepped foot on a farm until yesterday. I'm still trying to figure out how to get the smell of manure off my shoes. Being attracted to you makes no sense." She made a face. "Not that you smell bad."

"I'm sure I do." *This week at least.*

"You don't. I don't know how many times you have to shower to not smell, but I'm guessing at least three."

"I have found myself showering more than usual lately." I laughed, then sobered when I remembered thinking almost exactly the same thought she'd just expressed. We had nothing in common outside of our attraction, no reason to want to see each other after today. I needed it to stay that way.

"Knowing that you make a difference to those animals must make it all worth it."

"I suppose." I couldn't take my eyes off her profile or how she didn't hide her emotions. I'd dated many women who left me guessing as to what they were thinking or feeling. Crystal put it all out there. I couldn't imagine any other woman telling me she had an issue orgasming. In some ways it was as if Crystal didn't realize people wouldn't normally be so open. "Can you see yourself living on a farm?"

She took a moment to answer. "Honestly? Don't be offended, but no. I don't have to live in New York or Boston, but I need to know I can have a sandwich delivered at midnight if I'm hungry." She chuckled. "What I'm trying to say is that I like the convenience of a city, the energy as well. There's always something to do or see."

I told myself it didn't matter, but I asked anyway. "What do you think of Boston?"

"It's my favorite city. Right now my work keeps me in Maine, but my lab's been looking to expand to other cities, and that is one I would love to set up an office in. There's just something so charming about all the college areas and cafés. People sit outside for hours taking themselves very seriously while drinking high-octane espressos. It reminds me of Europe."

"So you've traveled outside the US?"

"Some. After my parents died, my uncle would often fly me out to wherever he was. It was his way of checking in on me." Her eyes darkened. "I don't know what I would have done if he hadn't come into my life."

"I'm sorry to hear about your parents." Her pain was a sucker punch to my gut. Either she was the most manipulative and gifted liar I'd ever met, or I was making a huge mistake. "Were you very young?"

"I was in college. Old enough to survive without them, but I don't think anyone is ever prepared to handle that kind of loss. It was a rough time." She met my gaze briefly.

"I can only imagine. My father has always been my rock."

"And your mother?"

"Not so much."

Her mouth rounded. "Oh, I just assumed you were close to both of them. Is that why they're not at the farm with you?"

The farm. Fuck. It was too easy to forget to lie to her.

Just like it was too easy to imagine spending the night showing her just how good sex could be with the right man. But that was another problem: I wasn't the right man.

Nothing about what we were doing was right, and I wasn't used to feeling that way about anything I did. I wouldn't consider myself eligible for sainthood, but the list of things I'd done in my life that I regretted was short. I was beginning to regret thinking I could step into Scott's life without repercussions.

It was the type of mistake my father would attribute to overconfidence with a dash of not understanding when something wasn't my business. I could almost hear the lecture he'd give me if he knew what I was up to.

And Crystal? He'd tell me to call it off before it went too far.

And he'd be right to.

"Crystal, stop at the nearest gas station or strip mall. I'll call for a ride. You should head back to Maine, and I need to get home."

She was hurt. I could see it in her eyes, but there was nothing I could do. Telling her anything would only lead to trouble. What would I do afterward? Ask her to not tell her uncle? Being honest would completely negate any advantage I had as far as negotiating for Scott. Or worse, the battle for Scott's farm could become personal.

Steadman would think Scott and I had played his niece. I didn't even have a niece, and I knew I wouldn't handle that situation well.

It was better to leave her guessing.

CHAPTER EIGHT

CRYSTAL

Leave it to me to screw up what otherwise might have been a wonderful day. I can't even do a casual hookup right.

"Sure," I said in a tight voice as I racked my brain for what I'd said that might have changed his mind. "Do you mind telling me what changed? Was it something I said?"

He looked out the window rather than at me. "You did nothing wrong."

"It was the orgasm thing, wasn't it? I made too big a deal of it."

His head snapped around. "What? No. God, no. It is a big deal."

I couldn't figure out how things had gone from hot to over so quickly. If he had had an orgasm, his reaction would have made sense. Some men lost interest afterward. But this was the reverse.

I went over our conversation in my head and groaned. It had to have been the mention of my parents' death. *He was trying to be all sexy and fun, and I started talking about sad topics that could kill any man's mood. And if that isn't bad enough? I moved on to question him about his parents.*

Because nothing says Take me now *more than grilling someone about his relationship with his mother.*

"I don't know what I said, but the running joke at my lab is that I don't get out enough and that I'm becoming socially awkward. They might be right. Sorry."

"Don't apologize." He rubbed his hands over his face. "You did nothing wrong. If it makes you feel better, I'm leaving because you did too much right."

"I don't understand." I pulled into a lot in front of a line of small shops, parked, and turned off the car. When he didn't get out, we sat there for several minutes without speaking. I'd never been particularly good with men, but I had no idea what to think of this one.

His earlier kisses had felt like a decadent promise, one that his talented fingers had started to make good on. He'd asked me to pull over, seemed to want the date to end, but wasn't getting out of my car. There might have been a better response, but me? I simply waited.

He released his seat belt and turned toward me. "I like you."

"Oookay."

"I realize you can't understand why that is a game changer, but it is. If I could be up front with you, you'd agree with me."

"Maybe, unless I thought you were wrong."

"I'm right." He frowned. "And wrong. It's complicated, but trust me, ending things now is what you'd want if you knew the whole story."

My mind raced. "You have something you're worried I'd catch."

"No." In a firmer tone, he said, "I'm careful."

"You're worried *I* have something."

"Do you?"

"No, I'm careful too." I brought a hand to my heart. "Are you . . . sick? Terminal?"

"It's nothing like that." He sighed. "I don't want to leave with you feeling bad about any part of this. As far as I can tell, you're a very nice person. I didn't want you to be, but you are, and it changes things. Sometimes things don't work out. That's how you should look at this."

"If you're a mass murderer or something, I want to make it clear that I didn't see any evidence of it."

He smiled. "I'm not, but that's good to know." He should have left then. One of his hands went to the door handle even while he held my gaze. "Why is it so hard to walk away from you?"

I searched his face. "Why do you have to?"

"It's already too late." He let go of the car door handle and raised that hand to caress the line of my jaw. "I don't see how this can play out without you ending up hating me."

I shouldn't have let him kiss me then, but in my defense, there wasn't an inch of me that wasn't craving him. His lips were gentle at first, then more demanding. I gave myself over to the pleasure of his touch. He cupped my face, plundered my mouth, made my body sing for his with nothing more than his lips and tongue. When he raised his head, I was shaking with desire for him. His eyes were dark with a hunger I welcomed.

He won't leave. Not now.

He swooped in for another kiss that he ended just as I was melting into it. I was still catching my breath when he opened the car door and said, "I wish we'd met under other circumstances."

He didn't wait for my response, just got out and closed the door with a finality that stung. Confused, angry, not sure what to do, I started up the car again and drove away. I didn't even check if I was going in the right direction. All I knew was that I needed to put distance between myself and the man who had made me feel better and worse than any man ever had.

I didn't like what it said about me that I didn't want to leave. Whatever his problem with me was, mine was worse. I'd just met a man I would have put my pride aside to have. I'd heard of them. Every woman meets one at least once in her life. If she's lucky, he either marries her or moves on before she has a chance to make a complete fool of herself.

He'd done me a favor by leaving the way he had.

I looked down at my cutoff shorts. I wanted to hate them, but I didn't. They weren't my usual choice of attire, but Ellie was right . . .

choosing something that made me feel beautiful had felt freeing. So had the orgasm.

I didn't want to feel bad about the time I'd spent with Scott. Sure, it had been confusing as all hell, but it had also been wonderful.

And thought provoking. No more Mr. Nice-But-Borings for me. The next man I chose to be with would have to make me feel what Scott had, or I wouldn't bother.

I called Ellie to tell her I was on my way back. She didn't ask how things had gone with Scott. She probably heard everything she needed to in my tone. I was coming home disappointed and more than a little sad.

In the lab I was known for being a tenacious problem solver. In chemistry things made sense, and when they didn't, there was usually an element of human error. How molecules interacted with each other was predictable. They followed rules.

People? Not so much.

Perhaps that was why I spent so much time at the lab. Little that was unexpected happened there. It was safe.

So were the men I'd chosen before Scott.

For the next couple of hours, I tried to convince myself that driving away was the only choice I'd had. Was it, though? I pulled the car over onto a side street. *I could have pushed harder for the truth from Scott.*

Or told him that it didn't matter.

I don't want to return to dating men I don't miss when they leave.

What would have happened if I hadn't given up so easily?

What if I never met anyone else who made me feel the way Scott did?

I'd survived losing both of my parents; if Scott told me tomorrow that he didn't want to be with me . . . I'd survive that too. Surely what we felt for each other was worth one more shot?

I circled back and drove by the parking lot I'd left him in. It was a long shot that he might still be there, considering how much time had passed. Possibly this was more about delaying taking a more daring step.

My uncle often spoke about the importance of knowing what you wanted and having the courage to go after it. I shouldn't have let Scott leave without finding out why he wanted to.

Didn't I owe myself at least that?

For all I knew, Scott felt bad about being with me because he knew he would turn my uncle's offer down. He might have thought it would make things difficult for me if he did.

He could be wishing we'd found a way to be together. There'd been too much emotion in his final kiss for him not to feel as gutted as I did.

I should have told him nothing mattered more to me than being with him.

I still could.

I could go to his farm and tell him that whatever he thinks is standing between us being together . . . it's not insurmountable.

The idea was so absolutely out of character and impulsive it felt insane in the most wonderful way. I'd never done anything even remotely close to it but decided that was why I had to.

I couldn't let it end this way, for me more than for him. He might tell me he didn't feel the same, but I'd know I had the courage to go after what I wanted.

CHAPTER NINE

JESSE

Rather than heading back to the farm, I called Thane and asked him to meet me for lunch in a suburb of Boston. The drive there gave me time to think, but in circles—nowhere productive. He asked if I wanted Scott to join. I said, "No." I needed to talk things out with the brother I knew well before addressing my concerns with the one I didn't. I could be honest with Thane and trusted him to give me solid advice. Scott? The more time I spent as him, the less I understood him.

I arrived at the diner before Thane and ordered a beer. He joined me halfway through the drink.

"That bad?" He nodded toward the bottle.

"Things could be better." I took another swig. "Thanks for meeting me."

"Anytime." He looked around. "Interesting choice." Most of the tables were empty despite it being lunchtime.

"I didn't want to run into anyone we know."

He picked up a paper napkin that had a visible smudge from someone's fingerprint on it. "Then this place is ideal."

I rolled my eyes. "You'll survive."

Thane placed the napkin to the side and ordered a coffee from the waitress. She gave us each a menu, then disappeared again. "You obviously have something weighing on your mind. Just to be clear, though, if you brought me here to tell me you need another day at the farm . . .

a meal from this place, no matter how much it costs, will not count as settling the bet."

"Don't be a snob. They say some of the best food can be found at diners."

"First, who are 'they'? And second, is the secret ingredient the unwashed silverware?" He held up a fork that still had egg stuck between the tines.

"Don't eat then. I need to talk to you about something."

Thane placed the dirty fork on the soiled napkin and pushed both to the edge of the table. "Speak."

"Things are getting complicated at the farm."

"I'm already aware of that." He sat back and nodded. We might not have been blood related, but I couldn't imagine having a closer bond to a brother. Thane had always backed me 100 percent, and there was nothing I wouldn't do for him.

"They've gotten worse. Scott is hiding something, and I'm concerned that it might be illegal."

Thane sat up straighter. "Illegal?"

"Drugs, maybe. I'm not sure. He's family. If it is something dangerous, I want to help him extricate himself from it, but depending on what he's mixed up in, things could get ugly. I don't want anything I do to jeopardize what you and I have built together."

He rubbed a hand over his chin. "I'd tell you not to get involved, but hell, even I would want to help now that I know him. What evidence do you have that he's hiding something?"

"When I told LJ that Crystal is a chemist, he said that wasn't good. He also told me to keep her out of the house. I've been racking my brain for what Scott could be into that LJ would know about and Steadman would send a chemist to investigate." I thought about Crystal and how her innocence didn't appear to be an act. "Or what LJ is worried a chemist would uncover. I don't believe that Crystal was asked to do more than deliver the proposal."

"You didn't sleep with her, did you?"

My face warmed as the memory of her orgasm in the car returned, but I shook my head. "No."

"Good, because this is already more complicated than I'm comfortable with. I asked Scott about Jarcisco. He said they became good friends right after the billionaire moved into his neighborhood. Scott said Jarcisco offered business advice in the beginning, but all Scott wanted help with was the barn chores."

"LJ told me the same. I don't believe it."

"I don't either. A tech mogul doesn't do much there isn't profit in."

"They could be laundering money. Or printing it."

"That seems more likely than drugs, but what is Steadman's interest? No way that's a coincidence."

"I'd ask Scott outright, but he would have already told us if he wanted us to know. This is likely going to require cornering and confronting. I feel like we need more information before we take that step, though. Remember that time I borrowed Dad's car and ripped off the back fender on a stone wall? I don't know if I would have ever told even you, but you came to me with a plan for how to get it fixed before he returned from his business trip. That's how I'd prefer this to go down."

"And if his hands are *really* dirty? If he's not the person either of us thinks he is?"

"I don't know, but I don't want to face that possibility yet. I'm hoping it's not as bad as the things we've considered so far. I just wanted to give you a heads-up. I've searched most of his home and found nothing, but if I do uncover something, things could take a downward turn fast."

"There's a chance he's not hiding anything."

"Do you believe that?" I didn't.

"No. Unfortunately, I don't. None of this makes sense unless there is something else going on."

"He keeps his basement locked. My gut tells me that's where he's keeping whatever it is he doesn't want us to know about."

"I'm glad you're the one with the twin, because you just completely creeped me out." He shuddered. "If there are bones down there, don't tell me." He raised one hand. "No, scratch that, do tell me, but I'd never babysit him for you again."

"Thanks, let's hope it doesn't come to that."

The waitress returned with his coffee and asked if we knew what we wanted. I ordered burgers and fries for both of us. After she was out of earshot, Thane said, "I can't remember the last time I had a hamburger."

"You need to expand your experiences," I joked.

He cocked an eyebrow. "Really? How is that laundry situation coming?"

Okay, so he and I had more in common than I cared to admit. I had planned to buy more clothing on the way back to the farm. "Completely under control."

"Mm-hmm." His expression turned more serious. "What were your initial thoughts on the proposal?"

I made a pained face. "I haven't looked at it yet."

He tilted his head to the side. "Did you bring it with you?"

"No."

"Because?"

Oh, what the hell. "Because initially I felt it was more important to spend time with Crystal."

"Crystal, the oil rep?"

"Yes."

"Oh boy."

I lowered my voice as I reluctantly admitted, "I like her. I've tried not to, but there's something about her. I know being with her would be a mistake, but one worth making."

"They never are."

"When I first met her, I thought she knew more than she was let-ting on, but now I'm convinced that her only role in all of this was to deliver paperwork to Scott."

"You realize Steadman could have hired a courier or had any of his employees bring it to you."

"That has all crossed my mind."

"But?"

"Even if he had motive behind involving her, if she doesn't know about it, she's innocent."

"That's a stretch."

"I know, but I don't believe she's capable of subterfuge."

"I hope you're right."

I took a swig of my beer. "It doesn't matter if I'm not. She's headed back to Maine. I doubt I'll ever see her again."

"Which is for the best."

"I wanted to spend time with her, but she thinks I'm Scott. I thought it might not matter, but then she was just so fucking nice. I had to end things before they went too far."

"They might have already. A little." He pinched an inch of air. "But you made the right choice."

"I couldn't tell her who I was."

"No, you couldn't."

"I don't want to continue lying to her. She thinks I'm this wonderful farmer who rescues injured animals. Me."

"You don't even like goldfish."

"That's not true." I frowned. "I like animals. I just didn't like the goldfish you kept in the bathroom window because it froze while we were on vacation and you went into some kind of crazy denial over its death. You thought it would start swimming again if we warmed the water, so you made me try to revive it on the stove. Dad came in and yelled at me for cooking your pet, and I got in trouble because he didn't want to hear our explanation. Does any of this ring a bell?"

Thane folded his arms across his chest. "I was six."

Those memories held no power to upset me, but I did enjoy giving my brother crap about them. "I was *five*, but I remember it clearly. You know why? Because getting grounded for boiling your brother's pet scars a child."

"I'll pay for therapy if you're still that upset about it." He shook his head. "Don't tell me you're planning on adopting one of Scott's animals."

"Of course not." While on the subject . . . "But I do want to get his duck a new prosthetic leg. Alphonse is a hoot. If I stay another day, I'm also going to have the vet out to see if Molly has a skin condition that requires attention."

"Molly?"

"Scott's miniature cow. She has anxiety issues. While I'm there, I may work with her on that as well."

Thane drummed his fingers on the table. "You came to me for advice, correct?"

"Correct."

"I think it's time for you and Scott to switch back. I understand that you want to help him, but you can do that as his brother. Being on that farm is messing with your head."

He was right, but that didn't mean I was ready to go back yet. "I need one more day."

"You've really lost it."

"What?"

"Our bet. Your mind. Seriously, why do you need more time? To uncover Scott's secret? The more I think about it, the less sure I am you should dig into his life. Best case? He's hiding nothing. Worst case? You're implicated in whatever he's doing. I don't want to visit both of you in prison."

The waitress interrupted with plates of burgers and fries. She looked down at the table, grabbed Thane's napkin and fork. "Oh my gosh, I must have seated you at a table that hadn't been cleaned. Hang on, let me get you fresh silverware."

She was back in a flash with another apology. "Not a problem," Thane assured her.

The grateful smile she shot him had just earned her a generous tip. Thane had high standards but was also quick to understand and move on. Both of us valued corrective action over excuses. We'd learned that from our father, who never had patience for those who brought problems to him without a plan to resolve them.

I said, "I can't leave without knowing if he needs our help."

Thane rubbed fingers over both of his temples. "I knew you'd say that."

"Want to hear something crazy?"

"I'm sure I don't."

"I feel really bad about how things went with Crystal. I believed she was someone with a hidden agenda, and I treated her accordingly. She didn't deserve that. I'm not used to feeling guilty about anything, but I do about how I handled the situation."

"Well, at least it's over."

I finished the last of my beer. "Yeah."

CHAPTER TEN

CRYSTAL

When I pulled into Scott's driveway, I saw his truck. It didn't mean he was there, but he'd had enough time to get home.

I parked and took out my phone. This was the single most impulsive thing I'd ever done. It was exciting as well as nerve racking.

There was a real possibility he might come out and ask me to leave. But what if he didn't?

What if going after what I wanted was something I should have done a long time ago? I sat in my car thinking that simply being there could be a turning point in my life. It was time to stop beating myself for wanting more.

Going to Scott's house was something I was doing for myself more than for him. Like with my outfit, I was choosing to value what I wanted over trying to please everyone else.

Even if he sent me home—this act of courage would be a win. I considered calling him to tell him I was there but decided it might be sexier to just appear at the door of the barn.

I practiced smiling seductively into my rearview mirror. My first attempt was too big, too toothy. My second—too forced. "Hi, Scott," I said until it sounded natural with a hint of *Please invite me inside.*

I made my way to the entrance of the barn, taking deep, calming breaths the whole way. Scott wouldn't have kissed me the way he had if he weren't interested. All I had to do was figure out what he thought was preventing us from being together. I was good at solving puzzles.

The animals were all still out in their paddocks. I leaned into the barn and called Scott's name. Nothing.

I turned and walked toward the house, then stopped at the bottom of his porch steps. A voice in my head whispered, *If he'd wanted you here, he would have asked you to be.*

I frowned. *If he didn't want me here, he should have kept his damn fingers out of my shorts. Talk about mixed messages. All I want is clarity.*

And to finish what we started—if that's what he wants.

I was halfway up the steps when a male voice called out, "What are you doing here?"

I spun around, nearly falling as I did, but steadying myself with the railing at the last moment. For just a second I thought it might be Scott, but it wasn't. "LJ?" I clutched the railing. "I'm looking for Scott."

"He's not here." He stepped closer. "So you definitely shouldn't be."

The aggression in his voice took me by surprise. "Do you know where he is?"

"I do not." He brushed past me, right up the stairs, and sat on the top one like a guard dog assuming a defensive position. "Did Scott ask you to meet him?"

"No." I backed down the steps and took out my phone. Whatever friendliness had been in him before was gone. Did he think I'd come back to rob the place? "I was hoping he'd be here."

"I saw the two of you leave together. Shouldn't *you* know where he is?"

I swallowed hard. "We had a little misunderstanding."

LJ's eyes narrowed. "I'll tell him you dropped by to see him. If he wants to contact you, he will." He leaned forward onto his elbows with his hands between his knees. "They may not be obvious to the naked eye, but this farm has surveillance cameras all over it. I knew the moment you came up the driveway."

"That's . . . uh . . . good to know. Safety is important."

"It is. A little security goes a long way when it comes to deterring people from doing anything they shouldn't."

I put my hands up between us. "I'm just looking for Scott."

"Sure."

I took a few steps backward. "But since he's not here, I'll head out."

"Good idea."

I walked to my car and paused to look back at LJ. Was his reaction due to my uncle's interest in the farm? He was acting like he'd caught a thief on the premises. Why? I remembered something Scott had said: *"Why would a man like Steadman send his niece into a situation that has the potential of turning ugly?"*

I loved my uncle, but there was definitely more going on at the farm than he'd told me about. I didn't like the idea that Scott might be involved in something shady or dangerous. Or that my uncle might be. I prayed it was a case of my imagination going into overdrive, but that wasn't the norm for me.

I was drawn to the tangible. If I could see it, touch it, test it . . . I believed it. If I couldn't, well, then I put it in a box with all the other questions I had no hope of answering and stuffed it away.

LJ waved to me, more to remind me that he was still watching me than as a farewell. The hair on the back of my neck stood up as I opened the door to my car. I should have stuck to Scott's plan, where we parted ways in one clean break. Sure, I would have walked away with questions, but going to his farm had tarnished what had otherwise been a romantic memory for me.

He'd been my broody, oh-so-sexy fantasy. Romanticized. More fictional than real, but definitely sigh worthy.

Our time together had been . . . orgasmic, at least for me.

I should have left things there.

A car pulled up behind mine. I froze, then turned in time to see Scott exit from the rear passenger door of a black sedan. My breath caught in my throat.

He looked from me to LJ on the steps and back to me. If I had the power of invisibility, I would have faded away right then. My hand tightened on the door as he approached.

In my fantasy of how this moment would go, his face had filled with joy at the sight of me. He swung me up into his arms and kissed me, murmuring an apology as he did.

That didn't happen. He strode toward me with an expression I couldn't decipher, but it definitely wasn't joy. "Crystal, what are you doing here?"

"Wishing I'd been a little less impulsive."

He stopped within inches of me. His presence alone was as exciting as an intimate caress. "I can't believe you came back."

Hope lit within me. "Me neither."

He ran his hand gently through my hair, then let it drop. "I shouldn't have left our date the way I did. I should have made sure you made it home safely."

I glanced at LJ, and a shiver rocked through me. "I can take care of myself."

He sighed. "I'm not handling this situation well."

What does that mean? Which part is he regretting? The orgasm or leaving? "I don't understand, but I want to. You said it was already too late—for what? Why do you think I'll end up hating you?" I shot a quick look at LJ again. I didn't consider myself paranoid by nature, but he was watching us like someone poised to take action.

But what action?

Scott followed the direction of my gaze and motioned for LJ to leave. LJ stood, dusted off his jeans, and headed into the house. For a moment Scott appeared to want to follow him; then his attention returned to me. There was desire in his eyes, but also sadness. "If this were just about me . . . but it isn't."

I had to ask. "Are you and LJ *partners?*" It would explain a lot.

A small smile curled his lips. "No. It's not that simple."

That would have been simple? Okay. Maybe I don't want to know what's going on. I told myself to walk away then. I couldn't. Had I been tasked to explain it in a thesis paper, I couldn't have. It defied logic. He drew me in, had my body humming with nothing more than a look, and I didn't want our time together to end. "I should go."

He pressed his lips together, then said, "You should." There was a hunger in him, though, that kept me right where I was.

No man had ever made me feel as desirable as I did then. The woman reflected in his eyes was young, sexy, and bold . . . me. Not the one I had been for too long but the one I wanted to be. I leaned closer. "Do you want me to?"

In a voice just above a whisper, he said, "No."

I'd been living carefully for so long I hadn't realized how small my life had become. I remembered a younger me, a more hopeful one, who had believed in happy endings and love. Scott might not have been my forever man, but he was reviving a side of me I hadn't realized had died along with my parents.

Temporary can be good.

I needed some good in my life.

I ran my tongue over my bottom lip. "Then ask me to stay."

His hands gripped my upper arms. The fire in his eyes fanned the one in me. "I can't."

Disappointment with a dash of embarrassment flooded in. Was I completely misreading the situation? I moved to take a step back, but he held me where I was.

"I'm sorry," he growled.

I yanked myself free. "No need to be. You didn't do this; I did. Sorry, I don't know what I was thinking. I don't usually follow men home." Head held high, I slid into the driver's seat of my car and closed the door before he had a chance to say more. Without lowering the window, I started the car and threw it in reverse. I needed to get away from him before I made more of a fool of myself.

I didn't look back as I drove away. I blinked away tears and told myself his response didn't matter as much as what I'd learned about myself today.

I'm capable of feeling more than I've let myself.

This hurts, but it's better than to be satisfied with feeling nothing.

CHAPTER ELEVEN

JESSE

For the second day in a row Crystal left me standing in the driveway battling a tsunami of emotion. The slam of the front door of Scott's house announced LJ's approach.

"She's gone," LJ said from beside me. "Good."

"She's gone." There was nothing good about it.

"I'm glad I was home when she arrived. Scott's security system alerted me."

I turned and frowned down at him. "Why does his system alert *you*?"

"With the way things have been lately, we thought it was a good idea."

"The way things have been? What does that mean?"

LJ rocked back on his heels. "People poking around. Someone broke into his house earlier this year."

"He didn't mention that to me."

With a shrug, LJ said, "He thought it might be some local kids looking for money. I encouraged him to put up surveillance cameras in case they came back. Since I'm the one who watches the animals when he goes anywhere, it made sense for me to receive alerts as well."

"But not me?"

"You weren't supposed to be here that long."

I didn't like that LJ knew more about my brother's farm than I did or how comfortable he was in his home. "What did you do while you were inside?"

LJ gave me a long look. "Your brother is the most trusting soul I've ever met. That's not a trait you share, I see."

"It is not."

"Scott asked me to pick up something for him."

"And did you?" I tensed.

"Yes."

"Give it to me, and I'll give it to him."

"No."

"I wasn't asking."

LJ stood his ground. "Not happening."

I stepped closer and lowered my voice. "When it comes to protecting my family, there isn't a line I wouldn't cross. Now, whatever it is, it'd be better if you gave it to me rather than making me take it from you."

LJ reached into his pocket. I readied myself for any possibility, standing close enough to knock a weapon out of his hand if necessary. He pulled out a phone and had it dialing Scott as he held it up. Scott answered almost immediately. "LJ, everything okay?"

"Not exactly. Your brother is all worked up. I'm hoping you can talk some sense into him." He put him on speakerphone.

"Jesse?" Scott called my name.

Perfect opportunity to check LJ's story. "Did you ask LJ to get something for you from your house?"

"Yes." Scott's tone was cautious. "He texted me when he saw the oil rep at the farm without you."

"What did you ask him to retrieve—your key to the basement?" It was just a guess, but one that made sense.

"Why would you—you haven't been down there, have you?"

"No." I watched LJ's expression, but it was carefully blank. "What are you hiding, Scott?"

LJ interjected, "This is getting messy, Scott. I told you it might. You need to come back."

For a long moment none of us spoke. Eventually, Scott said, "Show him the basement, LJ."

Not looking like he approved at all of Scott's suggestion, LJ turned partially away with the phone in hand. "I don't think that's smart. The fewer people who know, the better."

"What the hell are you into, Scott?" I demanded.

Rather than answering me, Scott addressed LJ. "Jesse is my twin brother. He's not just someone who walked in off the street. I trusted you, LJ, and have never regretted it. Give him the key and a tour."

LJ dug into another of his pockets and produced a key that he held out in my direction. "Only if he apologizes to me."

My mouth dropped open. "Seriously?"

He tipped the key back toward himself. "I've been nothing but nice to you. You practically threatened to off me. I believe that warrants an apology."

I held my hand out. "Give me the fucking key."

He placed it in my palm. "You get more bees with honey—"

"I don't want a bee; I want answers. Scott, this isn't how I was hoping we'd have this conversation, but if you're doing something illegal, it ends today. And before you tell me you can't leave it behind, there is always a way out. You're not alone."

With wonder in his voice, Scott said, "LJ, do you see what I mean? He's in my corner, just like you always have been."

LJ nodded. "Okay, let's do this. Come on, Jesse. Prepare to have your mind blown."

CHAPTER TWELVE

CRYSTAL

My drive home seemed longer because I'd doubled back to Scott's farm. It gave me time to clear my head, though. I came to some decisions and made a few vows to myself.

One, I would not allow myself to feel bad about taking a chance on Scott. I'd gone into it telling myself that the outcome would be unrelated to considering the action worthwhile. So much of what I did in the lab was trial and error, based on the best information I had. There were times when chemical combinations should have resulted in a pleasing taste but didn't. I didn't beat myself up over those attempts. My drive back to Scott's could have ended with me engaging in the best sex of my life. It hadn't, but that happened sometimes.

Two, I would not allow myself to continue to choose partners based on intellectual prowess. I wasn't quite sure how or why my taste had become men I wasn't attracted to sexually. There was significant evidence to suggest that I had played a role in maintaining a bland sex life. After spending time with Scott and feeling lust for the first time, I had sympathy for the men I'd dated. I'd chosen men I wanted to be attracted to. I'd thought passion would follow action. I was wrong.

Three, I wanted to feel more. Scott confused me, turned me on, angered me. Even though I was driving home alone, I felt younger, sexier, more alive, than I had in a long time. Looking back, it was simple to pinpoint the cause of my withdrawal into myself. Losing my parents

had shaken me to the core. I was proud of how I'd picked myself back up and gone on, but part of me had gone dormant.

From fear? I didn't know. I'd never been particularly good at self-analysis. Like my uncle, I tended to be action oriented. During the worst time of my life, I plowed through my degrees. I still worked longer hours during the holidays to keep myself occupied. Outside of having a career I was proud of, I didn't allow myself much. That was about to change.

I needed a hobby or a passion. Scott's duck came to mind. I still wanted to help him get a new prosthetic leg. Scott might not have been interested in me romantically, but my guess was that he wouldn't turn down something that would bring his duck comfort. It might be easy enough to create a prototype and send Scott the specs so he could print the proper size for Alphonse, but to do it right, I knew it would be better to find someone who knew more about prosthetics than I did.

Unless Scott no longer had access to a 3D printer. In that case it might be easier to simply give him the leg in different sizes.

I thought back to how defensive LJ had seemed about me going near Scott's house. *Mail. I'll definitely mail the prototypes. No more surprise visits for me.*

Four, I would not waste time wildly guessing about things. Scott had a secret he felt I couldn't accept. That didn't mean he was a criminal. It could be almost anything. When I took into account the reason for my visit to his farm, his reluctance to trust me still made sense. Had our roles been reversed, I might have questioned his motives as well.

Scott's secret might have been as simple as not wanting to have sex with someone he didn't trust. All things considered, that was a reasonable position to take. He was attracted to me; that much was no longer in doubt. His refusal to act upon it might have revealed an abundance of integrity rather than a lack of it.

There was no way to know his motivation without further information. Since the likelihood of seeing him again was slim, it didn't really matter what had changed his mind about being with me. All I had control over was my response to that disappointment—and more importantly, I had a choice about if disappointment needed to be part of the equation at all.

Meeting Scott could be the best or worst thing to happen to me, depending on how I interpreted the experience. *I may look back at Scott as the much-needed catalyst that jump-started a new and better phase of my life.*

Ellie was still at work when I got home. I took that as a gift from the universe. Yes, I had chosen to view my time in Rhode Island through the lens of optimism, but I wasn't sure if that positive attitude would survive questioning.

I stepped out of my shoes, placed my bags in my bedroom, and headed to the kitchen. I poured myself a tall glass of water and looked out over the counter at our apartment with fresh eyes. There were photos on the walls, but they were all of Ellie's friends and family. It was in that moment that I realized I had been dealing with the loss of my parents by not dealing with it. No photos. No treasured heirlooms. Everything I'd kept from them was still in storage.

I thought about my workspace at the lab. There was nothing personal in that space either. How had I not seen how I'd shut a whole part of myself down? I enjoyed my job and the friends I'd made through work, but what did I have outside of the lab?

Nothing.

If I moved out, the living room in the apartment I shared with Ellie would look exactly the same. Why? What had stopped me from making any part of it mine?

My phone buzzed with a text from my uncle. For a second I considered not answering, but he deserved better than that. I forced a smile and called him via video chat. "Hi. I was going to call you once I settled in. I just got home."

He didn't say anything at first, which meant he was assessing my mood. My uncle didn't make many moves without fully researching them. "I was beginning to worry."

I walked to the living room and sat on the couch, holding my phone up in front of my face as I went. "I'm sorry. That wasn't my intention."

"How did everything go?"

"Good." I made a face. I'd never lied to my uncle, never needed to. "Complicated. Eye opening. Possibly life changing."

He arched an eyebrow and cocked his head to the side. "Sounds like you did more than deliver the proposal."

"Yes and no." Heat rushed to my face. "But don't worry; he has the paperwork and said he'd read it over."

"Put business to the side for a moment and tell me about this 'yes and no.'"

I struggled to articulate the jumble of emotions I was still sorting through. Did any of it matter anyway? "I had no idea how attractive I could find a farmer, but sadly he didn't feel the same."

"Did he realize that before or after you spent a night down there?" His tone was protective, that of a man ready to go to battle for my virtue. It reminded me of how my father sounded when my prom date's car had broken down and I missed curfew. There was something comforting in both the memory and the knowledge that my uncle cared enough to want to keep me safe, despite my age.

"Before. Nothing happened, but I came to the realization that I might have been dating the wrong kind of men. I was all giddy and awkward around him." I sighed. "It was nice."

"How do you know he wasn't interested?"

I cleared my throat. "He essentially asked me to leave." That raised both of his eyebrows. I rushed to assure him, "Not in a rude way."

"Did you tell him you're a flavorist?"

"I believe I did. Also, that I have a PhD in chemistry." I groaned. "I hope he didn't think I was bragging about that. I said it because when people hear that I'm a flavorist, they imagine I'm a glorified food taster."

"It's not bragging to be proud of your achievements. What did he say when you told him?"

"He asked me where I went to school—said he likes to know who he's dealing with."

"Did he give you a tour of his farm?"

"Of his barn. He has all these rescue animals there. Alphonse is a duck who lost a leg to a fishing line. Molly is a miniature cow with anxiety issues. She only eats when he's there or her nearly blind companion donkey is with her. He also has chickens. Six, I think. Maybe seven. I don't remember all their names."

"No need to try. Did you see the rest of his farm?"

I shook my head. "Pretty much just the barn, but it was amazing. He has a female pig that weighs a thousand pounds. Someone imported her from China. Her name is Bella. Her owner thought she could be an inside pet, but she kept growing. She is as big as a polar bear but so sweet. I may never eat bacon again after meeting her."

"He's a vegetarian?"

I chewed my bottom lip before saying, "You know, I didn't ask. My guess would be that he is, but he didn't say anything."

"Outside of his rescue, did he talk much about his farm?"

I hesitated. My uncle wasn't normally so inquisitive. It made sense, I supposed, that he would be. He was looking to lease Scott's land. Of course he would want to know anything I might have come across that would help him with negotiations. What surprised me was how uncomfortable I felt answering. Scott was no one to me. My uncle was all the family I had. My loyalty was to him. I gave myself a mental shake and answered, "Not much. I do think there might be more going on at that farm than he was letting on."

"Oh, really? What gave you that impression?"

"Not much more than a gut feeling, but they seemed very concerned about me going into his house."

"They?"

"Scott and his volunteer, LJ. He helps out with the barn chores."

"So you didn't go in the house at all?"

"Never even made it to the top of the steps." While I was on the topic of what was weird . . . "He also has surveillance cameras all over his property. Seemed like a lot of security for a bean farm."

"Security systems are becoming more common. You never know when you might have a break-in." After a pause, he said, "If he calls you, I think you should give him another chance."

Never, not once, during our many talks had my uncle ever commented about the men I'd dated. "I don't see that happening."

"He'll call."

"Even if he did, we have nothing in common."

"No one knows that at first. You're careful, but don't be so careful you hold yourself back." His advice sounded so much like my own lecture to myself that I wasn't sure how to respond at first. "If he doesn't contact you, find a reason to reach out to him."

I gave him a long look. "Was there something you were hoping I'd find out while I was there?"

His eyes narrowed. "If I wasn't certain about a person or a situation, do you honestly believe I'd send you in?"

"No." He'd never done anything like that, and I couldn't imagine him not taking a more direct approach.

"Good. All I'm saying is that if meeting him was indeed 'complicated, eye opening, possibly life changing,' you might want to give him a second chance. Someone like that comes into your life once . . . twice if you're lucky. Find a reason to see him again."

I lifted and lowered a shoulder. "I was hoping to find someone who could design a new prosthetic leg for his duck."

"Need help?"

"No, I already have some ideas."

He nodded. "Call me after you see him again."

I smiled. "That probably won't happen."

"Just keep me informed."

I promised I would, then ended the call. Had telling my uncle about Scott been the right choice? I didn't owe Scott anything. Outside of the ridiculous idea of helping his duck, I had no reason to see him again.

I already felt foolish enough about how I'd gone back to his farm after he'd ended our date. I blushed as I remembered where his hand had wandered. My confusion was warranted, but I definitely wasn't going to call him. No, the next move would be up to him.

Finding someone to make a new leg for Alphonse didn't negate that. I didn't have to speak to Scott to find out if having someone make a prosthetic leg was even possible.

CHAPTER THIRTEEN

JESSE

With LJ a step behind me, I walked to the door of Scott's basement. Although I inserted the key in the lock, I didn't immediately turn it. Knowledge was power, but ignorance could also be bliss. Once I knew what Scott was hiding, there might be some immediate and difficult decisions that needed to be made.

Nothing about Scott's personality hinted at a life of crime. He was close with his adoptive parents. He had friends. If he was running some kind of drug ring out of his basement, I couldn't imagine why he would have agreed to switch places with me.

Unless he was a thief and was using the opportunity to case my life for what he could fleece me for. *God, I hope not. No one wants an evil twin.*

I turned the key and swung the door open. LJ stepped forward. "I should go first."

I gave him a hard look.

He threw his hands upward. "Unless you know where the light switches are."

Who could argue with that? I waved for him to proceed.

He switched a light on, and we made our way down old wooden steps into a musty cement-walled room. There was nothing immediately impressive about it, although I had finally located Scott's washer and dryer.

LJ walked ahead of me and turned on another light. He went to a second door and motioned for me to open it. In my younger years I'd enjoyed watching horror movies. Everything about the damp, poorly lit basement lent itself to a scene from one. It made me regret that I'd never gotten a concealed carry license.

I unlocked the second door and waited for LJ to enter before me. The burst of light after he did caught me off guard. It took my eyes a moment to adjust. I stepped inside and looked around.

The room was large, taking up most of the footprint of the farm-house. The walls were finished and light gray. One wall had a desk and several enormous dry-erase boards. The rest of the room looked like an odd mixture of a chemistry lab and a restaurant kitchen. There were at least ten refrigerators, endless cabinets, and cooking stations with machines that looked like large microwaves as well as a few ovens.

It was some weird shit. I held my breath and opened one of the refrigerators. *Don't let there be bodies in there. Anything. But. Bodies.*

The shelves were full of plastic food containers that were labeled with dates and strings of numbers. "What is it?" I asked.

"Bean-based meats."

I turned to see if LJ was serious. "That's already a thing."

"Not like this. He's cultivating a new strain of beans. Scott is close to changing what the world eats."

I removed a food container that appeared to have a piece of cooked steak in it and opened it. It didn't smell like steak. Thankfully it also didn't smell like flesh. There was little to no smell to it at all. "My guess is it looks better than it tastes."

"You're right. So far it does."

There had to be something I was missing. I closed the container and replaced it in the fridge. "You said I should prepare to have my mind blown. So far you haven't shown me anything I couldn't find at a supermarket."

LJ walked over to a dry-erase board that was covered with chemical equations. "On the surface it does appear that way, but your brother is on the cusp of a major discovery. When I met him, he had bioengineered an extremely fast-growing bean plant and was creating recipes that used them rather than meat. What caught my attention was that the meat product he made with his beans doesn't degrade. Raw. Cooked. Chilled. Room temperature. Packaged or not. It remains edible and in its original state. We refrigerate because we're playing around with additives."

We. I didn't like how invested LJ sounded in my brother's project. I made a sound of disgust and said, "Sounds *healthy.*"

"It could be. Think of the bean product as a stabilizing filler. It can be made into any shape and, with the right equipment, can assume the texture of all types of meat. It is resistant to bacteria and fungi but breaks down into harmless smaller molecules that pass through the body without being absorbed into it. During the digestive process, the body's enzymes release whatever vitamins, carbohydrates, or proteins we've added. Postdigestion, it reverts to a biodegradable substance similar to normal mammal waste."

"What you're saying is that this is not your run-of-the-mill bean chicken nugget."

"There's no comparison. If he succeeds here, he will have created a food source that would benefit both first and third world countries. Imagine being able to design foods that address the nutritional needs of any population. It could bring additional nutrients and fats to the starving, slim down the obese, regulate sugar intake for those with diabetes, and be a game changer for those with food allergies. With my help, your brother designed a food printer. This is the future right here."

I walked over to one of the appliances I'd assumed was a microwave. It had numbers on a keyboard and a glass front.

LJ opened the door of it, placed a plate inside, and hit a few of the buttons. The machine lit up, and a nozzle began to move quickly back and forth, much like in a 3D printer. Right before my eyes, what appeared to be an uncooked chicken breast appeared.

"Holy shit," I said, leaning closer to watch.

"It looks raw, but you could technically eat it this way. However, browning it will give it a texture you'd associate with cooked meat." It took several minutes to complete, but once it did, LJ removed the plate and took it over to the stove. He poured oil into a pan, placed the "meat" on it, then lit a flame beneath it.

"It doesn't smell like chicken," I said.

He shook his head. "It doesn't taste like it much yet, either, but it will. That's the next stage of development. We'll tackle that after we figure out the burning issue."

"Burning issue?"

"You have to be very careful when applying heat to it. In its raw state, if it begins to burn, it burns too hot and too long."

Hot and long enough to be a fuel source? If so, that would explain Steadman's interest. So much of what hadn't made sense was beginning to. "Who knows about this?"

"Scott, me, and his friend Remy. Scott has known him since high school. They had a falling-out when I got involved, though, and he hasn't come around since." He made a pained face. "Unless he was the one who broke in. We never found out who did it. Nothing appeared to be taken, but that doesn't mean nothing was. Scott doesn't tell me everything."

"What is your endgame?" I frowned. "Do you and Scott have an agreement or a contract?"

He shook his head. "I've made more money than I'll ever need. I'm in this for the future of humanity."

I threw up a little in my mouth. "Try again, but this time with the truth."

He sighed. "I'm in my sixties. Age changes a person's priorities. I've already had my face plastered all over the media, gotten awards, been called a genius . . . but I want to do something that makes a real impact. This is my gift to future generations." He looked me over. "What have you done so far that matters? Not to your bank account but to the planet? When you're gone, will it matter that you were ever here?"

I rocked back onto my heels and opened my mouth to respond, then shut it with a snap. My company would be part of creating what would be one of the planet's first recreational space stations, but I wasn't vain enough to claim that project wouldn't happen without my involvement.

Did that mean I believed him? Not really, but it did open my mind to the possibility that he might mean what he was saying. I'd still talk to Scott about the importance of protecting his work.

I looked around the room again before answering LJ. "No one else knows about this outside of you and Remy?"

"And you." Smoke caught his attention. "Shit." He turned the burner off and moved the pan to the other side of the stove. "It's fine. Close call."

"When you said it burns hotter and longer than it should, how hot are you talking about?"

"Let's just say Scott and I keep this out as a reminder to be careful with it." He held up a stainless steel plate that something had melted the center of.

I let out a whistle. "That's hot, all right."

"I've always told Scott if we can't get the flavors right, he could sell it as an alternative fuel source."

Yes. "I don't know much about beans, but I've never heard that they burn hotter than any other organic matter."

"Scott's plants are special, but there's also something about the soil on his farm. We tried to grow a few plants on my property, and the result wasn't the same. We've tested the soil but haven't found anything unusual. It might be the fertilizer his parents used to use or something we haven't thought to test for yet. That's another hurdle to make it over before we can attempt to mass-produce it."

Things were clicking into place in my head. "Did Remy know the results were different on your property?"

LJ tipped his head. "Not unless Scott told him after they had their little breakup. He wasn't around when we did the experiment."

Steadman had to know about the "special ingredient." That would be why he wanted the land so badly. If he couldn't steal or purchase it, he must have decided to settle for buying access to it long enough to figure out what the chemical makeup of the soil was.

Crystal's involvement was beginning to look a lot less like a coincidence again. I'd seriously underestimated Steadman. He hadn't sent just a beautiful woman but one with skills that were exactly what Scott needed. The combination would have made it too tempting for Scott to not share his research with her.

Her chemistry degree made her uniquely qualified to know what data was worth stealing as well as to gather and analyze a soil sample. *Steadman is a fucking genius, and I'm a fool for nearly falling into his trap.*

I didn't want to believe Crystal was capable of that level of deception, but the alternative was equally unflattering. Her uncle might have been manipulating her, but she had to be too intelligent to not see that.

I thought back to how difficult it had been to let her go—twice. Had she not bolted the last time, I might have changed my mind and let her stay. When I'd been with her, it hadn't seemed possible that she might be in on her uncle's plan. With the perspective of distance between us, it didn't seem possible for her not to be.

She was a conundrum. I wanted to see her again, but if she came back, I'd assume it was to poke around for her uncle. In that case, it would be better if I never saw her again. On the other hand, if I never heard from her again, it might mean she had no idea what her uncle was up to. In that case, never seeing her again would leave me wondering what would have happened if she'd stayed, we'd played, and I'd woken with her in my arms.

LJ cut a piece off the bean chicken breast. "You should try it."

I made a face. For more reasons than I cared to think about, being with her was a bad idea. "Didn't you say it doesn't taste like chicken yet?"

"I did."

I waved a hand. "No thanks."

He brought the cube of "meat" to his mouth. "Without flavoring, it doesn't taste like anything."

"So tempting, but I'll pass."

"Your loss." He popped the bite into his mouth.

It did feel like my loss—not the bean chicken but Crystal. No matter how I rationalized it to myself, I still hated how things had ended between us. I didn't like that she'd left looking upset. I didn't like that I was likely hiding as much from her as she was from me.

I walked away from LJ and gave the room another once-over. Everything there supported his story. "So this is Scott's big secret."

"This is it."

"I'm relieved, but I still think he's in over his head. Now that I know what Scott is working on, I can better understand Steadman's offers. It puts everything in a whole new light. You were right to be concerned about Crystal's appearance while I wasn't here."

"Said the brother whose motives might not be as altruistic as he'd like people to believe."

"You think I'm here because I knew about this?"

"I have no idea, but I've looked into you. You're a shrewd businessman and one with a lucrative new contract with Bellerwood. I wonder—what would make someone like you step away from his office?"

I folded my arms across my chest. "Family."

"So you keep saying." LJ held my gaze and mirrored my stance. "However, you've only just found out about Scott. Profit might outweigh loyalty in that case."

In a slow, tight tone, I said, "My relationship with my brothers is none of your business. Nice attempt to put me on the defensive, but it won't work. I know why I'm here. What comes out of your mouth is of little importance, since I intend to speak to Scott regarding his dealings with you. If your plans were for anything but what you say, consider them no longer an option."

LJ let out a slow breath. "God, I want to dislike you, but you remind me so damn much of myself." He lowered his arms. "Are you happy, though?"

I shrugged. "If this is the end of the tour, let's head back upstairs."

He smiled. "You don't even know, do you? You're too busy to stop and ask yourself what you want. My advice? Find yourself a good woman and make time for a family. I've made and lost and remade several fortunes in my life, but none of that matters anymore. After I lost my wife, nothing did. When I think of all the nights I worked late, all the life events I missed so I could get more done at the office—"

"Do I look like a fucking therapist?" I asked it both as a joke and because the mood was getting uncomfortably heavy.

LJ barked out a laugh and put a hand on my shoulder. "I'll miss you when you leave."

I shrugged off his touch. "I'm not going anywhere yet. What's Remy's last name? He and I need to have a little talk."

CHAPTER FOURTEEN

CRYSTAL

Seated at the workstation of my lab, I picked up my phone, then shook my head and placed it back beside the keyboard of my computer. Ellie stood and walked over. "Still no text from him?"

I turned back to face my computer screen. "I was checking the time."

"Really, then what time is it?"

I shot her the kind of glare someone does when their best friend won't allow the luxury of a pride-saving lie. "Fine, I haven't had a chance to tell you yet, but the craziest thing happened this morning."

Ellie pulled a chair up to my desk. "Spill."

"Okay, so remember how I said I was looking for someone who could design a prosthetic leg for Alphonse?"

"Scott's duck?"

"Yes. Everyone here had different ideas, but I wanted to get it just right. So I posted a question on a few sites."

"And?"

"And Wren Romano wrote to me. Romano. Her company designs robotic limbs for veterans as well as hospitals. They're kind of a big deal as far as being cutting edge with their technology. She offered to design a limb for me . . . I mean, Scott . . . Alphonse. Whatever."

"You're serious?"

"One hundred percent. For no cost. She said she could have a prototype within a week. All she needs is Alphonse's measurements and a video of how he currently walks. She sounded pretty excited about it."

Ellie leaned back and looked at the ceiling before meeting my gaze again. "You could forward her email to Scott."

"I could."

She searched my face. "But you want to talk to him again."

My shoulders slumped a little. "I do."

"If he'd contacted you at all, this would be such a sweet idea, but . . ."

"I know."

"So much of what you told me about when you went to his house raised red flags for me. I do think it's okay to cut loose and have fun now and then, but you also don't want to get caught up in something messy. The man said he couldn't ask you to stay . . . *couldn't*. When someone feels there is a reason something shouldn't happen, they're usually right."

I drummed my fingers on the table beside my keyboard. "You're right. So what should I do? Decline the Romano woman's offer?"

Ellie took a moment to answer, then said, "Fuck it, it's for a duck. Do it."

I laughed so loud everyone in the lab looked over. I waved for them to ignore us. "That sounds like a motto worthy of a T-shirt."

"It does." She laughed along, then said, "I'm sorry, now all I can imagine is a duck waddling around with a bionic leg. It has to happen."

"Right?" I picked up my phone and opened my messages. "I'll ask Scott to send me a video of Alphonse walking as well as the measurements of his legs. I did tell him I'd like to get something designed for him. This wouldn't come out of nowhere."

"And it'll probably be shipped directly to his farm."

I nodded. "No need to even see Scott again."

Ellie sighed. "I'm sorry it didn't work out with him."

I lifted and dropped a shoulder. "It happens. Honestly, I'm okay with it now." She gave me a look that had me amending my claim to,

"I'll be okay with it soon. It's getting easier. Hey, doing this might even give me the closure I need to get him out of my head."

When Ellie didn't say anything, I smiled and added, "Plus it's for a duck, so fuck it."

She chuckled and stood. "Exactly. Send that text so maybe, just maybe, you can get some work done today."

"I'll tell him about the offer and give him her contact information."

"Do it."

"And ask him if he still doesn't want to have sex with me." She shot me a quick look that had me laughing again. "Too much?"

She chuckled as she walked away. I was still smiling when I turned my attention back to my phone and typed: I couldn't stop thinking about Alphonse and his leg. I found someone who wants to make a robotic one for him if you're interested. No charge. I added Wren Romano's contact information.

A moment later a response came back: Crystal?

I groaned. Yes.

This isn't Scott.

I scrolled upward and checked if I could possibly have written to the wrong number, but my previous message to Scott, telling him I'd be a day late, was right there. Did someone else have his phone? Why were they answering his text messages?

Oh my God, is he married?

I'd never dated a married man, not even by accident. What if she asked me how well I knew him? Was it better to tell all or say nothing? I didn't want to be a home-wrecker, nor did I want to be an accomplice. I texted: Who is this?

Jesse. His brother.

Brother is better than wife. But why would he have Scott's phone? Is he okay?

His twin brother.

What the hell? I didn't know he had a twin.

No one did. That's what made it easy for me to step in and be him.

I put the phone down and stood up as a snippet from an earlier conversation came back to me.
"My friends call me Jesse."
"If we become friends, I'll remember that."
My hand went to my mouth. I sat back down and picked up my phone again. You were pretending to be your brother?

Yes.

I never met Scott?

Correct.

My hands shook as I typed: So everything you said to me was a lie?
I was so angry the screen of my phone blurred, but I could read his answer: Yes.

That must have been entertaining.

Far from it.

No apology, not even a halfhearted one. What was I supposed to do with that? Why?

I wanted to tell you, but it made no sense to.

No, why pretend to be your brother?

Because he is too nice to deal with what's going on here.

And you're not? Yeah, that's sadly easy to believe. I told myself not to ask, told myself I didn't care. What's going on?

I'm not able to say.

Of course not. Goodbye, Scott . . . oh, wait, Jesse.

Give your uncle a message for me. Tell him I know why he wants access to the land and it'll never happen.

Tell him yourself.

I tossed my phone back on my desk and let out a frustrated growl. Ellie motioned with her hands to ask if I wanted her to come to my desk again. I waved for her not to.

Scott wasn't Scott.

Scott was Jesse. Jesse who? I did a quick online search for Scott's twin and found nothing. No records. No photos. Nothing. Was it even true?

And his message to my uncle? Had the proposal not clearly outlined my uncle's intentions? Jesse had made it sound more sinister than that. I hated every part of this. I hated feeling like a fool, knowing that nothing that had happened at the farm had been real, and thinking that my uncle might have had an agenda he hadn't shared with me.

I jumped when Ellie's arms wrapped around my shoulders from behind. She hugged me. "You don't have to tell me, but I want you to know I love you and it'll be okay."

I blinked back tears and gave her arms a pat. "Thank you. I love you too. I'll tell you about it tonight. Right now I need to lose myself in some work."

She released me and stepped back. "I'm sorry it didn't work out. If you want, I'll call my mom for her anti-sex-drive recipes."

I spun in my seat. "Her what?"

"You know, the dishes you eat after a breakup that take the edge off so you can see the man again and not want him."

"How can you say that with a straight face?"

She tipped her head to one side. "Are you saying all mothers don't teach their daughters libido-lowering techniques?"

"That's exactly what I'm saying."

"Who knew." She went on in a serious tone, "She also has herbal combinations that produce the opposite effect."

I threw my hands up. "That would have been a nice share during my last relationship."

"It's for older men. The problem with that relationship wasn't a medical one." She made a face. "I can't believe I never told you about my mother's recipes. They're why I got into chemistry in the beginning. Fascinating stuff."

I rubbed my hands over my face, then stood up. The man I'd wanted to sleep with wasn't the man I'd thought he was, and my best friend had some secret, mystical food recipes. I shook my head. *If this is a dream, now would be a great time to wake up.*

Sadly, everything remained exactly as it was. "I'm going to call it an early day."

"Are you okay?"

I nodded. "Just tired. I might go for a walk to clear my head, then turn in early."

"Do you need something to help you sleep? My mother—"

"I'm all set."

Phone in hand, I grabbed my coat from the closet and announced I'd be back early the next day. Although on the outside I was calm, I was slowly losing it on the inside.

Jesse.

My uncle.

Ellie.

Did I really know any of them?

CHAPTER FIFTEEN

JESSE

Crystal was still very much on my mind a few days later when I was doing the evening barn chores. LJ had offered to help, but I'd become comfortable doing them myself. Plus when he wasn't there yapping in my ear, I found a certain amount of calm in the rhythm of the manual labor.

I was in Molly's stall, rubbing her neck absently while she munched on her dinner. When I paused, she pushed against my hand. I smiled. The veterinarian I'd had out to the farm to look into her skin condition had called it I-want-your-attention-itis. Apparently it was a chronic condition with only one cure—increased human interaction. The vet suggested I try talking to her more.

Sure. Why not? When in Rome . . . wasn't that the saying? Only, in this case, it was Rhode Island.

Molly paused from eating and looked up. I knew she couldn't understand me, but since it was doctor ordered, I said, "So Crystal contacted me. Said she found someone to make a robotic leg for Alphonse. Total bullshit, right? If I call Wren Romano, she'll probably never have heard of Crystal."

Molly returned to eating.

"Or maybe she has and it was a classic attempt at manipulation. Crystal wants to gain my trust so I'll give her access to the property again. I had to put her straight on who she was dealing with." Something was bothering me. "'Everything you said to me was a lie?' She actually said that. Like I was the one trying to steal her family's land and life's work and not the other way around."

Molly continued munching away.

"I didn't make her any promises or let things go that far. I'm the one who called things off. Me. She was perfectly okay with having sex while lying about her reason for being here, but I felt bad . . ."

My hand paused, and Molly gazed up at me again. It was impossible to look into those huge bovine eyes and lie. "I do like her. I know how insane that sounds. I've been with a fair share of women and never had a problem moving on, but I can't get this one out of my head." I gave Molly's neck a good scratch. "My father would say I'm making one of the biggest mistakes a man can—I'm letting my dick determine how I see the situation. That's how men lose their fortunes. He'd know. My mother walked away with half of his money because he was too in love to ask her to sign a prenup. He still calls her the most expensive fuck he's ever had."

You could say my father had never gotten over losing my mother, but we were pretty sure he missed the money more.

My mother—odd that I thought of her that way even though I didn't know her any more than the woman who had given me away. My father was jaded when it came to women. I'd never put a lot of thought into whether I was also, but doing barn chores gave me time to think.

I was raised to be goal oriented. Feelings got in the way of success, and there was nothing worth wanting outside of success. It wasn't as bad as it might sound. I couldn't remember ever being unhappy. Like Thane, I was so busy there wasn't time to think about much else.

I hadn't expected this time away from the office to change me at all, but I would return feeling dissatisfied even after the problem with Scott's farm was resolved. I was beginning to think my life was missing something. Molly looked up at me, and I chuckled. "Not you, Molly. I live in an apartment."

Crystal's face filled my thoughts. "I almost apologized to her. I didn't, but I don't like the idea that she might have been hurt by my deception. Her. Oil-company spy. I shouldn't feel guilty at all, but I do. What the hell do I do with that?"

"Who are you talking to?" a male voice asked from the door of Molly's stall.

My head snapped around. "Thane."

"Is someone else here?"

"No, I'm talking to Molly."

"Molly?"

"The cow."

"Is she answering you?"

"No." I couldn't blame him for giving me shit. Had our roles been reversed, I would have thought he'd lost his mind as well.

"Well, that's something, anyway." He looked around, and his face reflected how I'd felt the first time I'd stepped into the barn. He was dressed in a suit, which looked about as out of place in a barn as anything could. "Let's talk outside. How can you stand the smell in here?"

I took a deep breath and didn't smell anything bad. "In a minute. Molly hasn't finished eating."

"I'm worried about you, Jesse. When we spoke the other day, you said you needed some time to figure out what Scott's friend knew, but you've had time to do that. Why are you still here?"

It was a fair question and one I'd asked myself as well. "Remy is out of town. I'm waiting for him to return."

"When is he expected back? Today? Tomorrow? A week?"

"I don't know."

"Are you having some kind of breakdown? If so, we can get you help. Discreetly."

"I'm fine." I looked down at my soiled work boots and stained jeans. Strange how comfortable it all had become. I couldn't imagine wearing them for the rest of my life, but I wouldn't mind revisiting the farm now and then. "It's not as bad as you think. I'm sleeping better than I ever have. It might be all the fresh air—"

"There is nothing fresh here; trust me." Thane waved a hand in front of his nose, then looked down and swore. "Is that chicken shit on my shoe?"

I chuckled. "A common hazard, since they're free range."

He stepped away to wipe his shoe against a crate. "Then I have no idea why they're let out."

Molly gave her bowl one last nudge, then moved away from it. I took that as a cue that I was free to go and stepped out of her stall to join Thane. When I did, six chickens spotted me and came running. I opened a bin of mealworms I kept outside Molly's stall and threw some to them. "They keep the insect population down, and come on, look how happy it makes them to roam."

Thane gave me a long look. "Now I know you've lost your fucking mind."

"Maybe." I wiped my hands on my jeans and led Thane down the aisle. As we passed a white pigeon that was roosting off to one side, I said, "I'm not a bird person, but I like Winslow. He's a wedding-release survivor. He's not a good flyer and kept being 'rescued' by people who would find him in the road or their yards. Scott took him in when he heard the owner planned to cull him. Oddly enough, Winslow has never tried to leave the farm. He's a homing pigeon with no desire to go home."

Just outside the barn, Thane turned to me. "Fascinating, but let's talk about what *you're* doing here."

I smiled. *Is that how I sound? Wow, I really am an ass.* "You want to see the basement." It wasn't a question. Thane was a lot like me, in that he didn't believe much before he saw it with his own eyes.

"If there are no animals in it." Thane's humor was so dry people often missed how funny he was.

"Only the ones you can make with beans. Come on."

A short time later, after I'd given him a similar tour to the one LJ had given me, Thane was standing out on the porch with me. He hadn't said much, but that was his way. If a quick decision needed to be made, I was the one to come out of the gate with a strong opinion. Right or wrong, the path forward was always clear to me.

Thane took his time weighing all angles before moving forward. In business our differences complemented each other. He tempered my impulsive decisions. I lit a fire under his overcautious ass.

"There's something you're not telling me," he said.

I leaned against the railing and shook my head. "I have no reason to hold anything back."

He searched my face. "Scott is in way over his head."

"That's glaringly obvious."

"I don't trust Leo's involvement."

"I'm with you on that, but call him LJ." In response to the question in his eyes, I added, "It fits him better."

"Scott's recipes wouldn't be nearly as valuable without the food printer."

"I agree. How did it taste?"

One of his eyebrows arched. "You said you tasted some yourself."

"No, I said, 'This is where LJ offered me a sample.' I never said I accepted it."

Thane wiped at his mouth. "Thanks. For all we know, the secret mineral in the soil is arsenic."

I shrugged. "LJ ate it."

With a wave of his hand, Thane called for that topic to cease. "LJ is definitely a wild card, but Steadman is the one you'll need to be careful with. Oil companies don't like the idea of alternative fuels. Things could get dangerous—especially once he knows Scott brought in reinforcements. You shouldn't have—"

"I know."

"When you have the advantage of surprise, you don't just—"

"Do you think I'm not well aware of that?" I growled.

Both of his eyebrows rose. Thane and I disagreed on many topics, but we didn't raise our voices to each other. *Control of one's environment begins with control of oneself.* We'd both had that drummed into our heads from our Krav Maga training. There was a reason that style of fighting had been adopted by the Israel Defense Forces. Some people sent their children to study martial arts to learn discipline. My father signed us up for a real-world self-defense program that was derived from boxing, wrestling, judo, aikido, and karate. Awareness of a situation and ways to defuse a conflict were taught, but the efficiency of it came from the understanding that if engagement was unavoidable, there was no room for half measures. Fast. Brutal. Neutralized. Live to fight another day. The element of surprise was often a victim's greatest weapon.

Thane continued, "Even with this Remy. I'm surprised you didn't seek him out rather than wait for him to return. It doesn't make sense. I can't support your strategy here unless you share it with me."

"This isn't your problem, Thane."

He raised a finger in the air. "But it is. You and I just signed an extremely lucrative contract."

That had me straightening off the railing. "Do you need me back at the office?"

"Not yet, but I would feel a whole lot better if I knew where your head is at."

I sighed. If I had a good justification for my recent decisions, I would gladly have shared it. I didn't, so I said, "I'm surprised Scott didn't come with you today. Last week he was anxious to switch back."

"He's settling in, plus Leo . . . LJ updates him daily on the animals. When I heard you'd taken over caring for them, I had to come out and see it for myself. I still don't believe it."

I took a moment to choose the right words to describe how I felt at the farm. "I wouldn't want to live here, but I also wouldn't mind coming back. I'm so used to my thoughts focusing on one project after another.

I go to sleep thinking about what I could have done better at the office and wake up thinking about my work plan for the day."

"That's the focus that has gotten us to where we are."

"Yes, but I have nothing else. What do you do outside of work for enjoyment?"

His shoulders rose and fell beneath his suit. "There will be time to enjoy myself later."

"When? When is later?"

Thane frowned. "Are you intimidated by the size of the contract we signed? If so, you need to tell me. I can be the point person."

He would too. Thane always stepped forward to do what needed to be done. "That's not what I'm saying at all." I took a breath. "Stepping outside my life has given me time to ask myself what I want when I step back into it."

"And what do you want?"

I shook my head slowly. I was still figuring that out.

My phone rang with a call from a number I didn't recognize. Normally I wouldn't have answered, but I did. "Rehoboth."

A woman's voice said, "Hello. This is Wren Romano. I hope this is a good time to call. Crystal Holmes told me about your duck, and I'm excited to say I have designed what I hope will be the perfect leg for him. All I need are the exact measurements, and I could have the leg to you by early next week."

Wren Romano. Holy shit. Crystal didn't lie about contacting her. "That's incredibly generous of you. What measurements do you need?" I found myself smiling at the idea that Alphonse would soon have a bionic leg. He'd love showing it off.

She read off a list, then said, "Text me the info when you have it. This has been so fun to do. If it works out, we'd love to come by and see Alphonse use it in person. My husband, Mauricio, hates to miss a photo op."

"Sure. That would be great. I'll text you later today and keep you updated on how it works out."

"Thanks, Scott. I have so much respect for you and your animal rescue. It sounds like a wonderful place. We look forward to meeting you."

Scott. Not me. "Thank you, and you're always welcome here."

"Talk to you soon."

I pocketed the phone after the call ended. More confused than before, I sighed. The whole situation was a complicated mess. Why had Crystal followed through and found someone to make a leg for Alphonse? What did it mean? And why did the possibility that she wasn't a horrible person make me sad?

"Who was that?" Thane asked.

"Wren Romano."

"As in Romano Superstores?"

"Yes. She and her husband started a robotics company that specializes in prosthetic limbs. She's making one for Alphonse." When Thane didn't appear to know who that was, I added, "The duck."

"I had no idea you knew the Romanos."

"I don't. Crystal Holmes set it up. She met Alphonse, felt bad that he wasn't walking with a natural gait, and reached out to designers. The Romanos offered to create a robotic leg for him."

Shaking his head back and forth, Thane said, "There isn't one normal thing about this situation. Scott bioengineers a food slash new fuel source; then suddenly a tech mogul, an oil company, and now a robotics company begin to circle him. You're going to get yourself killed, aren't you?" He groaned and ran a hand down his face. "I'll be forced to either announce your death or let Scott continue to be you. I don't know which would be worse for our stock ratings. He still hasn't figured out how to work your shower without scalding himself."

I laughed. I couldn't help it. He looked so serious and genuinely more upset about how inconvenient my death would be than upset that I'd be dead. "I'm not going anywhere."

"You'd better not. I would hunt you down on the other side if you left me with Scott."

"That bad?"

Thane met my gaze. "I like him. He's just—not you."

That was so real it took me a moment to respond. "Thanks. I'd feel the same if you ever uncovered a twin."

He rolled his eyes skyward. "Please, God, no. One of us having a twin is enough." After a moment, he said, "What do you need from me? What can I do?"

"Hold down the fort? I need a little more time here."

"Why?"

There it was—the question I kept asking myself. "If I left now—"

"We could still protect Scott as well as his secret."

"It's not that simple."

"What? Is there something else going on here? If so, you know I have your back."

He meant it, which was why he deserved the whole truth. "My time here has felt like a journey, but one that isn't over yet."

"I don't understand."

"I don't either. You know me, though. I've always trusted my gut, and right now it's telling me this is where I need to be."

"To save Scott's farm?"

"That's part of it."

"What else could this be about?" He leaned his head back and sighed. "No, not the oil rep—Crystal, isn't it?"

I folded my arms over my chest. It would have been easier to confess that I'd murdered someone. "Yes."

"Have you heard from her again?"

"Not since we had the conversation where I told her to give her uncle a message from me."

He brought his hands to his temples. "I don't have to tell you what a bad idea it would be to get involved with her."

He wasn't saying anything I hadn't already told myself. "I know."

"At best, her loyalty is compromised. At worst, she's an outright spy for her uncle."

"Which is why I haven't reached out to her."

He shook his head. "No, you're doing worse than that—you're sitting here waiting for her to return."

"That's not what I'm doing."

He sighed. "Then tell me. What is this about?"

I lowered my arms and turned toward my brother. "When I met her, everything she admired about me had nothing to do with who I am. She thought I was the kind of person who collected and cared for broken animals—the throwaways."

"A sucker willing to take in the problems other people discard."

"That's how I saw them, too, but I don't anymore. Being here is changing me, Thane, and I don't think it's a bad thing. I care about our business and our contracts, but I don't want that to be all I am. I don't want to fill my social time with people I don't care if I see again, save money I'll never spend doing anything I enjoy, only to grow old alone. I want more than I've allowed myself to consider possible."

"Like love?"

"No. Yes. Maybe. All I'm saying is I want to care about things outside of work as well. That's it. Dad would be a lonely son of a bitch if he didn't have us."

"That's true."

"We're well on our way to being him, but a version of him without us. I didn't realize how much his lack of trust in some people influenced my own until I stepped away."

"Women, you mean."

"Yes."

"Which is why you told Crystal your secret. You're delusional if you think there's a chance she'll choose you over her uncle."

"Maybe."

"She may return, but you'd be a fool to believe anything she says if she does."

"That's true."

We stood there for several minutes without talking, and then he asked, "Do you really think she'll come back?"

"I have to give her a little more time to."

"What will you do until then?"

"Consider me on one of the vacations we never allow ourselves to take."

"Okay."

"Now help me find Alphonse. We need to measure him."

"I'm not touching a duck."

I smiled. Despite how nothing had changed, it felt like a weight had been lifted from my chest. "Someone has to hold him while I take the measurements."

"You're nuts."

"That's already been established." I turned and walked down the steps. "It would be rude not to at least send Crystal a text thanking her for helping Alphonse."

Thane joined me. "Thank her with flowers."

My eyebrows shot up. "I thought you said she was a bad idea."

"She is, but if you're going to do this anyway—at least do it right. A text leaves the door closed. Flowers fling it wide open."

"Flowers it is."

CHAPTER SIXTEEN

CRYSTAL

Early on a Monday morning, well before anyone else was due to arrive, I paused from working on a recipe for a college student I'd met at a party Ellie had dragged me to so she could finally introduce me to her boyfriend. I'd expected beer pong and togas, but I should have trusted that Ellie had better taste than that. Jonathan followed Ellie around like she was a goddess and he was helpless under her spell. I could see how addictive that could be. His friends were young but smart and motivated. Feeling completely out of place and so old despite our age gap not being that big, I sat down beside a young woman who thought I was a pharmacist like Ellie.

Her name was Kimberly, and she asked endless questions about a job I knew next to nothing about until I felt trapped in the lies. Ellie had introduced me to Jonathan's friends as someone who worked with her. I couldn't tell them that I was part owner of a very successful lab without outing her. So instead I spent about an hour layering lie upon lie and hating myself for being as fake as I'd judged Jesse for being.

In the middle of dark thoughts where I realized I was no better than the man I'd spent the last few days angry with, Kimberly told me she was caring for her grandmother while struggling to pay for school. With a self-deprecating laugh she mentioned that her dream was to take her ailing grandmother's yogurt-cake recipe, change it to nondairy, and use the funds from cake sales to hire a nurse to help with home care.

Time slowed, and suddenly it became clear what I should do. I offered to help her because, despite how I tended to view the world in scientific terms, there was a part of me that held out hope that there was a greater plan. If there wasn't, life was just a series of random, meaningless tragedies, and I couldn't accept that. Some things had to be more than a coincidence. I was meant to meet her. I told her I could put together a modified recipe she could use to make her dream a reality.

She asked, "Pharmacists know how to do that?"

"This one does." I offered to attempt a recipe at no charge. She was so excited and told me if she ever started her own company, I would definitely be the first person she'd hire. I smiled and thanked her. She had no idea how expensive my services were, but that was part of the magic of the moment.

The process was actually rather simple, since it was being done in a wide variety of yogurt brands already. The tricky part was re-creating the taste of her grandmother's homemade yogurt. That would take trial and error and time, because when it came to matching taste, I was a perfectionist.

The door of the lab dinged as Ellie entered. "I knew you'd be here."

I spun my chair toward the door. "Pharmacist hours."

She rolled her eyes. "Well, I'm here to help. It's my fault you got roped into this side project."

"I wasn't roped in—I offered."

"What are you thinking? Send me what you have, and I'll start mixing."

I sent the specs to her computer. "I've never done pro bono work. It feels good."

She logged in and read over my notes. "I agree. Looks good. Mind if I make a few tweaks?"

"Go right ahead." We worked together well because it was always more about the outcome than ego. Her modifications came up on my screen, and I nodded. "You're spot on, addressing the moisture differential during the baking process. Good call."

She shot me a smile. "Thanks."

We worked seamlessly side by side. I prepared the batter for a cake based on her grandmother's exact recipe. Ellie did the same for our nondairy version.

While we waited, she said, "I'm glad you came to the party last night. You needed to get out."

"It was nice to finally meet your workout partner."

She wiggled her eyebrows. "And?"

Jonathan was everything she'd described. Big, muscled, quiet. "He obviously has feelings for you."

She wrinkled her nose. "We understand each other. In bed, we're good—really good. For now, that's enough. The best part is that when it stops being good, we can just end it without either of us getting hurt."

After seeing how he looked at her, I wasn't sure he'd gotten that memo. "He was much more likable than I'd imagined he would be."

She nodded. "He's very nice."

"And he wants to be a physical therapist. That shows ambition."

"There's nothing about him I don't like, except that we're in totally different places in our lives. I feel old around him."

"You're not, though. You're just ahead because you finished school early. How much younger is he? Five years? In a decade that won't feel like much at all."

She smiled. "I love that you think we could be together that long."

"Are you so sure you couldn't be? You never know."

She sighed and came over to lean against one side of my desk. "You're still hoping your farmer will call, aren't you?"

I frowned. "He's not a farmer. Or maybe he is. I don't know. And it doesn't matter because I've already put him out of my mind."

Her expression said she didn't believe me. She picked up a pen off my desk and twirled it between her fingers. "I can't allow myself to get attached to Jonathan. I lied to him about my profession and have kept lying. It's not like I could just call him up and say, *Hey, I know I told you I'm a pharmacist, but I'm actually a pretty well-known chemist with my own lab.*"

"He might understand."

"Or he'd never want to see me again. I'm not ready for it to be over." She groaned. "I didn't think one little lie would matter, but it snowballed. You're the most honest person I know, and I even pulled you into this whole fake-pharmacist thing."

"It's okay."

"No, it's not. You felt guilty about it." She made a face. "I do too. Lying about my profession didn't matter until I started caring about Jonathan."

I froze.

No. That can't be it.

Jesse had pulled out of our date even though all signs had pointed toward us having sex that day. He'd sent me away and said we couldn't be together. I was already gone when he'd told me about switching with his brother. There was no reason for him to confess. He could have held to that lie.

Unless I mattered to him. That couldn't be it, could it?

My hand came up to my mouth. I'd felt awful lying to Kimberly, but loyalty could put people in situations they otherwise would avoid. Was that what had happened to Jesse? He'd claimed he'd switched places with his brother to help him.

There had been moments when I'd been so sure that our connection was real. Could it have been? Had his confession been a leap of faith? I hadn't stuck around long enough to find out.

I'd been so angry with him for lying to me that I hadn't given much thought to why he'd come clean. I looked Ellie in the eye. "You need to tell Jonathan. He deserves the truth."

"I know you're right." She searched my face. "I suddenly have sympathy for Jesse."

A wry smile twisted my lips. "Me too, but it doesn't matter. It's actually better if I don't hear from him again. With everything going on between him and my uncle, things are complicated even if we worked through the lies. Some things aren't meant to be."

She nodded, then walked to one of the ovens to check the cakes. "If I tell Jonathan, it'll be a lot easier to help Kimberly—even if he decides to never speak to me again. We have the connections to help her get a product in stores."

"We do."

"I know it's the right thing to do, but why can't I be a good person and still have good sex?"

"I'd like to think that's not the way it works." I chuckled even though I knew she wasn't joking. "You might be surprised how much forgiveness good sex gains you."

"I hope so." She checked the second cake. "I really hope so."

Soon after the cakes were finished, the rest of our team arrived. Without telling them the difference between the two, we gave each of them a sample. There was a slight difference in aftertaste, which meant we still had some work to do, but unlike the mess we were both making of our personal lives, this was the kind of problem we understood how to fix.

It was a long day at the lab but not a bad one. I was closing out of my computer when one of our interns rushed into the lab and said, "Dr. Holmes, come out to the front office. You have a delivery."

"You can bring it in."

She shook her head. "They're setting it up in the outer office."

I stood. "Setting it up? What is it?" She looked happier than one would expect an intern to be about a lab delivery. I was curious as to why.

When I stepped out of the lab and into the waiting room, my senses were overtaken by the scent and sight of carnations. Oh, so many. Boxes and boxes overflowing with them.

Two of the delivery people were putting together panels, then inserting the flowers into slots on them. My hand came to my chest when I realized they had built the front of a barn. Another man was pulling carnation farm animals out of boxes and placing them in front of the barn. It was easily the most adorable thing I'd ever seen, even if it was quickly overtaking the front office. I walked closer, my mouth rounding as I did.

Ellie appeared at my side. "A barn made of carnations? Oh my God, did you order that?"

"No."

The intern exclaimed, "Look, there's a pig over there and a duck."

A duck? I went over to it, my heart beating wildly in my chest. It might not have looked like Alphonse, but the coloring was unmistakably his. There was only one person this could be from. A small note hung from a string around his neck. I leaned down to read it.

Things didn't work out with you and Scott, but if you'd like to meet me, the real me, I'd like to try that date again. —Jesse.

I gently removed the note and read it a second time. Then a third.

Ellie read it also. "I might have just forgiven him a little." She turned her attention back to the barn. "Any man who would arrange something like this is worth giving a second chance."

I folded the note and placed it in the pocket of my lab jacket. "It is very thoughtful."

With a shake of her head, Ellie said, "Girl, if you don't call him and set up that date, I will."

"For me or for yourself?"

Her smile was shameless. "Call the damn man."

I laughed. "Okay. Okay."

As quickly as they'd arrived, the delivery crew left. Snapping photos with her phone, our intern said, "I'm sending this to my boyfriend. The half-dead bouquet he picks up from the gas station on his way over is no longer going to cut it."

Poor guy. This certainly does raise the bar.

A slow smile spread across my face. *Jesse wants to see me again.*

CHAPTER SEVENTEEN

JESSE

My family was never big on exchanging gifts. It was easier and more practical to simply buy whatever we wanted for ourselves. I'd sent flowers to women before. I'd even given jewelry to a few. What I'd never done was spent time with a florist designing something specific. This was the first time I'd ever sent something I was excited to hear a response to.

Would she love it?

Would she consider it too much?

Thirty minutes after I'd received notification that it had been delivered, my phone rang. In my rush to retrieve it from the back pocket of my jeans, I nearly dropped it in the paddock I was cleaning. "Hello."

I held my breath until she answered. "Jesse?"

"Yes." I'd almost asked who she thought would be answering my phone, but it felt too soon to test her humor with the situation.

"The flower farm you sent is beautiful. Incredible. I've never seen anything like it."

My face warmed. "I'm glad."

"How did you know where I worked?"

"There aren't too many Crystal Holmes flavorists in Maine. It was easy enough to find you." When she didn't immediately respond, I hoped that looking her up hadn't come across as stalkerish. "I also wanted to thank you for arranging the robotic leg for Alphonse."

"All I did was post a question on a few sites. I thought I'd receive advice. I had no idea someone like Wren Romano would offer to actually create something for him."

I took a deep breath. "Sometimes you have to put what you want out there, no matter how foolish it seems."

"Like us giving a first date a second try?"

"Exactly like that."

"I think I understand why you couldn't be honest with me about your real name. You were at the farm to help Scott and had to maintain the lie for his sake."

"Yes."

"And you didn't trust me."

This wasn't how I'd hoped the conversation would go. "Correct."

"Do you trust me now?"

That was a tough one. If the truth hadn't mattered, it would have been easy enough to say I did. I didn't want to lie to her again, though. "Not enough to have you at the farm but enough to want to see you again."

"Wow." She sounded insulted, and I mentally kicked myself for not softening the truth somehow. "If you feel that way, why do you even want to see me again?"

It wasn't a comfortable question to answer, but I'd never shied away from difficult tasks. "I can't get you out of my head. You're the first thing I think about in the morning. You're the last thing on my mind before I fall asleep. This isn't just about fucking you, although I've imagined that more than I should admit. You're the first woman I'm not okay with walking away from. There's something between us that feels worth trying a second or even a third time." Had I been too blunt? I cleared my throat. "Considering how we met, you probably will find this difficult to believe, but I'm known for being brutally honest."

"Actually, I can see that."

"And?"

Her voice turned husky. "I like that about you."

I smiled. "When it comes to you, I'm done pretending. No games. No more lies. Let's meet up, spend some time together, and see where this goes."

"Away from the farm."

"For now." It was all I could offer until I understood the situation better. "My original idea of Newport would be a long drive for you. I'd still like to show you around, though. I'll have my private plane at the airport nearest to you. Tomorrow . . . at ten a.m."

"I have a job."

"Isn't it *your* lab?"

"I am part owner, but—"

"One day, Crystal. Let's see how much of this is real."

She took a moment. "I can't tell if you're hoping it is or it isn't."

"Then we definitely need to spend more time together, because I've never chased a woman. If you said no to tomorrow, I'd call again with another suggestion. Not because it would be the right thing to do but because I wouldn't be able to help myself." The claim was a bit over the top, but after all the lies I'd told her, it felt right to be equally as honest. I wanted to see her again—even if that meant sending flowers and gushing a little.

The shaky breath she released was sexy as hell. "Sounds like you have it pretty bad for me."

"Or pretty good." There was nothing bad about how I was feeling in that moment, not when her voice held a hint of *yes* in it. "I'm sending that plane. I'll text you the info for where to meet it."

"I haven't said yes yet."

Yet was the key word. "See you tomorrow."

She let out a surprised laugh. "Oh, really."

"Really." I hung up with a smile and a hard-on.

CHAPTER EIGHTEEN

CRYSTAL

I stayed late at work to complete my current project as well as the recipe for Kimberly's yogurt cake. I'd already warned everyone I most likely wouldn't be in the next day. I didn't need to tell anyone why—the wall-to-wall flowers in the front office said it all.

Ellie would have stayed to help, but she didn't want to be late to her date. She said she'd try to come clean with Jonathan that night, but she looked nervous too. Thankfully, I'd see her before I flew out the next day.

If I decide to.

Oh, who the hell am I kidding? I want to meet Jesse—the not-Scott version.

I drove home, although I was so distracted I couldn't have said which route I took. After eating cold leftovers I didn't put a single thought into, I changed into pajamas, turned on the television in the living room, and started flipping through movie options.

Giving in to an impulse, I picked up my phone and texted Jesse: This is crazy.

He answered almost immediately. Every damn part of it.

No one has ever sent a plane for me.

I've never sent a plane for anyone.

I believed him. Yes, he'd lied to me about who he was, but it had been for a good reason. In his place I might have done the same. I want to go.

But?

I held the phone to my chest for a moment before typing: I'm not an exciting person. I don't take risks or fly off on a whim. I make plans and follow them.

I usually work twelve hours a day and spend most of my weekends traveling to meet potential clients. My time at Scott's farm is the closest thing I've had to taking a vacation since college.

I smiled. That's what I call a working vacation.

Oh, yes. Plus I can't smell the animals anymore and that scares me.

I laughed. It should. That farm stinks.

I'll take an extra long shower tomorrow morning and hope for the best.

The mental image of him naked beneath a spray of water temporarily wiped whatever I might have said clear out of my head. *Easy. There'll be time for that tomorrow if I decide to see him.* What do you do for work?

I'm in air conditioning and heating.

Mechanically inclined—I liked that. Do you enjoy your job?

Most days. It's a family business and that's important to me.

I nodded even though he couldn't see me. Do you have a big family?

It's just my father, my brothers and me, but that's enough.

I understood. My family had always been small but enough. Our conversation, getting to know him, was what I needed to be okay with seeing him the next day, but texting didn't feel like enough. Do you mind if I call?

My phone rang with a call from him. My heart thudded in my chest. It felt so easy with him, so right. It shouldn't have, not after how we'd started and not with what still stood between us . . . but it did. "Hi," I said.

"You're right; this is better. I love your voice."

Blushing, I sank back into the cushions of the couch. "Yours isn't so bad either." His deep answering laugh had me smiling and closing my eyes to savor it. After a moment, I remembered the topic I'd been curious about. "Did you lose your mother as well?"

"Not the same way you did. My mother found fidelity tedious and my father's money freeing. She divorced him when Thane and I were very young and gave our father full custody of us. As far as I know it was a decision she hasn't wasted a moment regretting."

That was terrible. Death was final, and any loss to it was painful, but abandonment must have a whole other layer of confusion and anger to it. "I'm sorry."

"It was a long time ago. Long enough that I don't remember her."

"That's so sad."

"Not really. My father is amazing. What I'll never understand is why she bothered to adopt two children if she didn't plan to stick around. I could understand if we were mistakes . . . we probably were,

127

just not hers. But if you go to all the work and expense of adoption, you'd think it would be hard to leave those children behind."

Especially children who had already been given up by someone else. My heart broke for Jesse and Thane. Wait . . . "I can't believe you were separated from your twin. Did they at least allow you to stay in touch?"

"I had no idea he existed until about six months ago, when someone showed me a photo of him online. They didn't know I was adopted and thought it was amusing that he looked so much like me."

"That must have been unsettling."

"You could say that. On some level I knew Scott was my brother as soon as I saw his photo, but I didn't allow myself to really believe it until after the results of the DNA test came back. We're identical."

"And you had no idea that you were a twin?"

"None. Scott didn't either. I was just as much of a shock to him as he was to me."

Wow. I struggled to imagine what that must have been like. "That explains why there were no photos of you together online." *Oh, crap, did I just say that?*

"You looked into me?"

Whatever. "I did."

"What did you discover?"

"A lot about Scott and his parents, but nothing about you. Not even your last name."

"So you have no idea who I am."

"You say that like I should."

"No. No, it's just nice. Usually, when I meet someone, they have a preconceived impression of me based on my father."

"Is your father famous?"

"Not unless you work in the industry we do; then he has a reputation for being a no-nonsense businessman. My father doesn't suffer fools easily."

"My uncle is the same." I thought back to how Jesse had been when I'd first met him. Now that I knew the truth, I couldn't believe I hadn't seen how un-farmer-like he was. "You seem like someone who's comfortable being in charge."

"It's what I was groomed for. Every dinner conversation we had growing up revolved around what we were doing to prepare for taking over when he retired."

"That's a lot of pressure."

"Or love. Some people make a distinction between biological and adopted kids. My father never did. We were his sons—period. You did not want to be the sorry soul who asked him if we knew who our real father was. My father didn't raise his voice often, but he made his feelings on that matter very clear."

"So you know nothing about your biological parents?"

"And I'm fine with that."

I wasn't sure I would be, but I could understand why he felt that way. His father's loyalty to him was something he'd internalized and valued. "Scott never wondered either?"

"He claims he hit the lottery with his adoptive parents. His father worked the farm. His mother baked daily and attended every football game he played. The photo album he showed me looked staged for a movie about a middle America Stepford family, but he says he had a wonderful childhood."

"Are you alike even though you were raised differently? It would be really interesting to see how the nature-versus-nurture debate played out in reality."

"We both hate cooked carrots."

"I'm not sure that's indicative of anything. I do too."

"Hey, we finally have something in common."

I chuckled. "It's a start."

After a pause, he said, "I can't believe how much I've talked about myself. I don't usually do that."

"I bet you say that to all the ladies."

"I bet I don't." That warmed me from head to toe. The smile I heard in his voice matched the one on my face.

"Good-looking businessman—you're not hurting for dates."

His voice deepened. "I never said I couldn't land a hookup, but is that what this is? Because that's not how it feels."

I'd never met a man who was as direct as he was. It was hot. "How does it feel?"

"Like something worth figuring out."

"Yes." I couldn't have described it better. It was messy and confusing, but I didn't want it to end before I knew what it was—what it could be.

He cleared his throat. "It won't be easy. We both have reasons not to trust each other."

"We do."

"I don't want you to get hurt in this. If there's a reason you can't be honest with me, don't come tomorrow."

I was only half joking when I said, "You mean if I'm only saying yes to try to get you to agree to my uncle's proposal."

"Or for any other reason. Maybe he asked you to do something while you were at the farm, and it didn't seem like a big deal, but he wanted to make sure no one saw you."

"What would he have asked me to do?"

"You tell me."

"He didn't ask me to do anything, and I don't really like what you're implying." Irritation with him as well as myself rose within me as I remembered feeling uncomfortable with my uncle's suggestion that I contact Scott again.

"Did you tell him I'm not Scott?"

"No." I didn't like what that admission implied. "But before you tell me not to say anything to him, that's not me. He's been good to me. I would never lie to him."

"So you didn't give him my message."

"Not yet." I sighed. "You already said you were turning down the deal and why you were there. No is no, right? I didn't see how it mattered if you were you or Scott."

"Thank you."

"I didn't do it to help you."

"Understood."

Neither of us said anything for a long minute. "Tomorrow would be a waste of time, right? How could we get past this?" I asked.

He didn't answer at first. "If a friend came to me for advice on a situation like this, I'd tell him to run. Relationships are hard enough without adding all the layers this one comes with."

"I'd advise the same thing."

"So why am I still hoping you'll get on that plane tomorrow?"

"Probably the same reason I'm considering going. I want to see you again."

"I want the same thing."

I covered my eyes with an arm. How was it possible to be as excited as I was to see him again? "What's your last name?"

"I'll tell you the next time I see you." With that, he hung up.

And I dropped the phone on the couch next to me.

Shit. Shit. Shit.

CHAPTER NINETEEN

CRYSTAL

The plane Jesse sent for me was a six-seater. Simply having his own plane said something about the man I was going to meet, as did having a private pilot and attendant. The plane was decorated in a masculine style with seats that faced a table with easily accessible outlets. No television or bar. The pilot who met me on the tarmac was polite but formal. The attendant was friendly enough, but outside of periodically asking me if there was anything I needed, she stayed out of the way. It was an airborne workspace, and the tone of the flight reflected that.

Not sure what to expect from our date, I'd packed a small bag of options. The slacks and shirt I wore could be dressed up or down. I was wearing the high heels Ellie had told me complemented my outfit, but I also brought sneakers in case Jesse suggested a long stroll. The weather in New England could be unpredictable, and anywhere near the ocean was always cooler, so I brought a jacket. The wind near the water could be brutal for hair, which was why I'd also packed a hairbrush. Although the flight was a short one, I'd brought my laptop so I could get some work done. If so much of the food I loved hadn't had garlic in it, I wouldn't have brought my toothbrush. A bathing suit made sense in case he chose to take me to a beach. I didn't have the kind of body that allowed me to simply grab something off a rack and feel good about it.

Last minute, I'd also thrown a handful of condoms in a small bag with some makeup. It was better to be prepared than not.

It wasn't until we'd landed and the pilot said he'd have my luggage brought to the car that it struck me that I might have brought too much.

Luggage.

I brought luggage to our first date.

I was still recovering from that realization when the attendant told me Mr. Rehoboth was outside waiting for me. I wanted to grab her by the shoulders, shake her, and say, *I've changed my mind. I can't go on the date. I brought* luggage.

Instead I set my chin at a proud angle and followed the attendant out the door of the plane to the top of the stairs. Jesse was down below, leaning against a car. Dressed in simple dark-gray pants and a deep-blue button-down shirt, he pushed off the car as soon as he spotted me.

I made my way down the stairs, taking calming breaths the whole way. The man who met me at the bottom of the stairs was polished and powerful. Confident. Dangerous.

So sexy I swayed toward him without saying one damn word. *Rehoboth.* His last name was familiar but not enough to matter to me then.

He cupped my chin with one hand and gave me a kiss I knew I'd remember for the rest of my life. It was a welcome, a promise, and a dare all in one. I doubted there was a woman alive who wouldn't have given herself over to the passion of it.

His lips brushed over mine. His tongue tempted my mouth to open. Once inside, his tongue set my imagination on fire with where else I'd love that kind of talent to wander.

It ended too soon.

I did my best not to look as shaken as I felt. *Holy shit, no matter what happens, I don't want to turn back. I want to know him—all of him.*

"You came," he said with a grin, dropping his hand away.

I let out a shaky breath. "Not yet, but I'm hopeful." In my head it had been a joke, but it came out like an earnest plea that had my cheeks blushing.

He laughed. "I like the way you think." His expression turned more serious. "No pressure. We'll see where the day takes us."

"Yes."

From behind him, the pilot asked, "Sir, would you like the luggage in the trunk?"

Jesse glanced back at the pilot, nodded, then met my gaze again.

I raised a hand and rushed to say, "Please don't ask. I like to be prepared. That's all that is. Walking shoes. A bathing suit. Also a change of clothes. Just in case. Not because I think I'm staying over or moving in. Oh my God, that sounds bad, doesn't it? It makes it sound like those are thoughts I've had, but I haven't. I don't want you to think—"

His kiss cut me off, and the anxiety that had been rising within me faded away. This kiss was tender and reassuring, just a sweet caress of his lips over mine. "I'm glad you're here."

"Me too."

His grin returned. "You brought luggage to our first date."

I gave his chest a shove. "Don't make me kick your ass."

"Kiss?" There was laughter in his eyes.

"You, sir, have poor hearing."

"A man can hope." His grin widened, and he offered a hand for me to take. I did and marveled at how natural it felt to have my fingers intertwined with his.

We made our way to his car. He opened the passenger door for me, keeping his arm over it as I slid in before closing the door for me. Before starting the car, he turned to me. "There's a walkway in an old area of Newport that skirts between the ocean and the mansions the area is known for."

"I've heard of it. It's called the Cliff Walk, right?"

"Yes. I thought we'd start there. Are you up for a walk? It's about three miles."

"I brought sneakers."

"In your—"

"Don't say it."

He chuckled. "It can be windy there. I suggest a jacket."

"I have one."

"You've thought of everything." Fire lit his gaze. "Just how prepared are you?"

There was a playfulness to the moment that I couldn't resist. "Protection for if you knock my socks off, a new book on my Kindle in case you don't."

His head tipped back, and he laughed. I joined in. When we both settled, he buckled his seat belt and started the car. "Ready?"

I buckled myself in as well. "Not really, but let's do this."

CHAPTER TWENTY

JESSE

Yes.

I understood then why she'd been impossible to get out of my thoughts—her touch felt right. Every heated look, every laugh I couldn't hold back, made me wonder how I'd ever settled for less. I refused to believe that anything I could feel so strongly about wasn't real.

As we drove, I said, "Last night I told you about my family. I'd like to hear more about yours."

She shrugged. "There's not much to say that I haven't already told you."

"I don't believe that."

"I'm not that complicated of a person."

"How did you become a flavorist? That's a job I never would have even thought of, although once you think about it, it makes sense that it's a thing."

"My father loved to eat, so my mother was always trying to figure out how to make what she cooked healthier. I paid attention. When I studied chemistry in high school, a light went on in my head. Formulas are simply complicated recipes. I understood them quickly and then better than my teacher did."

"That couldn't have gone well."

"It did, actually. Some teachers might be intimidated by students who challenge them, but Mr. Brown wasn't. He told my classmates to remember my name because one day I'd change the world. Then he called my parents and told them to sign me up for a college chemistry course. I credit him for teaching me more than chemistry—he taught me to believe in myself."

I took her hand in mine and gave it a squeeze. "That's incredible."

She nodded. "He was a wonderful man. I spoke at his funeral. A lot of his old students did. He refused to give anyone a perfect score on anything, but that was because he wanted us to keep reaching for more. When success comes too easily, there's no joy in it."

"Sounds like my father."

A tinge of sadness inflected her tone when she said, "Not mine. My parents celebrated everything I did. If I fell and skinned my knee, it was the most spectacular fall either of them had ever witnessed."

"That's how Scott describes his parents."

She sighed. "I miss them so much—every single day."

"Family is important to you."

She gave my hand a little shake. "I'm sorry I keep bringing up these heavy topics. Do you mind if we talk about something else?"

I was more than a little curious about her family, but I also wanted to enjoy the day. "Absolutely. Tell me about this lab of yours. You said you're part owner. Who did you go into business with?"

"My roommate, Ellie. We met while I was doing research for my dissertation. She was working as a medicinal chemist for a major biopharmaceutical company. She's brilliant, had her PhD in organic chemistry before she could legally drink, and was making good money, but she was bored. We hit it off right away, became friends, then roommates, then pooled our money and started a business together." Crystal smiled. "She says her mother inspired her to study hard, but I brought flavor to her career choice."

None of that sounded like someone who needed to spy for their uncle. "With your level of success, I'm surprised you still live together."

She raised and lowered both shoulders. "We get along, and I'm not as happy on my own. How about you? Do you live with anyone?"

"No." For clarification, I added, "I used to have live-in staff, but when I bought my apartment, I decided to have them only come during the day while I'm at work."

"You like things to be efficient."

I met her gaze briefly. "Doesn't everyone?"

"It's not a criticism, just something I noticed on the plane. It's an airborne office."

"Absolutely."

"Because you don't take vacations."

"Never had the time to." I shot her another look. "How about you? What's your favorite destination?"

"As an adult it's been my lab, but my parents used to have a trailer at a campground on a lake when I was a kid. We used to go canoeing and have campfires . . ." She cleared her throat. "Most of my trips since then have been to see my uncle. He flies me out to wherever he is. Always makes sure I have a nice room with a great view. Like you, he doesn't take vacations. He sees them as a waste of time."

I laced my fingers through hers. "That was what I believed."

"Until?"

With another woman I might not have been as honest. I wanted her to know me, even the parts that were still in progress. "Until I stepped out of my life and into my brother's."

She cocked her head to the side. "And decided you also wanted to be a farmer?"

"God, no." I wove in and out of traffic, doing my best to keep my attention on the road instead of her face. "I love what I do. It's just been a long time since I allowed myself anything else."

"I can understand. Without realizing it, we can get stuck in ruts. I'm here with you to actually pull myself out of one. I thought I was being careful, but somehow that led to avoiding all risks. I didn't even see that I was doing it." She let out a wistful sigh. "I don't want to live like that anymore."

I raised her hand to my lips and kissed her fingers. "I want to be a risk worth taking, though I have no idea where this is going."

The look we exchanged was intense and difficult to cut short, but I needed to focus on the cars around me. "I wish we hadn't met the way we did."

"I want to make it past that."

"Me too."

We arrived at our first destination. I parked the car on a side road that led down to the ocean. I released my seat belt and turned to her. "Until we do, there are things I can't tell you, but I won't lie to you, and I need to know that you'll do the same. That's all I ask of you."

She searched my face, then nodded. "I don't know what's going on between you and my uncle, and I don't want to. Don't show me or tell me anything you wouldn't want him to know about. I don't want to choose a side."

I believed her, and that made everything better and worse at the same time. "You may one day have to."

Her eyes darkened, and her voice sounded strangled. "I won't. I will never again choose between two people I care about, so don't put me in that position."

Her raw pain hit me like a sucker punch. A wave of protectiveness washed over me. I wanted to know who had hurt her, but more than that I wanted her to never feel that way again. I couldn't give her the promise she was looking for, though, because there was an element I had no control over—her uncle. I brought a hand up to caress her cheek as I spoke. "The only way I could ensure I won't do that is if we end things now—and I don't want that."

Her hand came up to cover mine. "I don't either."

She leaned in. I touched my forehead to hers. "This is so fucked up."

She chuckled without humor. "Why couldn't you be something easy, like too young for me?"

I raised my head. "Sounds like there's a story behind that statement."

She smiled. "There is, and I might just tell you, but I didn't fly here to sit in a car all day."

I laughed. She was a wonderful combination of strong and sweet, confident and unsure. Every time I thought I had her pegged, she showed me another side of her—and I liked it. "Then let's rummage for your sneakers under the kitchen sink you packed and grab that jacket because it looks windy out there."

"So bossy." She laughed. "Isn't a first date when you're supposed to be on your best behavior?"

"I make my own rules." I loved her playfulness. I bent close to her ear and growled, "Is that a problem?"

Her eyes widened and dilated. "I'll let you know." I was glad to see the shadows fade from them.

"I'm sure you will." I gave her a quick kiss before getting out of the car and walking around to open her door. She held on to my arm as she stepped out of her high heels and put on socks and sneakers.

After closing the trunk of the car, I took her hand and led her down the street toward the stone wall that flanked the ocean side of the path. She stopped and pointed to a warning sign that showed a person falling off the cliff. "'Stay on the paved path. Steep cliff. High risk of injury.' Have you ever taken anyone here before?"

I rubbed a thumb over my chin. "And had them live?" I pretended to count on my fingers, then chuckled. "No. This is a first. Apparently, be careful."

She gave me a long look, then tightened her hand on mine. "You too, because if I fall, you're coming with me." Her wink took my breath away.

I'm already falling. I didn't say it aloud, but the thought rocketed through me. The sun was bright on our faces, the wind from the ocean whipping her hair around, and I wanted to stretch that moment, that feeling, forever. "Then we'd better both be careful."

She held my gaze. "Or not—just this once."

A small group with children walked by us, effectively stopping me before I had the chance to say more than either of us would be comfortable with. I gave her hand a light tug and said, "Let's go. You didn't fly here just to read warning signs either."

We headed down some stone steps. The path had a chain-link fence on one side and a stone wall on the other. The cement path didn't appear all that dangerous, but I could see there were opportunities for poor choices. On the ocean side, there was a steep drop to rocks. Where land jutted out, people must have climbed the fence to sit on the other side. Crystal followed my gaze and said, "I don't know if I feel sorry for them for not valuing their lives more or if I envy them for being that level of free."

I could have made a joke or tried to get her out onto those rocks, but that wasn't how I'd been raised. "The view isn't worth it. I'm not afraid to risk everything, but I need it to be for a good reason."

"What would a good reason be?"

This was about being real. "Family."

She nodded.

I added, "If I saw a child headed toward the edge, that would also be enough for me to hop the fence."

She pointed toward a man who was backing up more and more to take the perfect selfie. "Not him?"

I shook my head at the arrogance of the man's actions. "My father would say you can't save stupid."

Her eyes widened. "I'm not sure I want to meet your father, but it does sound like he and my uncle would have lively conversations."

"No one is perfect, but my father checked all the boxes I feel are important in a parent. One, he stayed. Two, he doesn't say anything he doesn't mean. I've never wondered where I stood with him or if I was a priority. He definitely had high expectations for both me as well as Thane, but I'm a better man for it."

Her fingers gave mine a squeeze. "You'll make a wonderful father one day."

Had someone said that to me a few weeks earlier, I would have laughed and said neither a family nor having children was anywhere on my radar. Instead, I said, "I hope so." I glanced down at her. "How about you? Running your own lab is a full-time job. Can you imagine adding a family to that?"

"Adding, yes. Giving up one to have the other—no."

"I understand that. My goals are interwoven with my family's. They rely on me as much as I rely on them."

"You make me wish I had a sibling."

I pulled her closer to me, wrapping an arm around her waist as we walked. "It has its moments. Thane and I figured out early that we did better when we worked together rather than against each other."

"You sound like you're close."

"We are. We're different. He is someone who considers all possible outcomes before moving forward."

"And you?"

"I trust my instincts and for Thane to have my back when I'm wrong."

She shuddered beneath my arm. "Don't ever take him for granted. Not everyone has someone like that in their lives."

I stopped, bringing her to a halt beside me. There was so much I wanted to ask her, too much. So I kissed her instead. I hoped the gentle caress of my lips would reassure her, the tip of my tongue would entice her, and the warmth of my arms would bring her the sense of security she seemed to be yearning for. It was an emotion-packed kiss that she met hungrily, eliciting an answering hunger in me. As the kiss heated up, we moved to the side until Crystal's back was against the stone wall.

She arched against me, wrapping her arms around my neck. My cock strained to be released. It was heaven.

"Excuse me," a woman said loudly enough that I raised my head just in time for her to go past, pulling a wagon with a child in it.

The little boy asked, "Mommy, are they making a baby?"

"God, I hope not," his mother answered. "Don't look."

"Hi. They're looking at me." The little man waved at me, and I laughed as Crystal hid her face in my shoulder. I waved back.

As the woman and her child disappeared around the corner, I hugged Crystal closer and laughed again. "So that happened."

Crystal tipped her head back to meet my gaze. "I never thought I'd be *that* person."

"Me either."

She opened her mouth to say something, seemed to change her mind, then simply looked up at me. I could have pushed her to tell me, but that wasn't how I wanted things to unfold with us. I liked her, but there was no way to know where we were headed. Either we'd find common ground or we wouldn't.

I stepped back and held out my hand to her. "Let's keep walking."

Relief softened her expression. She placed her hand in mine. "Yes."

We didn't say anything at first as we walked, but it was a comfortable silence. We came across a grassy area and one of the first mansions that lined the path. "What building is that?" she asked.

"It's part of Salve Regina University. Ochre Court? These were summer homes. Hard to imagine putting that much work into a vacation home."

"The late 1800s. A.k.a. the Gilded Age—at least for the very rich. I read that many of these mansions were built as showpieces by the rich trying to outdo each other. Imagine being that successful and still that insecure."

"I cannot. The idea of endless parties full of people already planning how to make their own event more impressive sounds exhausting."

"I agree. I've never enjoyed big crowds, though. I'll go if it's work related, but given the choice, I'd rather remain behind the scenes."

"I don't mind being the point person on a project, and often that means I have to attend an event I wouldn't normally choose to. It's a necessary evil, though."

"What do you enjoy most about what you do?"

"Negotiating contracts—that's the adrenaline rush."

She glanced over at me. "You like to win."

"Who doesn't?" I lowered my voice. "If you were competing for a job with another flavorist, you can't even tell me you wouldn't get competitive. I don't believe you'd settle for being second best."

Her smile was a full admission. "You're right. We've gone up against bigger labs, even some in-house ones, and we win the jobs because we outperform them. We stay at the top by keeping informed of the latest research and striving to be innovative."

"That's exactly how Thane and I have moved our company forward." Since she now knew my last name, it wouldn't have taken more than a Google search for her to discover our next project, which was why I said, "In fact, we just signed a contract with Bellerwood to design their air-filtration system. It's exciting to play a part in something big like a space station."

She pulled me to a halt. "You're serious?"

"I am."

"That's fantastic!" Her happiness for me shone in her eyes.

I smiled. "Thanks." Her enthusiasm for my project took me by surprise. She seemed to genuinely care about how I felt about what I was doing and looked . . . *proud* of me? My heart thudded crazily in my chest. I felt capable of anything and everything when I looked into her eyes. Being with her felt so damn good.

She shook her head in amazement. "Really, amazing."

"Now we just have to make it happen."

Searching my face, she said, "How did I ever think you were a farmer?"

"I have no fucking idea." We both laughed. "Remember all those notes on the food bins at the barn? LJ wrote them for me because I had no idea what to do. I met the animals as I introduced them to you."

Her mouth rounded as she appeared to be going over our first encounter in her head. "Oh, so much makes sense now. You didn't know what you were doing either."

"No clue."

"Then why ask me to do it with you?"

"I was hoping to keep you off balance enough that you'd tell me something I could use."

"Something about my uncle."

"Yes."

She slid her hand out of mine. "How do I know this date isn't about that as well?"

And that was our greatest hurdle—trusting each other when we both had reasons not to. "You don't. All you have is my promise that I won't lie to you again."

She blinked a few times. "This is hard."

"It sure is."

Her chest rose as she took a deep breath. "If you're with me hoping I'll tell you more about my uncle, I won't."

"Good, because I would use whatever I learned about him to protect my family even if that meant ruining your uncle. He won't get Scott's farm—not the rights to it, not access to it, nothing."

"If you went after my uncle, I'd do whatever I could to stop you— even if that meant ruining *you*."

"Then we need to make sure we don't get to that place."

She was all eyes as she asked, "And how do we do that?"

I took her hand in mine again. "I don't know yet, but my gut tells me we can . . . and my instincts are good."

"Except when they're wrong."

"It has happened." I conceded the truth of that with a nod. "If trying to figure us out is too complicated, tell me and we'll call this off. No hard feelings. We tried."

Her hand tightened on mine. "You'd be okay with that?"

"If it was what you wanted—yes." I dipped my face closer to hers. "Just be clear about what you want."

She went up on her tiptoes, threw her arms around my neck, and gave me a kiss that rocked me back onto my heels.

That's clear enough.

CHAPTER TWENTY-ONE

CRYSTAL

Holding back wasn't possible with Jesse. I was on fire as soon as we touched. I opened my mouth, deepening our kiss, and writhed against him. Desire licked through me, making everything else fade away. Powerful. Primal. It was a hunger that didn't want to be denied and one that I was eager to feed.

I dug my hands into his hair.

His touch was rough and sure as he held me even closer.

Had we been anywhere private, I would have torn his shirt and shed mine without hesitation. When his mouth left mine to trail kisses down my jaw to my neck, I moaned and gave myself over to the sheer pleasure his mouth wrought.

I'd never understood how people went back to lovers they'd broken up with. *This. This would be enough to weaken any woman's resolve.*

Breathing raggedly, Jesse raised his head. "We have to stop before I get way too excited to care about anything beyond dragging you off to a room somewhere."

I bit my bottom lip, then said, "Would that be so bad?"

"No, but"—his grin sent a flutter through me—"I actually put thought and effort into planning this date."

He made it sound like that was novel for him. I laughed. "You poor man. And here I am thinking only of myself."

"Exactly." He kissed me briefly, then put me back from him. "Now stop distracting me. I want to do this right."

Right? Everything we were doing felt pretty damn right to me. Still, his tone was serious, and I didn't want to rush and ruin whatever this was either. I strove to keep it together on the outside, but my insides went into full-blown chaos. All I was capable of was a nod.

He offered me his hand, and we started walking again. In an attempt to calm myself, I asked, "So what do you have planned?"

"Something you'll either love or hate."

"That's vague."

He met my gaze. "Are you the type who needs to know?"

I didn't want to be—not anymore. "No."

He smiled. "Good."

We walked farther, past a few buildings. The path now had a black chain-link fence on both sides. Behind it on one side, a large stone home appeared. I exclaimed, "It looks like an Italian castle."

"That's the Breakers, and I believe that was the look the Vanderbilts were shooting for. It's heavy on classical Greek and Roman architecture."

"Amazing." We made our way past the house to a street where we found the entrance to the mansion. "This is really interesting."

"I'm glad you like it." We entered through a huge iron gate and walked down a gravel driveway to where a private guide was waiting for us. The ornate limestone exterior of the building had been beautifully kept up, as had the lush gardens that surrounded it.

My jaw dropped open just inside the mansion when we entered the fifty-foot, two-floor marble great hall. Murals covered the ceilings. Corinthian pilasters ran from the first floor well above the second floor. The detailed carvings on the moldings blended with stunning accents that were both overpowering and stirring at the same time. The architect had designed not just a room but an experience. A large burgundy-carpeted staircase curved beneath a stained glass skylight. Simply stunning.

At my side, Jesse soaked it in as well. Neither of us paid much attention to the tour guide, who ushered us from the hall to one of the rooms off it. There was too much to see.

Once the initial awe faded and we made our way through one luxurious room after another, I began to feel sorry for the family who had built it. Had I lived there, it would have felt more like a cage where I was put on display than a home.

"What are you thinking?" Jesse asked.

I told him, then added, "Not that it's not beautiful. It's a piece of art. I just can't imagine ever being comfortable in it. Not one single room in it says, *Kick off your shoes and relax, because you're safe here.*"

"Is that what you're looking for? Somewhere safe?"

"Isn't everyone?"

He nodded slowly, then tucked me to his side and kissed my forehead. "Hard to believe I doubted your intelligence when we first met."

My head snapped back. "What?"

He held my gaze without blinking.

Meanwhile memories of our first meeting flashed through my head. I rolled my eyes skyward. "That blouse was perfectly modest that morning when I left the house."

His grin was a tell that it hadn't been by the time he'd seen it. "I'm also partial to that skirt. It made it difficult to remember why you were there."

I batted my eyelashes. "Why, sir, did you just give me a compliment?"

"I did." He bent and growled into my ear, "Even though wearing that outfit was an obvious ploy."

Leaning back so I could look him in the eyes, I said, "It was not."

He frowned. "You don't have to deny it. All's fair in love and . . . business."

I stiffened in his arms. "I'm denying it because it's not true. I spend most of my time in a lab coat and slacks. I wanted to look business professional, and that's the only reason I wore that skirt and blouse."

"It doesn't matter."

"It does to me." I pushed out of his arms. "You expect me to believe you when you say you won't lie to me again. Trust goes both ways. I haven't lied to you, but you still think I would."

The air became thick with tension.

Our guide came over and asked, "The next room is the kitchen. Would you like to hear the rationale for putting it off in a wing by itself?"

Without looking away from each other, in unison we both said, "No."

He cleared his throat. "I'll stand by the connecting door—whenever you're ready."

The standoff between us continued even after we were alone again. I wanted to be with Jesse, but not if he had a low opinion of me. He looked as if he was waiting for me to say something first, but I was doing the same.

Eventually, Jesse released an audible breath. "You're right."

Some of my tension eased. "Thank you."

"We keep coming back to this place."

"And we might continue to—until we get it right."

"I'm used to dating being easy, but things tend to be when you don't care about the outcome."

That sent my heart racing. It fit how I felt perfectly.

He stepped closer. "I wasn't aware that I was holding on to a negative slant about how we met. I'll work on that."

My smile was tentative. "Trust takes time."

His answering smile had me wishing I could launch myself into his arms again. "We should probably go hear about why the kitchen has its own wing."

Without looking away, I said, "It's to contain the burn in case of a fire."

Placing his hands on my hips, he lowered his voice. "Fire has a mind of its own. Can it really be contained?"

I shifted closer and placed my hands on his chest. "I used to think it could be, but now I'm not so sure."

His mouth came down until it hovered over mine. "What changed your mind?"

"You." I ran my tongue across my bottom lip.

"My answer to that question would be the same." He brought a hand up and ran his thumb over the same path my tongue had taken. "You and I shouldn't make sense, but when we're together, we're all that does."

"Yes."

His kiss was brief but bold, and I swayed into it. When he raised his head, he said, "I should have chosen somewhere more private for our first date."

I framed his face with my hands. "No, those instincts you trust were spot on. We need time to get to know each other."

He turned his face to kiss one of my hands, then stepped back. "I do feel a little sorry for our guide. I haven't listened to a word he's said. All of my attention has been on you."

I took him by the hand and began to lead him toward where the guide was standing. "It really is an impressive mansion."

"Mansion?" He looked around as if he hadn't realized where we were. "What mansion?"

I laughed and hugged him. "I love you."

He tensed.

I groaned. I wasn't in love with him, but I was with the moment. I could have said, *I love being here with you.* Or *I love how easy it is to laugh with you.*

Or I could have avoided the L-word altogether. That would have been best.

But no, I had to voice a declaration I didn't even mean.

Awkwardly frozen in time, I forced myself to meet his gaze. "I don't—*love* you. I don't know why I said that."

He blinked a few times, then said, "It's okay."

Telling myself that throwing up would not make the situation better, I swallowed hard before adding, "I meant it like when a person says they love ice cream. I know we're just starting to get to know each other, and it's way too soon to really know how we feel at all. I'm still trying to figure out if I even like you—"

"Crystal."

I stopped and swallowed again, fighting a minor panic attack. "Yes?"

"Breathe."

I gulped in air and deliberately released it slowly, then repeated the process. "Sorry. I just don't want you to think—"

His mouth claimed mine with the sweetest kiss he'd given me to date. Gentle. Reassuring. I shuddered against him as my panic subsided.

His voice was deep and rough when he raised his head to say, "Want to know what I think about when I'm around you? This. You in my arms, those soft lips of yours anywhere and everywhere you'd like them to go on me, and how much I want to know the taste and feel of every inch of you. That's it." His smile returned. "Also, sometimes I wonder how many condoms you packed. I'm curious to see how optimistic you were."

"I don't know. I grabbed a handful."

"I take anything more than one as a compliment." His smile was infectious.

"I never thought of that. How many did you bring?"

"Three. I knew one wouldn't be enough. A whole package seemed like too much."

"I take anything less than the whole package as an insult."

His eyebrows shot up, and I laughed.

He joined in.

We hugged, and everything seemed on track with us again. Against his chest, I murmured, "I really don't love you, but I do like you—more than I expected to."

His arms tightened around me, and he kissed the top of my head.

CHAPTER TWENTY-TWO

JESSE

I didn't consider myself an overly emotional man—definitely not a sentimental one—but the woman in my arms was pulling at all my heartstrings.

I wasn't normally comfortable with relationships that had expectations, but I wanted to promise to be her safe harbor in any storm. I was quickly becoming addicted to how good it felt to hold her, touch her, have her mouth meet mine eagerly.

Even as I told myself to tap the brakes while we figured each other out, it was insanely easy to forget there was any reason for caution. There was no doubt that we'd have sex, but the how and when were slowly killing me. I wanted her so much I ached, but I also knew that things that were rushed into often fell apart just as quickly.

I didn't want that.

Her declaration of love had shaken me, but not for the reason it normally would have. Usually, those three words were my cue to begin to pull back. I'd never allowed myself to get attached and hadn't looked for a commitment from my dates. I'd always been clear about that.

When she'd said she loved me, I didn't want to withdraw. I wanted her to mean it, and although I wasn't in that place yet, I wanted to be able to say it back.

Crazy.

Scary as hell.

Over Crystal's head, I caught the guide checking his watch and looking worried. I understood why. I had something special planned for Crystal, and there was a chance it was already upstairs waiting for us. I felt some sympathy for our guide. We couldn't have been his easiest tour, but I also knew the generous tip I'd give him would ease any annoyance with us. "We should get going."

She nodded and stepped back, slipping her hand back into mine as naturally as if we'd been a couple for years. I resisted the temptation of one last kiss but just barely. It was only the lure of wanting to see her expression when she realized what I'd arranged that had me ushering her toward the guide.

Just outside the kitchen I spotted a Nason radiator. Crystal followed my gaze and smiled. "That's the first radiator I've seen here. I was wondering how they heated the mansion or if they even did, since it was a summer home."

As if excited that we might have finally come across something that interested us, the guide turned and said, "The original Breakers was a wooden home and burned down in a fire. To ensure it wouldn't happen again, the kitchen was built in its own wing, and the boiler room was built underground a good distance away from the house. Pumps moved the water through tunnels to the radiators in the main rooms. Some of the system has been removed and updated, but I could give you a brief tour of what remains if you'd like. Would you like to see the system?"

Would I like that? Hell yes. Even as technology moved us forward, there was wisdom to be found in the ways things had been done before. So much had changed, and yet little had. Whether on land, at sea, or circling the planet in a space station, air quality and temperature mattered.

I took a deep breath.

But not on a first date and not while my surprise for her cooled.

Crystal tugged on my hand. "You don't get an offer like that every day. Let's do it."

My job frequently involved looking at older heating/cooling systems, but never one like this. The Vanderbilts would have gone beyond what was necessary to create a wow factor for that time period. Some might've even been unique to the Breakers. I made a sound deep in my chest as I fought an inner battle. I could always come back. "Another time."

Brushing her breasts temptingly against my arm was enough to scramble my thoughts, but the smile she shot me completely did me in. "You know you want to."

I wanted a lot of things that weren't possible right then.

I shook my head and tried to remember how to speak. In a thick voice I finally said, "You don't want to tour a dusty basement."

She looked me right in the eye. "I do if you do. This date isn't just about me."

A man could fall for a woman like that.

This man was in real danger of it.

A few minutes later we were on our way into the basement, and I found admiration for the architect of the Breakers. Throughout the basement, accessed through cast-iron doors, were indirects inside brick structures big enough for several people to stand in. A series of terracotta sleeves came up through the floor in hydronic catacombs. I'd never seen anything so beautiful—except possibly the woman beside me, who looked just as fascinated by the ductwork. Time had necessitated updates to the system, but they had been perfectly integrated into the original one. When I heard that the initial designs for the system had been burned after it had been completed so it couldn't be easily recreated, I couldn't help grinning from ear to ear. *That's one way to make sure no one steals your secret.*

Crystal smiled up at me. "Aren't you glad you said yes?"

"I am." I pulled her to me for a kiss. Glad that I'd said yes to seeing her again. Yes to giving us a chance to work things through. Life was full of so many moments that didn't matter, but every single moment I'd spent with her felt like it would stay with me forever.

The guide cleared his throat. "If you'd like to see what's left of the original boilers, we have to go outside. I would have said that was where things really heat up, but you two don't seem to have a problem with that."

Crystal and I broke off the kiss, both laughing. She was apologetic. I was not. I did share a look with the guide, though, and he was more amused than judgmental, man to man.

Remembering what we were already late for, I said, "I hear the view from the second-story loggia is beautiful."

The guide nodded and checked his watch. "It's also a good time of day to be up there. I'll take you up the servants' stairway. It's not as grand, but it's impressive in its own way. The house required over twenty servants when the family was here, and they needed to be invisible. The architect made sure that was possible."

We followed him up countless stairs, then down a long hallway that was closed off to the public. The staff had hidden the loggia with dark privacy screens. When we were led through a side entrance, Crystal gasped and turned toward me. "You did this?"

I smiled. "It would be odd if I didn't but we claimed it as ours anyway."

She hugged my chest before pulling me by my hand to a table that was set for two beside one of the arches. "This is like a dream."

She was a breath of fresh air. So many people I knew were impossible to please. So far Crystal had only seen the table and was over the moon. "It gets better."

She hugged me again. "I can't believe you did all this."

I wrapped my arms around her. "We didn't meet in the best of circumstances. I wanted to replace those memories with some good ones."

A waiter appeared and held out a chair for Crystal. She took her seat; then I took mine. The waiter returned with a silver tray with two blindfolds on it, and Crystal gave me a surprised look.

I laughed. "You're going to love this. I hope."

She picked up one of the blindfolds. "What did you plan?"

I took mine from the tray and thanked the waiter. "Do you trust me?"

She looked around. No one could see into the area where we were, but we also weren't in private. "I want to."

We shared that feeling, and it was one of the reasons I'd thought this experience sounded like a good place for us to start. I put my blindfold on first. "It's just as hard for me to lower my guard with you."

I heard her nervous breath. "Okay. I have it on."

There was only the sound of staff moving around us. I said, "I do feel a little ridiculous right now."

She laughed, and I felt her hand touch mine. "I'm glad you said that. I do, too, but I also don't want to take off the blindfold and ruin whatever you've planned."

I laced my fingers through hers. "Hopefully it goes as I imagined."

A male voice began to speak beside us. "Welcome. I'm Chef Goumell. It is my pleasure to present to you a meal identical to one served more than a century ago in this very house, had you been invited to a weekend with the Vanderbilts. Creating such a feast is a labor of love and how I honor the past. Many of the cooking techniques my staff uses have been forgotten by modern kitchens. As you sample each dish, imagine you've been transported back in time. Let the sound of the ocean take you back. Feel the pulse of history with each bite. We will pair the dishes with different wines to complement them. Neither of you have food allergies, correct?"

"Correct," we both said. I wished I could have seen Crystal's face, but I heard the excitement in her voice and felt it in the way she held my hand.

"On your napkin to the left of your plate, we have placed a thinly sliced piece of bread with a dab of freshly made butter. To the right of your plate you'll find your glass of wine. Are you ready for your first dish?"

I waited for Crystal to answer. Hers was a tentative "Yes."

"Then bon appétit, and remember the reason for the blindfold is to enhance your other senses. Take the time to soak in the aromas. Don't gulp the food down. Let it rest on your taste buds. Enjoy the moans of pleasure you hear from your dining partner."

It didn't take more than that for my cock to decide the future needed to include a repeat performance of this with Crystal somewhere more private.

A moment later a waiter introduced himself, and there was the sound of plates being placed before us on the table. "Raw oysters. The chef suggests you don't swallow them without chewing at least once. Those who swallow them whole never fully experience their full flavor."

Crystal made a nervous sound. "I've never eaten a raw oyster, and I have to say it's scary to think about doing it while blindfolded."

It was an opportunity I decided not to miss. "I've eaten my fair share of them. I could guide you through it."

She laughed nervously, then said, "I'm game, but if I dump it on the front of my shirt and you laugh . . ."

"I promise not to laugh, although I can't promise I won't wear some of this myself. I've never eaten them blindfolded."

She gave my hand a squeeze. "Jesse?"

"Yes."

"I've done a lot of food tastings. In fact, it's a large part of what I do, but I've never done anything like this. Thank you for arranging it."

"You're welcome." I released her hand and felt around the table for the correct utensil to use. "There's a small fork next to your plate. I would pick it up with your right hand."

"I have it."

"Now hold one of the oyster shells with your other hand. You don't have to lift it off the plate for this part."

"Got it."

"Use your fork to move the oyster around a little in the shell. You want to loosen it."

"Done."

"We'll do the first one 'naked,' which means with no sauce or lemon. Ready?"

"I think so."

"Raise the shell up to your mouth and slide it onto your tongue. But don't swallow. As the chef said, rushing doesn't allow you to taste the full flavor of it. Bite into it once or twice. Let the juices of the oyster fill your mouth, then swallow."

"Want to do it together on the count of three?"

I chuckled. "Sure."

"One. Two." She paused. "Oh God. I'm surprised how nervous I am. Flavors, both good and bad, don't tend to bother me."

"Our senses are heightened and focused. That's probably it."

"Blindfolds might need to become part of our lab uniform."

"That's not where I was hoping you'd want to use them."

"Excuse me?"

I laughed. "Did I say that out loud?"

"You did." Humor flickered in her tone.

"Three," I said and lifted the oyster shell to my mouth.

The little sound of pleasure she emitted after tasting hers sent my senses into overload. I wanted to rip the blindfold from my face and carry her off to the nearest bed or secluded hallway. At the same time, I didn't want to rush the experience of being with her. Every moment of it was too good not to savor.

She gushed, "That was fantastic. Briny with a hint of melon. I didn't expect that second flavor."

"It's common to put a light butter sauce in the shell. Should we try another?" I felt around the plate until I located a lemon wedge. "This time we could squeeze a little lemon on it."

"I'd like that."

CHAPTER TWENTY-THREE

CRYSTAL

It might have been the amount of wine I consumed as we moved through the courses, but I'd never tasted a better meal or eaten more in one sitting. The oysters were followed by a delicious mushroom-and-lobster broth. Red mullet with a delightful sweet brandy aftertaste. Sweet. Bitter. Sour. Salty. Each dish took my taste buds on a journey of more than one flavor. The main course was duck, followed by fresh fruit with a light glaze.

The chef returned at the end of the meal to tell us we could remove our blindfolds. "How was everything?"

I blinked several times as my eyes adjusted to the light. "Like nothing I've experienced before. Thank you so much."

"It was truly spectacular," Jesse added as he placed his own blindfold onto the table. Spectacular. Yes, that was how it felt to be with him.

"I'm honored to hear you enjoyed it. Stay. Have some coffee. Now that you can, please take in the view," the chef said. "Do you have any questions before I go?"

I almost didn't voice any. A romantic date wasn't really the place to unleash my inner chemist, but I was curious. "I do. Just a few." I met Jesse's gaze. "If that's okay."

He smiled. "Ask away. I was hoping you'd find this interesting."

"'Interesting' is an understatement." I turned back to the chef. "You said you used some techniques that have been mostly forgotten. Could you give me some examples?"

The chef pulled up a chair and spent the next thirty or so minutes talking to us about how food that was cooked over wood had a more distinct flavor than anything prepared over gas or electric heat sources. The heat was usually lower, and dishes spent more time simmering. Also, the type of wood mattered: applewood, mesquite, and almond wood each left its own flavor fingerprint on a dish. The art was in knowing which wood worked best with each food.

I was fascinated.

Even better, Jesse appeared to be as well. He asked if those flavors would infuse vegetables as well as meats. I hadn't expected him to be as interested in the topic as he was, but we were both smiling when the chef finally stood and thanked us for giving him the chance to share his passion for antiquated menus with us.

Alone again, without the distraction of food or the waitstaff, we shared a quiet moment. I remembered my first impression of him as a broody farmer and compared that to the smiling, polished man across from me. Flavor was better when it had nuances that unfolded during the experience. Extremes such as the ones I'd seen in him could make for a memorable, pleasant taste, but not always. Sometimes one flavor masked another.

"What are you thinking?" he asked.

"About oranges and toothpaste."

He cocked his head to one side. "Now, see, that was not where my thoughts were wandering."

I smiled and shook my head. "Sorry."

He leaned forward. "No need to be, but I need to hear more about this toothpaste tangent before I worry that it's a not-so-subtle hint that I should grab a mint."

"Oh no, it's nothing like that." I hesitated. Things were going so well I didn't want to bring up anything that might diminish it. "Have you ever brushed your teeth after you've had a glass of orange juice?"

He made a face. "Unfortunately, yes."

"The detergent molecules tamper with the membranes of your taste buds. It inhibits one's ability to taste sweet and makes tart taste bitter."

"Okay."

"There's also a glycoprotein, miraculin, that can make something sour taste sweet."

Jesse sat back and rubbed a hand over his chin, then said, "You're worried that I may not be what I seem."

"All of this has been so nice . . . so thoughtful. If I hadn't met you at the farm first, I wouldn't have doubts at all."

His lips pressed together, and he didn't say anything at first. "There's nothing I could say that would change how we met or the situation we're in. All we can do is try to ride it out or call it a day and go home."

I felt like the least grateful person on the planet. "God, why do I have to be so difficult?"

He leaned in again. "Not difficult—intelligent and honest. Lies are easy. Many people go through life turning a blind eye to anything they don't want to deal with. You face things head-on, and I like that about you."

Not since I'd lost my parents had I felt so accepted for who I was. "Because you do the same."

"Yes . . . according to Thane, I'm often more direct than I should be. Okay, that may be according to a lot of people." He smiled. "Either way, I don't see the point of dancing around a problem. Bring it into the light, shake it out, see what it's made of, and deal with it."

That took real confidence. He'd said he trusted his instincts, and I envied that about him. He thought we were similar, but I didn't have nearly as much confidence in my decisions as he did. Could I get it back? "I used to be more like that, but now I wait until I have all the information and have had time to weigh my options."

"And how is that working out for you?"

To some that might have seemed like a rude question, but I felt it was sincere. "Not fun, but I'm working on it."

He gave me a long look, then stood. "There's so much more to see in Newport than the mansions. Let's get out of here."

I rose to my feet, then placed a hand on his arm. "Thank you—for all of this—and for understanding."

He winked. "Don't tell anyone. I have a badass reputation to uphold."

Chuckling, I went on my tiptoes and whispered in his ear, "I believe you."

"Hey, what's that supposed to mean?" His head shot up, but he was smiling.

Doing my best to mimic his voice from the first day we'd met, I said, "'You have nothing I'm interested in.'"

He made a face. "Ouch, did I say that?"

"You did."

"I was shooting for unapproachable."

"You hit the mark." Although my words were harsh, my tone wasn't.

He took my hand, tucked it into the crook of his arm, and began to lead me out of the loggia. "It was your fault. I had a plan, but you had to go and wear that blouse. What you witnessed was my attempt at damage control."

I stopped and looked up at him. "I'll take that compliment even though it's bullshit."

He turned me toward him, then yanked me flush against him. "What part of this is bullshit?"

The kiss he gave me—deep, demanding—removed all doubt about how attracted he was to me. This was raw hunger. His touch was bold. Impatient. It brought an answering desire in me that had me winding myself around him.

There was the loud sound of someone clearing their throat. "I was going to ask you if you'd like to see the bedrooms on this floor, but it's probably best if we skip that part of the tour."

Jesse laughed against my lips, then raised his head. "What *is* he implying?"

"I have no idea." I laughed as well, hugged Jesse, then stepped back. "But he's probably right."

CHAPTER TWENTY-FOUR

Jesse

I was tempted to head from the Breakers straight to the nearest hotel with Crystal, but I wanted her to see Newport . . . and then the sunrise from my arms. I'd taken the liberty of booking an oceanfront suite near the docks in Newport. If we didn't use it, we didn't use it, but if things remained hot and heavy, we now had a place we could go seamlessly. Digital keys were a genius invention.

Since it was a beautiful summer day, we drove downtown and parked at Brick Market Place. We explored several of the shops, then made our way to the more historic Thames Street. Conversation was light and easy. Shopping-wise, she was by far the least expensive date I'd been on in a while. Although she enjoyed wandering through the stores, she didn't seem keen on buying anything. At first I thought she felt odd about spending my money, but that theory was disproved when we visited the arcade. We spent more there than I would have thought possible but had a great time.

Afterward, we bought ice cream and continued our walking tour of the area, then stopped for drinks at an outdoor bar near the water. I had been to Newport many times before, but she hadn't, and I loved seeing it through her eyes. We found an open bench on the dock and sat for a while, watching sailboats come in and out.

"Have you ever been sailing?" she asked.

"Not since college."

"Did you enjoy it?"

"I did. Very much. I just haven't had time."

She nodded.

I shifted closer to her and ran my hand through her hair. "How about you? What would you like to do that you haven't made time for?"

She turned to face me. "This. I had fun today, and that's something I haven't allowed myself in a long time. It was a perfect day. I saw new places, learned some things, tasted an oyster for the first time . . . blindfolded . . . every part of today was incredible."

I leaned in and kissed her cheek. "It's not over yet."

Her face flushed, and her eyes lit with desire. "Are you suggesting that I won't be reading my Kindle during my flight home tonight?"

Our eyes locked, and my heart started thudding wildly in my chest. "Not unless you want to?"

She laid a hand on my thigh. "What's my other option?"

I bent, brushed my lips gently over hers, and whispered, "Stay."

"At the farm?"

"I was thinking someplace here would be better. Some have suites with amazing views of the ocean." I hated that I wasn't sure if she'd push to return to the farm. If she did, it would change things. I didn't want that to happen, but there were aspects of this I had no control over.

She took a moment to search my face, and I held my breath. There was something on her mind, and she looked like she was about to share it. *Don't ask to go to Scott's farm . . . not after how good today was.* She tapped a finger on my chest. "Why do I have the feeling you've already booked a place?"

I waited for more, but when none came, I let out a relieved breath. "I may have."

Her eyebrows rose. "*May* have?"

I grinned. "Okay, I did."

She leaned forward, ran her hand higher up my thigh until it brushed the edge of my hardened cock, and growled, "Then what the hell are we still doing on this bench?"

"Wasting precious time." I stood and pointed to a hotel. "Thankfully our hotel is right here."

She gasped. "You're serious?"

I tried to appear innocent. "A lucky coincidence."

She wagged a finger at me.

I laughed. "Do you think you're the only one who likes to be prepared?"

With her tucked to my side, we made our way through the hotel lobby and to an elevator that would take us to the top floor. She was in my arms the moment the door closed behind us. I kissed her with all the need building within me. She made these delicious little noises and writhed against me.

When we reached our floor, the elevator opened right into the suite—which was a good thing because although I'd never been big on public displays of affection, I couldn't have held back.

Without breaking off the kiss, I freed her from her shirt and bra. She yanked my shirt up and out of my trousers, removing it from me just as eagerly. Backing her against the wall, I kissed my way across her jaw, down the curve of her beautiful neck, over one of her shoulders.

She wrapped her arms around my neck, dug her hands into my hair, teased my chest with her bare nipples. I kissed my way lower, over the curve of her breast. Every woman was different, but I knew a few tricks that tended to please. I took my time, using the heat from my breath to warm her skin. With my tongue I circled and teased.

She moaned and arched, but I didn't rush. I undid her pants and slid them down over her long legs, then moved my attention to her other breast while my hands ran up and down the glorious expanse of skin I'd exposed.

When her breathing became erratic, I began to flick my tongue back and forth over her nub. Her hands came up to clutch my shoulders. I gave her other nipple equal attention, slowly, like we had all night—because we did. A flick. A light tug. A graze of my teeth. I brought it all out until I found what drove her wild, and then I took her higher.

Her hands were feverishly undoing my belt when I took the kiss lower, and her hands fell away. With her back to the wall, I spread her legs and sank to my knees between them. I hitched one of her legs over my shoulder and parted her sex with two of my fingers. Just as deliberately slow, I began to tease her clit. Some women were a slow burn, but with patience, man, could they burn. I sucked on her clit gently while easing a finger into her. The hot warmth of her as well as the scent of her excitement wasn't new to me. I sought the rhythm of a stroke that had sent her over the edge the first time. She'd told me she'd had problems coming when she wasn't alone. I'd make it my mission to ensure that was never an issue with me.

With me.

I paused, not liking the idea that another man might find pleasure with her after me.

After me. When would that be? Did it have to be?

She dug a hand into my hair and begged me not to stop. I resumed pumping my finger in and out of her. Deeper. Harder. Faster. All the while I worshipped her clit with my tongue.

When her hand fisted in my hair and her release rocked through her, there was only one thought going through my head—*mine*.

That was what I wanted her to be.

Somewhere on the floor my phone announced a call from my father. I ignored it, choosing instead to kiss Crystal's stomach while lowering her leg back to the floor. The phone announced a second call from him, and I groaned. My father didn't call twice in a row unless it was an emergency.

Looking beautifully flushed, Crystal straightened off the wall as I stood. I took a moment to soak in the naked perfection of her. She wasn't thin; she was better—curvy, lush, so damn tempting I wanted to break my phone when my father's third call came.

"That's my father. I have to take it to make sure he's safe."

With a smile that said she was still floating down from her orgasm, she assured me that was fine. I suggested she find the bedroom and said I'd meet her there in a minute. She gave me a hot kiss and a slap on my still-clothed ass and told me to hurry.

Hell yes.

I answered my phone while Crystal was gathering her clothes from the floor, bent over in a way that made it nearly impossible to form a coherent thought. "Hello," I croaked.

"We need to talk."

Crystal disappeared through a door. *Not now we don't.* "Are you okay?"

"No, I'm not. You and Thane are suddenly 'too busy' to see me. I know you just signed a huge contract, so I'm fine with it—but then you stop returning my calls. So I dropped by your office today to see you."

Oh no.

"And I had the most interesting conversation with you—but it wasn't you."

"What?"

"Thankfully I know about your twin, or I would have thought you'd had a stroke or something. When I asked how your project was coming, nothing that came out of your mouth made any damn sense."

Shit. "He's not supposed to leave my apartment or talk to anyone I know. That was our agreement."

"Apparently he didn't get that part of whatever agreement you two made. He was in one of your suits and was looking pretty damn comfortable in your office."

"Dammit. I'll talk to him. Thane is supposed to be watching him."

"I want to know what you've gotten yourself into. I called Thane first, but he was tight lipped."

I'd have to thank Thane for that. It wasn't easy to stand up to our father. "I asked him not to say anything." I gave my father a brief overview of what had brought about the switch. All he really needed to know was that I was there to help Scott save his farm. "We were originally going to switch only for a few hours, but then things got—complicated."

"You met a woman."

"Yes. No. Yes, I met someone, but no, she's not the reason we didn't switch back yet. That's not entirely true. She is part of the reason, but there's also LJ, the beans, the oil company, Remy, and now I'm waiting on a bionic leg for a duck."

"You're not experimenting with drugs, are you? Haven't I always warned you how easy it is to lose everything if you go down that road?"

"I'm not doing drugs, Dad."

"Whatever you're playing around with, it's time to get your ass back here and make sure you don't lose everything you've worked for."

I sighed. I didn't work for my father anymore, but I did respect him. He sounded angry because he was worried. I regretted not telling him what I'd planned or letting him in on where I was once those plans changed. "I can't, Dad. Not yet. I'm kind of in the middle of something."

"What's this one's name? Wait, it doesn't matter because you never introduce me to the same one twice. You've always been smart like that."

"Crystal. Her name is Crystal. And she's different."

"They all seem that way in the beginning."

I definitely wasn't ready to have this conversation with my father, but it also felt important to defend Crystal to him. "She could be the one."

"The one? There's no such thing."

"I don't want to argue, Dad, but I also don't agree."

"You don't find it oddly convenient that *the one* shows up right after you sign a lucrative deal for your company? Money is a woman magnet."

I sighed. That wasn't Crystal—not if my instincts about her were right. I'd never doubted the loyalty of my father or Thane. We were family and that was unshakable, but were we the only kind of family that could be like that? Not all women were like my mother. Crystal was loyal. She was honest. I couldn't imagine her walking away from her children. "If you want to help, Dad, keep Scott away from the office. Take him golfing or something."

"I don't golf. You know that."

"Find something you could do together. You might enjoy getting to know him."

"If you need me to."

"I do." I almost didn't, but I added, "Don't be as blunt with him as you are with Thane and me. He wasn't raised that way, and he wouldn't understand it."

"Is that your way of saying I sound like an asshole?"

"Only when you care. And I'd judge you for it, but I sound the same way."

He made a *hmmph* sound, then said, "You're going to do what you want, but don't rush into anything. You've come too far to piss everything away on a woman. Have a little fun, then get your brain out of your pants and back on your company."

To end the circular trajectory the conversation was taking, I decided to infuse some humor. "I was trying to get it out of my pants, but you called enough that I was worried it was a real emergency."

He didn't laugh, and I didn't dare make another joke. Finally he said, "I don't like that you and Thane did this without consulting me. There's more going on there than you're telling me, isn't there?"

"I'll tell you everything, Dad, but you have horrible timing. I'll be back in a couple of days."

"This isn't like you, Jesse. You don't keep things from me."

"I know, and it wasn't deliberate. Originally it wasn't worth mentioning; then it got so messy I didn't really want to discuss it. But I'm following my gut on this, and I have a handle on it now. I'll be back at the office before you know it, but right now I'm where I belong."

"For God's sake, don't get her pregnant."

I smiled. "Good night, Dad."

"Call me tomorrow. I'm worried."

"I know. I'm sorry, and I will."

"I love you."

"Love you, too, Dad."

After the call ended, I dialed Scott's number. When he didn't answer, I called Thane. After updating him on where Dad had found Scott, I asked Thane if he needed me to come back.

"No, no," Thane said. "I'll talk to him. He's been going out more and more, but I assumed it was because of the woman he said he'd met. I'll track him down and figure out what's going on."

"He met a woman as me? You're not supposed to let him go anywhere."

"That was easy to enforce when you were switching for a few hours—even a couple of days. When you decided to hunker down in his life, just what did you think would happen over here?"

I sighed. "I didn't think about it. Is he still anxious to switch back? We could now. I could track down Remy as myself."

"I'll ask, but Scott's been looking pretty happy lately. My guess is you have time to figure out that side. I'll just make sure I clarify with him that he can't go to the office. I have no idea what he was doing there."

"I asked Dad to spend some time with him."

"You really think that'll be less trouble?"

"It would be nice for Dad to know him."

"I guess." He chuckled. "I'll join them the first time. It should be entertaining to watch."

"Keep me updated."

"Hey, how was your date?"

Thane had started checking in daily. There was nothing he didn't know. "Wonderful, actually. In fact, it has the promise of getting even better if I can get off the damn phone."

He laughed. "Go. We'll talk tomorrow."

"Bye." I ended the call, turned the ringer off, and dug the condoms out of my pants pocket. On the way to the bedroom, I shed my clothing until all I was wearing was a big smile. The last few minutes had been a speed bump, but it didn't take more than the memory of Crystal coming in my mouth for my engines to be fully revved. My heart was thudding, my blood rushing downward, and I was imagining just how good things were about to be. The room was dimly lit, but I made out the outline of Crystal beneath the comforter on one side of the bed.

Asleep.

Snoring.

I looked from her to my cock, which was waving eagerly in the air, and shook my head. *Not tonight, buddy.* I let out a pained chuckle. I'd known from the moment I'd met Crystal that she was different. This was different.

I walked over to the bed, turned off the lamp, slid beneath the comforter, and wrapped my arms around her from behind. She didn't wake, and I was okay with it. I wanted her, but she affected me on more levels than I was used to. As much as I was turned on, I also felt protective of her. We'd had a long day; it made sense that she was tired. It might have been all the fresh air or that round of drinks, but soon after resting my head on a pillow beside hers, I fell asleep as well.

CHAPTER TWENTY-FIVE

CRYSTAL

I woke slowly, smiling, savoring the feeling of strong arms wrapped around me and the warmth of . . . oh my God . . . *Jesse.*

My eyes flew open and struggled to adjust to the darkness of the room. I lay there, going over how the night had ended. I remembered floating to the bedroom in a postorgasm euphoria, celebrating when I saw that the hotel supplied small vanity kits so I could brush my teeth, and hoping Jesse had remembered to bring his condoms with him because mine were still in his car. Naked, I'd first waited for him on top of the comforter in what I'd hoped was a sexy pose. When he hadn't joined me, I'd slid beneath the comforter and relived both orgasms he'd given me while touching myself.

There's no shame in sneaking out an orgasm if a man makes you wait. He would do the same in a heartbeat.

It was good, but not as good as the one I'd hoped to soon experience. Still, it was enough to relax me right into a slumber.

I wanted to wake him and ask him how his father was. I regretted not staying awake long enough to pose that question the night before. *I hope he doesn't think I don't care.*

I hope it wasn't bad news.

Was that why he didn't wake me?

If it was really bad, he wouldn't still be here.

Unless he needed comfort.

And, ugh, all he found when he came in was me sleeping.
At least I don't snore.

I snuggled closer to him, loving how his arms tightened around me. His cock stirred against my bottom, and it put a tantalizing idea in my head. I turned in his arms. He might've still been asleep. "Jesse?"

"Mmmm?"

"Was everything okay with your father? I'm thinking of how much I enjoyed last night and returning the favor, but I don't want to do anything if you're not in the mood."

"Yes, it was nothing important." A sexy smile curled his lips, and his eyes opened. "I can only speak for myself, but I can't imagine not being in the mood for you to 'return a favor.'"

Performing oral sex had never been on my list of things I loved to do, but I'd also never been on the receiving end of it done well. The idea of bringing him the same kind of pleasure he'd brought me made it suddenly exciting.

As he had done with me, I took my time. I kissed him slowly, running my hands up and down his muscled chest. When he would have deepened the kiss, I shifted lower, kissing my way down his neck. His hands caressed my back, my arms, then slid between us to cup my breasts.

I moved lower still. According to what I'd read, men's nipples could be as sensitive as women's. I'd never felt confident enough to test that theory. Jesse's techniques had worked so well on me that I tried them on him, moving from one of his nipples to the other before raising my head and asking, "Do you like that?"

"I like everything you're doing."

"So it's good?"

He took one of my hands and wrapped it around his rock-hard cock. "What do you think?"

He generously filled my hand in a way that had me eager to feel him inside me, but not yet. First I wanted to take him where he'd already taken me twice. I let the kisses I rained on his chest be my answer, kisses I trailed lower and lower.

He tossed the comforter aside and ran a hand through my hair. I took my time, pumping my hand ever so slowly up and down his shaft. Lower still, I kissed his abdomen, his thighs. He shifted his position so I could reach him more easily.

I knew what he wanted, but the anticipation was exciting me as much as it was him. I began to flick him with the end of my tongue. Little teasing licks that encircled his balls, ran along the length of him, then tasted the tip of him.

He moaned, and I gave him what he craved. I took him deep in my mouth, as deeply as I could. There was a freedom with him, a desire to experiment that was uninhibited by concern that my pleasure would be an afterthought. He'd already made it good for me, and unless he threw me out of his bed, I was sticking around in hope that he'd do it again and again.

Up and down, swirling, sucking. I let my hand explore him as well until I found exactly how to drive him wild. Only then did I increase my speed, each time taking him as deeply as I could. It wasn't my first foray into giving a man oral sex, but it was the first time I was excited by doing it.

He ran a hand down my back, over the curve of my ass, then between my legs. His finger slid between my wet folds and thrust inside me. With his thumb he moved back and forth over my clit while pumping in and out of me. When he thrust a second, thick finger inside me, it stretched me in the most delicious way. I gasped and paused, taking a moment to enjoy the waves of heat shooting through me.

Strong. Forceful. Unrelenting. He fucked me with his fingers while I began to move up and down over his cock again. I felt his orgasm nearing as his balls tightened. Rather than moving back, I took him deeper into my throat and swallowed the splash of him as he came. As I did, his hand roughly, mercilessly took me over the edge as well.

Gasping for air, I rolled onto my side, collapsed, and murmured, "That was fucking fantastic."

He lifted me upward to rest against his chest. "I didn't know you were a mind reader—that's exactly what I was thinking."

"I could get used to this." I snuggled closer.

"Me too." He kissed the top of my forehead. "Unexpected perk of being with you? I'm saving a ton on condoms."

Too comfortable where I was, I laughed without raising my head. "So you're a funny guy."

His chest puffed with mock pride. "I'm a man of many layers."

My hand slid down to encircle his already hardening cock. "Thankfully none of them are clothing."

His chest rumbled with a laugh. "I'd like to apologize now for how soon nothing I say will make any sense. You're killing my ability to think about anything but burying myself inside you."

I cupped his balls, then moved my hand up and down his shaft. "You say that like it's a problem. Where's the complaint department, because the service in this hotel is sooooooo slow?"

He rolled so he was above me. "Please don't file a formal complaint before giving me a chance to make things right." He positioned himself between my legs, spreading them wide, and sheathed himself while poised above me. I tensed a little, turned on but surprisingly hesitant. His humor was replaced by a kiss so sweet and promising that whatever nervousness I had fell away.

Once again he used that talented tongue of his, those strong and sure hands, and now the bold tip of his cock to bring me to a frenzy of need before he entered me. When he did, though, it was with the same skilled force I was beginning to expect from him. His thrusts were powerful and deep—somehow almost too much and not enough at the same time. His mouth was everywhere. His hands owned me. I wanted more of him, and with each thrust he gave it to me.

When I thought it couldn't get better, he couldn't get deeper, he pulled out and hauled me to the edge of the bed. From there he wrapped my legs around his waist, lifted my ass off the bed, and pounded into me until I was crying out his name and clutching at the bedsheet on either side of me. This. This was what it was like to be fucked.

Wild.

Raw.

He let go, and his hands turned rough and demanding. I came with a wave of pleasure unlike any I'd experienced before, the kind that brought tears to one's eyes. And still he continued. I was riding a wave of bliss, shattered but in the most amazing way, when he gave a final thrust and came as well.

He pulled out, cleaned himself off, and returned to beside me on the bed. He yanked the comforter over both of us, and I tucked myself to his side. He didn't say a word, and neither did I.

When anything was that perfect, no words were necessary.

CHAPTER TWENTY-SIX

JESSE

Sex was sex, but this was something different. I wrapped my arms around Crystal and breathed her in. Having never felt this way before, I struggled to make sense of it. Somehow, with a woman about whom there was still so much I didn't know, I'd glimpsed forever.

Shit like that didn't happen to men like me.

I wasn't the romantic type.

I didn't believe in *happily ever after*.

Hell, half the women I'd dated would probably say I had a heart of stone. The other half would assert I didn't have one at all. None had touched it.

Crystal had not only found it, but she'd ripped it out of my chest and claimed it as her own. How? How the hell did that happen?

Was I supposed to fight it? Revel in it? How could I make sense of wanting to never let this woman go when I'd always been the type to never let a woman stay?

She rolled over in my arms so we were eye to eye. "What are you thinking?" she asked.

"Thinking?" It was a weak response, but at a time like that a man needs time to gather his thoughts.

She searched my face. "Would it freak you out if I said it's never been like this with anyone else?"

I closed my eyes briefly and hoped to God what I felt in that moment wouldn't fade when we left the bed. "No, because it hasn't been like this for me either."

Her smile warmed me to my toes. "I'm glad you're not the asshole I thought you were when we first met."

I tucked her hair behind her ear. "Oh, I'm that man, too, just not with you."

Her expression turned more serious, and I regretted being so honest. "Do you really think we can do this?"

I pulled her closer, bare skin to bare skin, but sated. "Too late to ask if we should. I'd say we're already doing it."

She brought a hand up to caress my cheek. "I don't want to be that woman . . . the one who needs to know where things are headed. I'm not looking for a promise, but I need to know—after I go home today, will I see you again?"

It was a conversation I'd had with women before and one I usually fielded with ease, letting them down as gently as I could. None of my usual smooth lines fit how I felt. Had she been anyone else, I would have felt there were too many unknowns to rush into anything. Instead I cupped one of her breasts with my hand and said, "You're a short flight away. I have my own plane."

She lifted her head and arched an eyebrow. "Is that a yes?"

I hated that I wasn't better at articulating how I was feeling. "That's a hell yes."

She seemed to mull that over. "If we did this—if we saw each other again—would it be just for sex? It's okay if it is. At least, I think I'd be okay with that. The sex is really good. I just like to know what my options are."

Holding back a smile, I shook my head. She'd told me she'd become careful and liked to have all the facts before moving forward with anything. She'd also told me she wasn't happy that way. "This is more than a hookup. I have no idea where we're heading, but I know I want to go there with you. It's a crazy leap of faith for both of us, but it's one I'm willing to take."

The deep breath she took moved her nipples deliciously against my chest. I swallowed hard and tried to focus on the subject at hand. "Me too. I'm scared, but I want to see you again, and I'm not ashamed to admit it."

I gave her a quick kiss before saying, "Good, because there should be no shame with us. I want to see you again and again and again. Let's make it happen."

"Just like that?"

"Just like that."

She nodded. "I'm in."

"Me too." I was—all in.

CHAPTER TWENTY-SEVEN

CRYSTAL

Late the next evening, my flight home was oddly formal. I wanted to tell the attendant, *Smile—you might be seeing a lot of me from now on,* but I didn't. Would she, though? Men said all kinds of things they didn't mean postsex.

Some men.

I didn't know enough about Jesse to guess at his next move. He might play the "wait game" and not call me for a couple of days. Or he might not call me at all.

On my way to see Jesse, he'd sent a car to collect me from my apartment. A car also met me at the airport upon my arrival back in Maine to return me home. The driver wasn't the same one from the day before. Yet like the pilot and the attendant, he, too, was professional and polite. He offered to carry my luggage up to my apartment for me, but I declined.

As I took the elevator up to my apartment, I smiled down at the bag. Jesse had kindly gone to the car to retrieve it for me so I would have a change of clothing. Or it might have been because we'd used all the protection he'd brought. I sighed happily. I'd had more sex in the last twenty-four hours than I'd had in the last year.

Inside my apartment I placed my bag beside the door and looked around. Something was off. There were open food containers on the coffee table next to a large pile of tissues. On one end of the couch Ellie peeked out from beneath a thick blanket. Her face was swollen and red. I rushed to her side. "Are you okay?" I touched her forehead. It wasn't warm. "Are you sick? You should have called me. I would have come back earlier."

She blew her nose, then threw the tissue in the pile. "I'm not sick. I'm just stupid."

I sat down beside her. "No, you're not. What happened?"

She reached for another tissue and sniffed. "I told Jonathan the truth."

"Oh."

"Too much of it."

"He didn't hurt you, did he?"

She shook her head. "No. Worse. I hurt him."

"I don't understand."

"Last night I told him about the lab and that I lied about being a pharmacist. And he handled it better than I thought he would."

"That's good, right?"

"It was. He ended our date early but said it was because he was tired. He promised to call me this morning."

"Did he?"

After blowing her nose again, Ellie said, "Yes. After a night of thinking it over, he said he only had one question he needed the answer to."

"What was it?"

She closed her eyes and covered them with her hands. When she opened her eyes again, there were fresh tears in them. "He wanted to know why I'd lied."

"Oh."

"I told him I didn't think it would matter in the beginning because I didn't think we would matter. He said he doesn't know if he can believe anything I say, so we're better off over." She hugged the blanket to her.

Not knowing what else to do, I gave her back a supportive pat. "I'm sorry."

"It's not your fault. I'm the one who lied to him."

But I was the one who encouraged you to be honest with him. "He'll call you. He probably just needs some time to work through his feelings."

She shook her head and wiped at the corners of her eyes with the heels of her hands. "I'd love to think you're right, but I think it's over. His tone was so cold. He'd never spoken to me like that before. He wasn't looking for a fight . . . he was just done."

My phone buzzed with an incoming call. I checked the ID—Jesse. Holding up my phone, I asked, "Do you mind if I take this?"

Ellie waved me away. "Go. I'm fine, and I'll be right here when you're done."

Jesse's call went to my voice mail while I was hugging Ellie, but I walked from the living room to my room and called him back. Even though my heart was breaking for Ellie, that didn't stop it from also racing in anticipation of hearing Jesse's voice. "Hi."

He sounded happier than I did when he answered, "Hi, yourself. Just wanted to make sure you made it home."

I sat on the edge of my bed. "I did, thank you. Everything went smoothly. I'm hoping, though, that one day I can get any of your staff to open up and talk to me."

"Were they unresponsive to something you requested?"

"Oh no, they were wonderful. Very professional. It's just that I can tell that when you travel, you must have instructed them not to speak to you."

"I do prefer not to be interrupted when I'm working."

I smiled. "I can tell."

"If you'd like to engage in conversation with them, I can direct them to be more personable."

"Don't. That would be worse. They were all perfect. Please, I shouldn't have said anything."

"I want to know when you're not comfortable with something." After a pause, he said, "I didn't realize how little I was investing in my relationships with women until I met you. This is all-new territory to me, so I may not get everything right, but if you meet me in the middle, I might not get it all wrong either."

His words mirrored how I felt. I thought about Ellie and Jonathan and how fragile new relationships could be. No one was perfect. I was so sad Jonathan couldn't see that the good in Ellie far outweighed how much her honesty had stung. "Could I get your male perspective on a situation?"

"Sure."

I told him about Ellie and Jonathan—both about how good things had been between them and about how suddenly they had ended. I briefly went over how she'd told Jonathan she was a pharmacist, even had me lie about my profession, then confessed. "She only lied because she felt strange about their age difference and didn't want him to think she was out of his league. I understand that he's upset that she wasn't honest with him, but do you think he'll be able to move past that?"

Jesse cleared his throat. "Is this a roundabout way of asking if we can get past me telling you that I was Scott?"

"No." It wasn't. Not at all. "I understand why you did that. I guess that's my point. We started with a lie, but I don't feel that I can't trust you."

"Which is a good thing." He sighed. "I don't know Jonathan, so I can only guess at how he feels, but he's young, and it sounds like he fell for your friend hard."

"When I saw them together, that's how it seemed to me."

"He's scared."

"Of being lied to again?"

"Of having his heart ripped out and trampled. Men may not express it the way women do, but they often take breakups just as hard. My father is still hurting over my mother's desertion, and it's been over twenty years. When you meet him, if he says something wildly offensive about women in general, keep that in mind."

That explained some of what I'd sensed from Jesse when we'd first met. "That couldn't have been easy for you."

"I don't put much thought into it."

"Because when things are painful, it's easier not to?"

"Because I don't believe in wasting time thinking about things I have no control over. I let my anger toward her go a long time ago, but I can't make my father forgive my mother."

"Forgiveness can be tough. I'm still angry at my parents for how they died." God, I was a broken record. Was I determined to drive him away?

His voice lowered. "Why?"

I lay back on the bed. "I'm sorry. You're probably already sick of hearing about them."

I thought he'd deny it, then change the subject. Instead he gently ordered, "Tell me."

"You don't want me to open that door. It's dark and sloppy back there."

"Crystal, I want to know you—the good, the bad, the sloppy. If we can't be real with each other, then what are we doing?"

I inhaled a shaky breath. He was right. I let myself go back to the night that changed my life. "I'd stayed on campus that weekend even though my parents had said they wanted to see me. I was working on a project, and the deadline for it was tight. When I received a call from a number I didn't know, I almost didn't answer it, but it was the hospital telling me that my parents had been in a car accident and were both in critical condition." I paused as memories from that night overwhelmed me. "I should have been there with them that weekend. If I had been, we all would have been home."

"Or you would have been in that car with them."

I shook my head. "No, they went out to buy a few items for a care package they were going to send me. My mother had a thing for socks. No matter what the occasion was, she would buy me a pair to match it. One year she bought me a pair that said *Fuck off* to wear when I'm angry with the world." I wiped a tear from the corner of my eye. "My mother told one of her friends that I'd sounded stressed, so she and my father were going to surprise me with a package of snacks and silly socks. They never made it to the store."

"You can't blame yourself for an accident."

"Oh, I can and I did—but I've worked through most of that." I sniffed. "What I can't get past—what I can't shake—"

"Yes?"

Was it too much to share? He'd said he wanted to know all of me. I'd kept it in for so long. Was that why it was bubbling out? Maybe it was time to put a voice to what was circling in my head. "When I went to the hospital, both of my parents were touch and go. My mother had flatlined. My father's vitals were dropping. They were in separate rooms. I was in a panic but also a little numb, if that makes sense. I didn't believe my parents could be as bad off as the doctor warned me they were. A nurse asked me which one I'd like to go in to see. I chose my mother. Not because I put a lot of thought into it but because I didn't understand how bad off my father truly was." My throat closed up, and I had to take a few calming breaths before I could continue. "I held my mother's hand while she died, and I will always be grateful for that moment. But I never got to say goodbye to my father, because he was gone by the time I left my mother's side. I hate that my father died alone. I hate"—I sniffed again—"that I had to choose between them." I wiped my hands over my eyes again. "I wish I'd known my father had so little time . . ."

"You didn't choose between them. You were put in a no-win situation. I can't speak for your father, but if I were him, I would have wanted you exactly where you were," Jesse said in a voice thick with emotion.

I hadn't really thought of it that way before. I hadn't talked about that night with anyone because I had a difficult time every time I relived it. Jesse's words freed a part of me that had been trapped in guilt. I blinked back tears. "My father was that kind of man. He would pull over if he drove by someone struggling even in their own backyard. You did not want to go for a drive with him in the winter. Guaranteed you would end up helping him shovel out some elderly couple's driveway. He was that standard I try to live up to." I sighed. "I hate that I wasn't able to say that to him before he died."

"He knows how you felt."

"You really believe that?"

"I don't know, but what's the alternative? That we simply cease to exist after we die? That nothing we do here matters? I'm not a religious person, but I believe there are many things we don't understand. And maybe we aren't meant to."

I nodded. "I was so angry at first. I couldn't understand how something so horrible could happen to people like them. I still don't, but I've stopped asking questions there are no good answers to."

He sighed. "Sometimes that's for the best."

"You *do* understand."

"I didn't lose anyone the way you did, but I understand having questions I'm sure I don't want to hear the answers to. That about sums up why I've never asked about my biological parents or my adoptive mother."

"You don't think you'll ever change your mind about that?"

"I don't know why I would. Thane and I talked about it once. Our adoptive mother knows where we are if she ever has an interest in knowing us. There's a slim chance our bio parents might have been wonderful people who simply couldn't keep us. The more likely scenario is a darker one and, frankly, probably disappointing. I am glad I found

Scott, though. Even though the situation is more complicated than I ever would have imagined."

I wasn't sure what that meant. "So what is Scott doing while you're him?"

Jesse groaned. "Now that is the million-dollar question. He was supposed to lay low and not interact with anyone who would know me, but my father caught him at the office yesterday."

"No."

"Yes."

"What was he doing?"

"Nothing, according to everyone I asked."

"That's what he said as well?"

"Not exactly. He said he is trusting me with his life, so I should trust him with mine."

Wow. "Do you?"

"I don't believe Scott would *deliberately* do anything to mess with my reputation or our company."

Ouch, but probably accurate. Scott had been raised on a farm in a small town. He might not have known how to fend off the business sharks that seemed to spawn in large cities. "Sounds like you should switch back soon." I wondered what that would mean as far as us seeing each other.

"Soon, but not yet. I have some unfinished business at the farm."

"With my uncle?"

"He's part of what I'm working through."

"Do you want to talk about it?"

He was quiet for a moment, then said, "Not yet, but soon."

"Okay." His honest answer stung a little. I thought about Jonathan and how he'd reacted to Ellie's confession. Ignorance was bliss, but honesty was the foundation of anything real. My conversation with my uncle echoed in my head. He wanted me on that farm. I thought about LJ, who'd stood on Scott's porch like a guard dog. My work was based on formulas and research, but it also involved a certain amount of guess-work. "Is there something in the farmhouse you don't want me to see?"

"This isn't about what I *want*."

But there *was* something. "Does my uncle know about whatever it is?"

"I suspect he might."

I took a moment to digest that. I had to ask: "Is it illegal?"

"Would anyone answer that question honestly?"

"You would." I believed that.

"I would—*for you*." He made a sound of frustration in his throat. "Even if it made no damn sense to. It's not illegal, but it's also not my secret to share."

"LJ knows about it as well."

"He does, but not from me."

"It's why the farm has security cameras all over it."

"Yes."

It had to be something someone could steal; otherwise none of the rest made sense. What would a farmer have that my uncle would want so badly Scott thought he might steal it? What would leasing the land give my uncle access to?

My heart skipped a beat at that. Being with Jesse felt like we were each standing on opposite sides of a ravine, stretching across it to touch, and being almost but not quite able to. The potential of a fall was real, but we were so close—if we both stretched a little more. There was comfort in knowing he was risking as much as I was . . . and he was still there.

He couldn't say more, so I didn't ask the questions that were racing through my head. I hugged an arm around myself and asked, "How do we do this, Jesse?"

"One day at a time. I have some things I need to work on here, but would you like to spend the weekend together? I'll come to you."

"I don't live alone, and Ellie is probably still going to feel a little too fragile to have you stay here."

"I'll get a room somewhere. I don't care where I stay as long as I get to see you."

Nothing beyond seeing him again mattered. "Yes. I'd love that."

"I've never been the call-every-day kind of guy."

"That's okay."

"But I'd like to start tomorrow with hearing your voice."

He was quickly becoming someone I couldn't imagine not having in my life. This had to work out. "I head into the office early, but if you call before eight, I'll have time to talk."

"Good night, Crystal. I'm good with how things are, but I also wish I were there."

"Are you a mind reader? Because that's exactly what I was thinking."

He chuckled at my use of his earlier claim. "Talk to you in the morning."

"Yes."

We ended the call with that, and I sat there with a big goofy smile on my face, wiping tears from the corners of my eyes. Emotionally I was one hot mess, but I'd never felt so alive.

I was on my way to the bathroom to freshen up when my phone buzzed with a text from Jesse.

I forgot something.

Yes?

I put a little gift for you in the side pocket of your luggage.

He could have said *bag*, but he was busting on me. Still smiling, I rolled my eyes and headed back out to the living room. There, in the second pocket I checked, I found a small gift-wrapped box.

Ellie's eyes caught mine from across the room. I held up the gift. "It's from Jesse."

She looked calmer than earlier. "Open it. After the flowers he sent you, I'm really curious."

I ripped off the paper and opened the box. A handwritten note read: *For our next date. —Jesse.* I moved the note aside, revealing two black velvet blindfolds.

"What is it?" Ellie asked.

I held one up. "A bold suggestion."

She laughed. "I like this one."

Me too. Cheeks flushed, I texted Jesse. Planning another food tasting?

If that's what you want to call me exploring every inch of you with my tongue—sure.

I fanned my face with the blindfold. You're not making it easy to wait for the weekend.

Good.

That was all he wrote—the little shit. When nothing else came through, I decided the most playful response to that was nothing, so I tucked my phone in my back pocket.

Ellie gave the couch cushion beside her a pat. "Get over here and tell me all about your date. Obviously, it was amazing."

I hesitated, but she genuinely seemed to want to hear about it. "If you don't feel—"

"I want to hear everything. It'll actually be good for me to think about something else. Start with the flight. What was that like?"

I curled up on the other side of the couch and told her everything, except that Jesse was hiding something at Scott's farm. As Jesse had said, it wasn't my secret to share.

When I finally headed to my room, I placed the blindfolds in the drawer next to my bed. It was impossible to think of anything beyond us tangled up wearing only them. I changed into sleep shorts and a T-shirt and padded to the bathroom to brush my teeth. When I saw my face in the mirror, I stopped in my tracks.

My eyes were bright and shining. My face was flushed, and I was smiling. I recognized the expression on my face even though I hadn't seen it in a long time. *This is me happy and excited about something. Someone.*

I'd shown Jesse a part of myself I concealed from the rest of the world, and it hadn't scared him off. I looked myself in the eye and said, "Don't do anything stupid like fall in love. There's a high probability that this will end as badly as Ellie and Jonathan." *Unless it doesn't. What if this is it, and he's the one?*

My parents said they knew right away that they were meant for each other.

I leaned forward onto the sink as the smile left my face. If my parents were alive, I would be at their house, snuggled up to one of them, asking them to tell me again how they'd met. I needed to hear a love story with a happy ending.

Theirs had ended so suddenly—but that didn't mean it was any less wonderful. I could say that with certainty because they'd shared their happy ending with me. I was part of that loving tale.

I loved the expression on my father's face whenever he looked at my mother. His love for her was always right there for all to see.

They argued sometimes, like everyone. I remembered hiding around the corner once when they were arguing about a bill my father had forgotten to pay . . . which had somehow become an argument about the new car my mother wanted. I was too young to truly understand what they were upset about, but their voices boomed through the house. My mother stormed into their room and slammed the door. My father headed outside onto the porch and did the same. I sat there—afraid—until I heard both doors reopen.

My mother said, "I love you."

My father said, "I love you too."

"I'm sorry."

"And I'm an idiot who should know not to put mail in my car instead of the mailbox."

"My idiot," my mother said with humor.

My father laughed.

I learned some things that stayed with me—love wasn't easy, but that didn't mean it wasn't real. Arguments happened, but they didn't have to get hateful. I'd spoken to my mother once about that day, and she said, "Marriage has its ups and downs, but when you love each other, you work things out. It's that simple."

Does that work for dating as well?

How do Jesse and I work out a problem if he won't tell me what it is?

CHAPTER TWENTY-EIGHT

JESSE

The next day I finished the chores in record time. I stood at the entrance of the barn and breathed in the fresh morning air. There were emails waiting for me, but I'd been able to handle most of them remotely, and I'd be returning feeling refreshed. For now, Thane had the helm.

I called Crystal. "Morning."

There was a smile in her voice. "You don't happen to know where I put my purse, do you?"

As a joke, I said, "It's next to the couch."

She chuckled. "Imagine if you were right?" A moment later, she said, "I shouldn't tell you because you'll get a big head, but it actually is on the floor beside the couch."

"How's Ellie today?"

"A little better, thanks. She's getting dressed; then we're heading to the lab together. We usually each drive by ourselves, but she could use the company."

I had yet to find a side of Crystal I didn't like. Our conversation the night before had only added to my feelings for her. She'd gone through something that would have broken many people, but she hadn't let it beat her. She was strong, intelligent, resilient, yet also in need of a shoulder to lean on. I wanted to be that shoulder. "Then we'll keep this short and simple—I miss you."

"I miss you too." She cleared her throat. "Today will be a busy one here. Ellie and I have a new client—Airdale Ice Cream. They want to start a line of no-sugar, lower-calorie flavors. They've done work in house, but so far the feedback from their focus groups is not positive. Since they pride themselves on having a secret recipe for increased creaminess, I'm curious to see how much they'll share. I'm willing to sign whatever nondisclosure paperwork they require, but there's not much we can do for them if they don't give us full access to their recipes."

"Is that a common situation to be in?"

"It does happen. Thankfully, Ellie and I have built a reputation for being worth the risk."

"You definitely are." I was referring to my feelings, but it fit.

"How about you? What are your plans for the day?"

There were some things I couldn't tell her yet but a lot I could. "I'm still trying to track down someone who's proving elusive. I need to speak to Scott—get a clearer view of what he's up to. I'm also seriously considering going fishing."

She chuckled. "Tough day."

"I'll put in a few hours of work as well. I don't want Thane to claim all the credit for the space station project."

"Hang on." She asked Ellie if she was ready, then said, "I have to go. Have a great day, Jesse."

"You too." It was a quick, friendly end to our conversation and didn't feel like enough. I stood there, holding the phone, wondering what the hell was wrong with me.

When my phone rang, for just a second I thought it might be Crystal calling back, and my heart started racing. "Hello?"

"Hi. It's Wren Romano. I hope this is an okay time to call."

I put my disappointment aside. "Absolutely. Just finished feeding all the critters."

"I have Alphonse's leg ready. Mauricio and I would love to drop by with it. If it requires tweaking, it would be easier to see the issue in person."

"Sure. When?"

"Tomorrow? Is that too soon? We would come by in the evening."

"Not a problem."

"Will Crystal be there? I'd love to meet her."

Her question had my stomach instantly in knots. I wanted to say Crystal would be. I hated that there were valid reasons why it would be better to keep Crystal away from the farm. *At least for now.* "Unfortunately, this is a busy week for her." That was true at least.

"Oh, too bad. Understandable, though. I'll text you when we're close."

"Thank you. I look forward to your visit."

Replacing my phone in my back pocket, I groaned. If being with Crystal only put me at risk, I probably wouldn't have given it another thought. There had to be a way to move forward with her and protect my family. I refused to believe there wasn't a solution. I walked over to the fence and leaned forward to rest my forearms on it to think while hitching my foot up on the lowest board.

"You look more like Scott every day," LJ said.

I didn't bother to turn to greet him. He walked around Scott's farm like he owned the place, but since half the time it was by Scott's request, there wasn't much I could say about it. "Morning."

"How was your date?"

I would have asked him how he even knew about it, but how much Scott was telling him was annoying. I rolled my shoulders before answering. "You and I are not friends."

"I respect that, but I can't stand back and not tell you you're playing with fire."

"You can. You absolutely could keep your thoughts to yourself."

196

He didn't seem bothered by my suggestion. "Technically, yes, but you and I want the same thing."

Now he had my attention. I looked over at him. "And what is that?"

"To help Scott. Maybe save the world. Classic midlife crisis hero stuff."

"I'm neither middle aged nor looking to be a hero."

"Then why are you still here?"

I shook my head and turned back to look out over the paddock.

LJ said, "I'm glad you at least took my advice about keeping Crystal away from the farm."

"If you weren't rich, I'd offer you money to stop talking."

"Is that why you don't like me? Do I intimidate you?"

I straightened and turned to face him. "I don't trust you. I haven't figured out what your role is in all of this yet, but I will. And for your sake, I hope it's what you claim."

LJ shrugged. "The differences between you and Scott are actually fascinating to see. I had to warn him he shouldn't trust everyone with his discovery. He has no idea how ruthless people can be when money is involved. You, on the other hand, wouldn't believe me if I told you the sun came up this morning. Nature versus nurture. Have you wondered how much of who you are has to do with who raised you? How different would you be if you'd been raised by Scott's parents instead of yours?"

"Have you wondered if a person could speak if they couldn't breathe? Oddly, that's something I ponder whenever you're talking."

With a chuckle, LJ took a step back. "I'm a techie, not a fighter. I did actually come by to tell you something, but now that I know you don't want to hear my voice, I should let it be a surprise."

"Should let what be a surprise?"

Smiling, he took another step back. "Suddenly you care what I have to say?"

"I can't be the only person who wants to strangle you."

He raised his pointing finger. "Not nice. I would leave without telling you, but I care about Jill and Ryan."

"Scott's parents? Has something happened?"

"In a sense. They heard you were here, so they turned their RV around and headed home. If I'm right, they should be arriving . . ." He paused to check the time on his watch. "In about an hour."

"An hour? Jill and Ryan?" Although I'd spoken to them on the phone, I hadn't yet met them in person. No. No. No. This wasn't happening. "Does Scott know?"

"He's the one who told them you were here. Said something about having so much fun with your father he thought he'd return the favor." LJ brought a fist up to his smile and cleared his throat. "Brothers are tough—am I right?"

I rubbed a hand across my forehead. "I'm going to kill him. It's like he wants me to fail here. Is that it? Does he actually want to lose his farm and his work along with it?"

LJ's smile faded. "I have thick skin. You can say almost anything to me, and I really don't give a shit. Be nice to Jill and Ryan. I have a feeling they will love you even if you do nothing to deserve it. Try to deserve it."

With that, he turned and walked away, leaving me in a state of mild panic. Scott's parents were everything my family was not. They would ask a million questions and likely get in the way of anything I tried to do. *This clinches it—we need to switch back. Scott is the one the Romanos want to meet. I can't have them here with me and Scott's parents—they probably keep secrets as well as he does. This is all going to shit.*

I took out my phone to text Scott but found myself sending a text to Crystal instead. Scott's parents will be here within an hour. They want to get to know me.

Her answer came back almost immediately. That's awesome.

Is it?

198

I guess it'll be what you make it.

Why don't I want to meet them?

My phone buzzed with a call from her. "Jesse. I can only imagine what you're feeling."

"Hey." Really, it was just good to hear her voice. "Sorry. You told me you had a busy day. This can wait."

"No, it doesn't have to. I take breaks just like everyone else. Now, to your question—you're the only one who could answer that."

"And I don't know. I felt good about coming here to help Scott. The issues that I've encountered have only made me more determined. Why does the idea of meeting his parents make me want to run back to Massachusetts? I'm not the type to avoid confrontation. I meet problems head-on. What is so hard about this?"

She was quiet for a moment. "Facing feelings is more difficult for some than taking action. At least, for me it is. I received my PhD for a dissertation I defended fearlessly, but I don't ever visit my parents' graves. Never. I'd rather face a shark with a bloody steak strapped to my leg than drive by the house I grew up in. Not sure that helps."

"It does, and it's quite an image." I let her words sink in. My father had drilled it into us that fear was wasted energy, but was that what this was? What could I possibly be afraid would happen? "The way Scott describes his mother—"

"Yes?"

"She's so . . . motherly."

Crystal laughed. "I don't know what that means."

"She'll ask me if I'm hungry. She'll want to know how I feel. Probably want to hug me."

In a more serious tone, Crystal said, "She's what you never had."

I didn't like how close that was to the mark. "I have a great life. I've never wanted for anything."

"Except maybe that hug she'll want to give you."

I shook my head. "That's not who I am."

"That's who everyone is . . . on some level. It doesn't make you weak to want that. In fact, it takes more strength to risk letting someone in than keeping everyone at a distance."

I'm a real piece of work. I blurted, "Wren Romano is coming tomorrow. You should be here to meet her."

"Do you want me to be?"

Honesty was the only way this worked. "Yes . . . and no. I can usually see the path I want to take clearly, but lately I—"

"Jesse, when you sent me the carnation barn with animals, that really touched my heart. I thought it was a gift that would be hard to top, but this call . . . it's a million times better."

I didn't see how it could be. "Sharing that I have no fucking idea what I'm doing is a gift?"

Her next softly spoken words took my breath away. "This is real, Jesse. It's the stuff that matters. I loved how we spent yesterday, but knowing that you're willing to show me when you're confused or hurting—that makes me feel like I mean something to you."

My throat tightened. "You do."

"My father used to say that he and my mother were friends above all else. I've always wanted that but never glimpsed anything close. When we figure this out, Jesse, you might just become my best friend."

Holy shit. What she described was so far removed from my experience with relationships that I wasn't sure it was possible. "How are you not upset that I don't fully trust you yet?"

"Because my uncle suggested I find a reason to see you again. He wants me to know you . . . well . . . Scott. I love my uncle, but I don't know why he wants me at the farm. If I have questions, how could you not?"

"You haven't told him who I really am yet?"

"No, and I don't like keeping anything from him. He's been so good to me. So, see, I understand how you feel. I don't know what to do either. But knowing I can be honest with you makes it somehow okay."

Yes. "I'm not going to lie to Wren Romano. I'll tell her who I am and that I'm watching Scott's farm for him."

"And if you want, I'll come to the farm but stay outside."

"I'd like you there. I want to say that second part wouldn't be necessary."

"Someday it won't be."

"I'll send a plane for you in the morning."

"You don't have to—"

"Let me do some of this right."

She chuckled. "Fine. I won't be able to stay, though. I really do have a lot to get done at the lab."

"You know what makes a great workspace? A plane that was designed to be one."

"But does it have a kitchen?" she joked.

"No, but my next one will." Although my tone was also humorous, my declaration took me by surprise because it sounded like a promise. I didn't make those to women.

But with her I wanted to.

"I'll see you tomorrow morning, Jesse."

"Yes."

"Good luck with Scott's parents."

Oh yeah, I almost forgot about that. It's happening. Talking it out with Crystal had removed my desire to bolt. "Thanks. For everything."

I smiled after we ended the call as I remembered something she'd said: *"You might just become my best friend."*

I wanted to taste her again.

I wanted to trust her completely.

But more than anything else, I wanted to be her best friend.

I'm in love.

CHAPTER TWENTY-NINE

CRYSTAL

Despite having signed a contract for a project that had a tight deadline, I told Ellie I was stepping out for lunch—alone. I needed to have a conversation with my uncle, but outside the possibility that anyone might overhear. I texted to confirm that he was available to talk. He was, so I dove back into work until our scheduled time.

Inside my car was the location I chose to video call him from.

"Crystal." His smile welcomed me, but there was concern in his eyes. "You don't normally call me in the middle of the day. Should I send someone for you?"

"No. I'm fine." His unwavering support warmed my heart but made the questions I had harder to voice. "I just wanted to talk."

He frowned. "Are you in your car?"

"Yes."

"Why?"

I swallowed hard. "I didn't want to risk anyone overhearing our conversation."

"Are you in some kind of trouble?"

"No. No." I took a deep, calming breath. "It's about Scott."

My uncle's face hardened. "What has he done?"

"Nothing." I waved a panicked hand in the air when I realized how that sounded. "But I'm in love."

A smile returned to his face. "I had a feeling you would fall for him. As soon as I heard about his magical beans, I did a full background check on him. Everything I learned about him sounded like someone you need in your life. He's a nurturer—like your father was. A little naive when it comes to how the world works, but we could help him with that. His parents are liked by their community. His mother bakes pies to raise money for their town's animal shelter. This would be a good family for you."

"What are you saying?"

He pressed his lips together in a straight line, then said, "I wasn't there for you when you were a child. Your father and I disagreed on many things, and my pride kept me away. I've done my best to be the family I know you need, but I can't change who I am. You need to be celebrating the holidays with people who don't see that as a waste of time. Losing your parents knocked you down, and although you've done well in business, you're not me. Work alone won't make you happy. You want what your parents had."

"I do, but—"

"And who better to find that with than a man who is in desperate need of a flavorist? The two of you were meant to be."

"I don't understand."

"He didn't tell you? I was sure he would have."

"Didn't tell me what?"

"How much time have you spent with Scott?"

I grimaced. I didn't want to lie to him, but was being honest a betrayal of Jesse? The conflict within me gave me a better understanding of the one that must have been going on within Jesse. I resented feeling that I had to choose between them, and that surfaced in my tone. "So what you want me to believe is that the reason you encouraged me to see Scott again is because you were playing matchmaker? You?"

His eyes darkened. "I'm insulted by the insinuation that I would lie to you."

"Then tell me the truth. All of it, not the part you think I can handle. You didn't send me to Scott's farm because you were hoping we'd be a match. You were already trying to buy his land, or lease it if he wouldn't sell. He has something you want, and you were willing to use me to get it."

"I have never lied to you, Crystal. Scott has all the qualities of a man I'd like to see you with."

"But this is about more than that. What did you say he had—a magical bean? What is that?"

"No one knows, and that's what's so intriguing about it. Late last year I was contacted by a man who said he had seeds from a fast-growing bean plant that, when processed, burned slow and hot enough to rival oil as a fuel source. Of course I wanted to learn all I could about it. I tried the processed sample, and it was impressive. I bought the beans from him. Unfortunately, my people couldn't reproduce the substance he'd sold me. When I tracked him down and asked him why, he admitted he'd stolen both the substance and the seeds from Scott Millville. I contacted Scott directly, but it was . . . let's just say . . . a less-than-productive conversation."

"So you offered to buy his land?"

"I was hoping he could be swayed by money."

"And when he wasn't?"

"There was a possibility that access to the land itself would reveal the reason we couldn't re-create the substance ourselves. My people thought it might be something in the soil."

"Then this wasn't about me at all."

My uncle held up a hand. "Crystal, I'm a practical man. My secret to success is my ability to create win-win situations. Scott isn't interested in using his beans as a fuel source. He's trying to create plant-based meat substitutes that taste horrible right now. He's idealistic—thinks he can change the world. If things work out between the two of you, you could help him reach that goal."

"And his discovery wouldn't become a fuel source at all." *Because what oil company wants a cheap, renewable fuel source to be discovered?*

"Correct."

"What if I didn't fall for him? What would you *win* in that scenario?"

"He's not known for keeping secrets. I figured he would tell you all about his substance and likely share what might be unique about how he grows the beans. A chemist like you might be shown his notes and understand what not many others would. From there we could determine how the substance would best be developed. There is profit in both applications of it."

"So your plan B was that I gather intel for you so you could steal his discovery."

"I was looking for information if the opportunity presented itself. Sure, I'd make a profit from it. Listen, imagine if electricity had been discovered by someone who wanted to use it to only create toy fireflies. The world would still be a very dark place. I have no intention of stealing anything from Scott, but if he's sitting on something that could indeed feed or fuel the world, someone has to help him along."

"Help him? Or help themselves?"

"When 'helping' is done right, everyone is left in a better situation than they started."

"Your whole plan was unethical."

"Ethics are subjective. There are people in the world without enough food to eat. Are you currently feeding them or ignoring their existence because you feel nothing can be done about it? What if something can be done, but it requires your view of right and wrong be modified?"

"I'm not spying for you."

"So if you end up marrying this small-town farmer, you'll keep his secret? Let the world stay cold and hungry—just so you can feel good knowing you stood by him."

"Don't even try to twist this. You may know a lot, but you don't know everything. Don't count Scott out when it comes to changing the world. He already has influential people in his corner. When I said I'm in love, I didn't mean with Scott. I meant with his twin brother, Jesse Rehoboth."

"Who?"

"You heard me. I guess your background check missed a few things."

"I guess it did. Who the hell is Jesse Rehoboth?"

"I'm sure your people will fill you in on the details, but what you need to know is that he is important to me. You need to back away from his family. Leave Scott alone. If you really do care for me, you'll do this. Don't ask me about him or his magical seeds or whatever he's growing. And I won't tell them why they should watch their backs around you."

"I've done nothing illegal."

"That doesn't make it right. None of this."

"You're letting your emotions cloud your objectivity."

"No, it's my morality that's doing that."

"You're beginning to sound like your father."

What he'd voiced as an accusation brought another piece of me to life, and some of my anger left. "Are these the types of arguments you had with him?"

"Your father had a narrow view of the world, and it held him back."

"I don't agree."

"I know. You and I are not the same people. It's why I can never be that perfect little family you're yearning for."

I rubbed my hand over my eyes. "I need time to process this. I love you, but right now I can't decide if you're a hero or a villain."

He laughed. "You watch too many superhero movies if those are the only two choices you feel you have. The world is more complicated than that. I would never consider my life more important than another's. In theory, no one ever should. Generals send men into battle every day knowing that some of them won't make it out alive. Even if they have a good reason to, they've chosen one life over another. Is that evil? Heroic? Even historians can't decide."

"Stop." I shook my head. I couldn't see the world that way. "I feel like this will lead to me choosing between you and Jesse. I don't want to do that. Just say you'll stay away from his family."

"Someone will come for what he has."

"As long as it's not you. Promise me it won't be you."

I wasn't sure he would at first. My uncle could be hard to read. With a nearly imperceptible nod, he said, "I put family second to what I wanted for a long time, and not a day goes by that I don't regret that I didn't call your father and tell him that nothing we'd argued over mattered as much as he did to me. You're all the family I have, Crystal. I want you to be happy. I want that for my brother but also for you. If that means helping you protect a man who's foolish enough to think the world will let him keep his secret in his basement, then I guess that's what I'll do. When something happens, and it will, call me. I'll bring whatever leverage or power I have to help you save him."

"It may not come to that."

"God, you are your father's daughter."

My response was instant and emotional. "I'm okay with that."

CHAPTER THIRTY

JESSE

It's not every day a man realizes he's in love for the first time. I was still somewhat shell shocked when I heard an RV pull up Scott's long driveway. My jeans were dusty from the barn, but I'd at least changed my shirt. As I stepped out of the house to meet them, my hands were cold and sweaty. I'd met with billionaires to discuss business deals and been less nervous than I was meeting Scott's parents.

My conversation with Crystal was fresh in my head as I came to a stop at the bottom of the steps. Rather than pushing how I was feeling aside and denying it, I chose to be as honest with myself as I'd vowed to be with Crystal.

I want to like them.

I want them to like me.

The driver and passenger doors of the RV flew open at the same time. The woman who came rushing around the front of the vehicle without taking the time to close the door was a tanned, jeans-and-T-shirt-clad woman, with short curly brown hair and a huge smile. She didn't have a speck of makeup on but looked a good twenty years younger than I'd heard she was. Her husband was easily my height, with thick gray hair, and would have made a good advertisement for the health benefits of an outdoor lifestyle. He closed the vehicle door behind him, then walked over to close the one his wife had left open.

I forced a smile and held out my hand to greet Scott's mother.

She ignored my hand, raising both of hers to cup the sides of my face. "I've seen photos of you. I didn't believe you'd look so much like Scott, but you do."

"Jill," Scott's father said as he walked up behind her. "Give the boy a moment to get to know us."

She gave my cheeks a squeeze. "I can't." Tears misted her eyes. "I have to hug you. May I?"

"I—uh—" The intensity of the moment was overwhelming. "Yes?"

She wrapped her arms around me and hugged me like I was someone she was welcoming home after years away rather than someone she was meeting for the first time. "You have no idea how much meeting you means to us. When Scott told us you were here . . . we couldn't not come back. It feels like I have another son."

Wow. That's . . . that's . . . I didn't know how I felt about that. It was way too much and somehow everything I'd hoped our meeting would be. I tentatively put my arms around her and gave her a pat on the back. "This means a lot to me as well."

Ryan put a hand on his wife's shoulder. "Easy there, Jill. Jesse *has* a mother."

Jill stepped back, wiping at the corners of her eyes. "You're right, Ryan. Sorry, Jesse."

"I'm right?" Ryan asked with humor. "Where's the calendar? I need to write this date down."

She swatted at his chest and sniffed. "Stop. I told you this would be emotional for me."

He put his arm around her and kissed the side of her head. "I know. Just don't want you to scare the poor boy off before we have a chance to get to know him."

When Jill's attention returned to me, the yearning in her eyes reached past every defense I had. She was a ball of love and enthusiasm, like a puppy instructed to sit that was struggling to contain its excitement. That was the only explanation I had for why I said, "Actually, I have no memories of the woman who adopted me. She left while I was very young, and we've had no contact with her."

Fresh tears filled Jill's eyes, and she shared a look with her husband. "Did you hear that?"

"Now you've done it," Ryan said lightly. "I hope you like this farm, because don't think you can escape without visiting it often now."

Jill wrung her hands in front of her. "I don't want to make you uncomfortable, but I do want you to know that there was a part of my heart that opened to you the moment I heard Scott had a brother."

In a deep voice, Ryan added, "I'm trying to appear cool about all of this, but I felt the same way. You don't know us, so this must be incredibly awkward for you, but I'm tempted to give you a hug myself. We're a huggy family."

My father was never big on touching, and if someone had described how Scott's parents would be with me, I would have said this would make me uncomfortable. That wasn't how it was, though. It felt like— an early-morning sunrise. Fresh. Pure. Full of hope. I stepped toward Ryan and did something I couldn't remember doing with another man: I held out my arms for a hug. His hug wasn't nearly as long or teary as Jill's had been, but it left me wondering what it would have been like to have been raised by people who gushed affection like my father gushed advice.

When we parted, Jill and Ryan were both beaming smiles at me. I found myself smiling back. I cleared my throat and said, "You must both be tired. What do you need brought into the house? I'll carry it in."

Jill hugged her husband tighter. "He even sounds like Scott."

A little shadow settled over the moment. They needed to know something. "Scott and I may look the same on the outside, but we're very different people. If you're looking for similarities beyond our physical appearance, you'll be disappointed."

After searching my face for a moment, Jill asked, "Are you hungry? If you help Ryan bring in our bags, I'll start lunch."

For a moment I wondered if she'd heard me, but when I saw Ryan nod with approval, I realized she had and was not acknowledging any disappointment was possible. I'd seen that same optimism in Scott when we'd first discussed the troubles at his farm. I'd dismissed it at the time as lack of comprehension of the situation, but now I saw it for what it was—a decision to remain positive in the face of the unknown. Action followed intent. I utilized that philosophy myself when it came to choosing goals for our company: imagine a positive outcome, then make it happen. It wasn't how I'd ever navigated personal relationships, but I was beginning to see merit in it.

I'd already taken steps in that direction with Crystal. To have a future with her, I needed to believe we could.

And I did—so we would.

I smiled. "I am very hungry. Ryan, show me what you need taken inside."

"Absolutely." As we made our way to the RV, Ryan said, "So Scott tells me you have a girlfriend. Will we be meeting her as well?"

"Her name's Crystal, and she's coming by tomorrow." How did that not sound insane anymore? "We have something being delivered, and she wanted to be here for it."

"That's great." He opened the side door of the RV. "What's being delivered?"

"A robotic leg for Alphonse."

Ryan turned, looked me in the eye, then laughed. "That damn duck. A robotic leg, huh? Fancy. Don't tell me Scott is getting into robots now. Not that I blame him for moving on from those bean products to something with more promise. Have you tasted what he and LJ consider 'meat'?" He shuddered.

"I have." I smiled. "I agree it needs some work."

"I keep telling him he needs to get out of that basement, meet someone, maybe give us some grandchildren while we're young enough to enjoy them. I made a good living simply farming this land. He could do the same and still have time to tinker on the side." Ryan kept talking as we entered the RV. "I'm sure your father says the same."

"Not exactly." I tried and couldn't imagine a scenario where my father would suggest Thane or I start a family over expanding our business. "My father is a lone-wolf type."

Ryan nodded. "I was like that once." He laughed again as he began to pile folded clothing into a bag. "I'm kidding; that was never me. I was raised by two sisters who doted on me—they still do. I'd love for you to meet them while you're here. They're both married with kids and living in Massachusetts. They might stay over if they come down."

"I'm from Mass. It's only an hour away."

"As a rule, we always bring luggage when we cross state lines. Now that we have the RV, we've been as far as Ohio. I swear Jill thought we should bring everything we own."

That made me smile. "She's going to like Crystal."

Ryan zipped a bag closed, then turned to me. "About Jill—thank you for being kind to her a moment ago. She's been looking forward to meeting you ever since we heard about you."

"No problem."

He reached for another bag. "We tried to have children for years, tried to adopt a baby for even longer. There's never been a day when any of us were hungry, but we don't have the kind of money it takes to adopt an infant. We considered fostering, were in the process of getting certified for it when a private adoption agency out of New York contacted us. They were willing to waive their adoption fees if we agreed to let them come out once a year to ask Scott a few questions."

"My parents adopted Thane and me from the same agency. My father mentioned that the agency had been meeting with my mother and us once a year to check in, but he ended that as soon as he found out about it."

"We would have agreed to almost anything after we held Scott for the first time. When we heard about you, we regretted not trying to find out more about Scott's original family." He sighed and handed me one of the bags. "Did you look into them?"

"No, nor do I have any interest in doing so."

He nodded. "I understand. We're Scott's family. Of course if he wanted to find out about his biological parents, we'd support that choice, but he never has." A smile returned to his face. "We're glad you found each other, though."

I looked him in the eye, and all I saw was the soul of a good man who loved his family with his entire being. "Me too."

CHAPTER THIRTY-ONE

CRYSTAL

Jesse met me at the plane the next morning with a big smile and a kiss so tender I nearly burst into tears when he raised his head. Rather than stepping back, I laid my head on his chest, hugged him tightly, and breathed in the scent of him. His arms swept around me, and he held me to him while tucking my head beneath his chin.

"I'm glad we didn't wait until the weekend," he murmured.

"I brought the blindfolds just in case we can find a room this evening before I go back."

"In case? I think you mean *when*."

"A girl can hope." I smiled against his chest. "They're in my luggage."

His chuckle rumbled through me. "Of course they are." He gave the top of my head a kiss and stepped back, taking one of my hands in his as he did. "No need to hope; there are some things you can count on happening." His wink was sexy and full of promise.

I floated beside him to the car. "You look as happy as you sounded last night. Aren't you glad you stuck around to meet Scott's parents?"

He opened the passenger side door for me. "I am, but I'm not surprised it went well. When I first stepped out of my life, I couldn't understand how Scott could be happy in his—but I do now. I'll be returning to Massachusetts soon, but with a better appreciation of how I was raised, as well as how Scott was. Jill and Ryan welcomed me into their family in a way I hadn't known was possible. I hope my father is being as good to Scott."

I waited until Jesse was belted into the driver's seat and pulling away from the plane before I said, "I'm sure he is. If he loves you like he says he does, he'd never hurt anyone you care about."

He shot me a side glance.

I looked out the window and sighed. I hadn't told him yet that I'd spoken to my uncle. I'd wanted to the night before, but he'd sounded so happy about how things had gone with Scott's parents. I knew I had to tell him—but when?

"Everything okay?"

I gave his hand a squeeze and forced a smile before turning to face him. "Sorry, yes. I had to rush around this morning, and it must have put me in a mood."

He didn't look convinced, but he brought my hand to his lips. "I'm glad you're here."

My heart started racing in my chest. "Me too."

"It's only ten. I told Scott's parents we'd have a late lunch with them."

Warmth began to spread through me as I wondered if his thoughts were filling with the same ideas mine were. "So we have hours."

His smile was all sex and heat. "Enough time to find a place where we could try out those blindfolds and work up an appetite."

"Did you already book a room?"

"You know I like to be prepared."

My mood lifted. "How far is it?"

"I'll drive fast."

A short time later, we pulled into the driveway of a small house. I'd expected a hotel, and my surprise must have shown on my face. "You rented this place for the day?"

He shrugged. "For what I wanted for today, I thought a house would be fun."

My eyes widened. "Should I worry?"

"Only if you don't trust me." After parking, he popped the trunk open, and without coming around to open my door, he headed back there to get the luggage. "Do you?"

"I do, but you look suspiciously like you're up to something."

His grin was shameless as he approached with my bag. "Dig out the blindfolds. We'll start with you wearing yours."

I did as he asked, but I'll admit my adrenaline was high as I did. With the blindfolds swinging from one hand, I followed him to the door of the home. When he began to put a code in to unlock the door, I touched his shoulder. "There's no one else in there, is there?"

He looked back at me. "Do you want there to be?"

"No," I said in a rush. "And no cameras."

He turned and ran a hand gently down my cheek. "Good, because that's not what I have planned at all." Leaning down to just beside my ear, he growled, "I should have asked if you're okay with toys."

My breath caught in my throat, and I warmed from head to toe in anticipation. "Totally okay."

"Good." He kissed me deeply, bringing me flush against his excitement. "Then put your damn blindfold on."

He released me so I could, and I stood there, feeling a bit silly. I heard the door open and the rustle of him moving my bag. He guided me through the door, and it clicked shut behind me.

"Strip for me," he ordered.

Part of me wanted to move the blindfold aside just enough to make sure we were indeed alone, but not knowing added another layer of excitement to the experience. I gathered my courage and whipped my shirt up and over my head. Without giving myself time to start questioning if I should, I unhooked my bra and let that fall away as well. My courage wavered at the button of my pants, but when I felt the hot caress of his breath on my bare nipples, I slid my shoes off and stepped out of the rest of my clothing.

"You're so fucking beautiful," he said just before he took one of my breasts into his mouth. I shivered with pleasure and began to caress his shoulders, but he raised his head and said, "No, I'm in control this time. No touching for you until I tell you to." Against my parted lips, he murmured, "When it's your turn, you can make the rules. This one is for me."

"Okay," I said in a breathless voice. There was nothing I wasn't loving about how he took his time exploring my body with his mouth and hands. God, the things that man knew how to do with both were sinful. I was wildly turned on and wet for him, and we were still just inside the doorway.

He licked and teased one of my nipples until I was moaning and writhing, then moved on to the other. Meanwhile one of his hands claimed my sex and simply cupped it at first while his other hand massaged my bare ass.

"Come with me, but don't touch the blindfold," he said as he led me forward into the home. The floor went from tile to carpeting beneath my feet. The scent of roses greeted me.

"You got me roses?"

"I did." He came to a stop, and it sounded like he moved a chair aside. He placed both of my hands on what felt like the flat surface of a table, then guided my foot up to the seat of a chair. "Climb on up there and stay on all fours faced away from me."

What? No one had ever asked me to do anything at all like this before, but maybe that was why I had so few good memories of sex. With that in mind, I crawled up onto the table. Realizing the surface was covered with rose petals evaporated what was left of my hesitation.

Once I was settled, he said, "Spread your legs wider for me."

I did.

He nipped at each of my buttocks as he ran his hands up and down the outside and then the inside of my thighs. Those talented fingers of his teased and dipped into my sex until I was ready to beg for his cock.

I contained myself to a sound that revealed my level of excitement and need.

I nearly wept when his hands dropped away, but then I heard the buzz of a vibrator being turned on. I'd never felt so vulnerable, exposed, powerful, and free. He dipped the tip of it into my sex. I bit my bottom lip and pushed back against it, wanting it to fill me.

He moved it in and out slowly, deeper and deeper each time. A second part of it tickled at my clit each time it delved deep inside me. Teasing flicks became a constant wondrous vibration that sent an orgasm crashing through me.

It was almost too much when the vibration continued after my orgasm, but I was willingly going wherever he wanted to lead me.

"I could spend a lifetime watching you come."

I would have answered with something witty had I been capable of speech. Instead I gasped for air and marveled at how quickly my body was revving up for more pleasure.

He pulled the vibrator out, turned it off, and told me to turn over onto my back. Blindfolded, that was a trickier feat than I'd anticipated, and I wasn't necessarily graceful about it, but that didn't seem to bother him in the least.

The sound of him stripping was one of the most erotic experiences I'd ever had. The ripping of a condom package being opened was my hint of what was next, and I splayed my hands on either side of myself when he pulled me to the edge of the table and wrapped my legs around his waist.

His hands were rough and impatient. His huge cock thrust deep. I gasped and arched against the table. He pounded into me powerfully, mercilessly, and I cried out his name along with a few curses as our mating turned animalistic. The man was a machine. He kept up the pace as warmth spread through me again. Not quite an orgasm but something wonderfully close.

I pushed myself onto my elbows. He swooped an arm behind my waist and lifted me. A few steps, and he was fucking me against a wall. There was nothing but him and how he was claiming me. His kisses were heated and everywhere. When his mouth found mine, fireworks burst in me, and I moaned into the kiss. He came with a final, deep thrust.

Slowly, he lowered me to the floor before giving me a gentle kiss and stepping away. I sagged against the wall and lifted the blindfold. In all his naked glory, he was walking back toward me. "I love you," I burst out. "And this time I mean it."

"There you go, reading my mind again." He pulled me into his arms and gave me a kiss that shook me to my soul. "I love you too."

I burrowed into the warmth of his embrace. This was how I'd always dreamed it could be with a man. I didn't want to return to reality. "Can we stay in this house forever?"

He moved an arm and said, "Forever? No. But we have almost two hours left. Less if we leave time for a shower and travel."

I glanced around. It wasn't just the table that he'd filled with flowers. The entire living room was full of bouquets of roses. I gave him another tight hug. "You're not playing fair. How could I possibly top what you just did?"

He smiled and wiggled his eyebrows. "Men are simple creatures."

I laughed. "Seriously? Is the blindfold even necessary then?"

"Only if you want to wear it again."

CHAPTER THIRTY-TWO

JESSE

I'm not saying a man can't be calm without several orgasms; I'm just saying it sure doesn't hurt a man's mood. By the time Crystal and I were on our way back to the farm, I felt at peace with the world in a way I hadn't in a long time.

"I hope they like me," Crystal said out of the blue.

"The Millvilles or the Romanos?"

"Both. Mostly the Millvilles. What did you say their names were again? I can't believe I forgot."

I took her hand. "Don't worry. They're going to think you're wonderful. Hell, Jill and Ryan like *me*, and I'm not even as nice as you are."

"Jill and Ryan. I can remember that."

"They're a lot, but not necessarily in a bad way. They're going to hug you. Jill will probably ask you a thousand questions about what you do. I'd be honest with them, but I'd go easy on how much you tell them. I get the feeling Scott has left them in the dark as far as what's been going on."

"Interesting. What do they think you're doing at the farm?"

"I told them my original plan was to help Scott deal with unwanted offers to buy the farm." I gave her hand a squeeze. "That it was supposed to be a brief switch; then I met you."

"Plausible."

"And true."

Her head snapped around, and our eyes locked briefly. "You stayed to protect Scott."

I had to look back at the road. "I could have done that from anywhere."

Her hand shook in mine. "You stayed for me."

"Yes, even though I didn't see it at first. I wasn't looking for a relationship. I grew up hearing that they were nothing but a distraction. That's not what you are to me. You made me question what I thought I knew about myself. Was I living the life I wanted to? If I wasn't, what was it that was missing? What I'm discovering is that this was what I was looking for." I raised our linked hands between us. "I work hard, and I'm damn proud of what I've accomplished, but it's an empty win if I don't have someone to share it with."

When I glanced her way, she was all eyes. "This is what I was missing as well." She let out a shaky breath. "Jesse, there's something I should tell you."

"Hang on." While pulling onto a side road that led to Scott's farm, I noticed a car parked on one side, enough off the road that it was suspicious. I slowed my vehicle as I passed it and noted there was no one inside. I slowed the car even more. My gut said something was very wrong.

I stopped my car in the middle of the road and turned to Crystal. "I need to check this out. Someone's been causing trouble for Scott, and this could be them. Go on to the house. That path connects to Scott's land. Keep your phone near you. If it's something, I'll call the police and have you move everyone into the house. It's probably nothing, though. Probably someone thinking they can hunt on his property."

She shook her head. "I'm not leaving you here. That's not happening."

"You're not coming with me."

"What if neither of us go? We'll go to the house and call the police from there. They can check it out."

"They could be gone before the police get here. If they're up to something, I want to catch them in the act."

"I don't like this plan."

I undid my seat belt and opened the car door. "I'm going."

She grabbed my arm. "Even if I ask you not to?"

I gently pried her hand off. "Crystal, you're not going to lose me. I have no intention of confronting anyone, but I do want to see what they're up to."

She blinked a few times. "Let someone else do this."

"Protect my family?" I felt her pain, but my gut told me the answers I'd been looking for were in those woods. "I can't do that. You're what I stayed for, but this is what brought me here. I need to solve this for Scott."

"You don't know whose car that is."

A dark thought occurred to me. "Do you?"

Her mouth rounded in shock. "No. Why would you ask me that?"

I frowned. "Is there something you haven't told me? Did you talk to your uncle again?" Her guilty expression knocked the air out of me.

"Yes, but—"

"Did you tell him who I am?"

"This wasn't how I wanted to tell you. It wasn't like that."

"So he knows everything, doesn't he?"

"Yes."

"And you do now as well."

"About your brother's beans? Yes. Jesse, I was going to tell you. I was waiting for the right moment."

I wanted to believe her. "Go to the house. We'll talk later." I exited the car, not waiting for Crystal to move to the driver's side or to say anything more. I was angry—at myself as well as at her. As I headed through the woods in the direction of the parked car, I went over the conversation I'd had with Crystal again and again. She'd spoken to her uncle without telling me. The right moment? We'd just spent hours together alone. She should have told me. The questions I was wrestling with were if I could trust her and, if I couldn't, how much it would change how I felt about her.

I didn't know what their conversation had been about because I hadn't given her time to tell me. I'd stormed off. I stopped and looked over my shoulder. My car was gone, along with my anger. She hadn't lied to me, and she was worried for my safety.

We did need to talk, though.

Near the car I spotted footprints leading into the woods and onto the path toward Scott's land. I made out two sets of prints. They'd gone onto the path, then off and through a field of tall grass at the edge of the woods. There, I crouched down and scanned the area. A movement behind one of the tractors caught my attention. There, in broad daylight, was a man shoveling dirt from a corner of Scott's bean field into a bucket. Was this the same person who'd broken in? Information on something like what Scott was working on would be worth a lot of money. Selling that information would require proof, though. And proof was what the man seemed to be shoveling into a bucket.

I took out my phone and began to snap pictures of him in the act. Proof was also what would put an end to his illegal activities. A sound behind me had me straightening and turning quickly. The click of a gun being cocked followed.

Shit.

"Don't move," a male voice said from behind a tree. "I don't want to shoot you."

"That's good, because I don't want to be shot."

"Throw your phone over here."

"Where?" I asked, even though I had a very good idea of where he was. I scanned the wooded area around me. He sounded young. And scared. People did things out of fear they normally wouldn't. I needed to be careful.

The man partially stepped out from behind the tree and waved a hand. "Right here. Throw your phone over here."

I almost felt bad for him. He was far from a hardened criminal and definitely not someone who should have been waving a gun around. "It's a new phone. Please don't steal it. It's not insured."

To my surprise he seemed sympathetic. "If you let me delete the photos, I can give it back to you, I guess."

Really? The more the man spoke, the younger he sounded. Some young people put a high value on their phones, and that appeared to be the case with him. "Could I just hand it to you? Really, I don't want any trouble. But I just got this phone."

"Okay, but don't try anything." The young man stepped fully out from behind the tree. He was all legs and arms—likely midteens. He kept the gun pointed in my general direction with a hand that was shaking so much I thought for sure he'd shoot me without meaning to.

I took a step toward him with one hand extended, holding the phone out as if for him to take. "You'll need my code to get into the phone. Should I put it in, or do you want to?" I stepped even closer.

He didn't look sure and lowered the gun ever so slightly as he seemed to debate which would be better. I took advantage of his stance and threw my leg up and around, kicking the gun out of his hand. When he lunged forward, I hit his jaw with an uppercut to stun him, then swung my other fist around in a hook that sent him sliding to the ground. Confrontation was something I'd been taught to avoid, but if a fight was necessary, survival often depended on disabling an opponent before they had time to consider retaliating. All those years of Krav Maga were finally paying off.

My adrenaline was still pumping as he lay there bleeding from his mouth. As he struggled to sit up, I bent and grabbed the handgun from the ground, clicked the safety on, and stuffed it in the back of my jeans. "You're too young to be doing whatever this is."

"We're just getting some dirt, Scott. It's not a big deal."

Ah, his sympathy for me made sense now. He knew my brother. "Then why the gun?"

"No!" The expression on the young man's face turned to horror, and I understood why too late. A crack of something to the back of my head sent me to my hands and knees. For a moment I was too stunned to do more than shake my head. The gun was yanked out of the back of my jeans as I fought to not face-plant in the dirt.

"You were supposed to be watching for people," another male voice snapped.

"He came out of nowhere."

"Well, you really fucked up this time. He saw us. What do you think he'll do if we let him go? I'm not going back to jail."

"Don't hurt him. It's Scott."

"Doesn't matter. I can't *not* hurt him. I finally have a good thing going. I could have helped you pay for college. I still might be able to, but you've got to start thinking. Get up, take this shovel, and go dig a hole. We can't let anyone find his body."

Holy fuck.

There were moments in a person's life that put everything else into perspective. This was not where I would die. I had too much to live for—my family, Crystal, the family we would start together. No. I refused for this to be the end.

"Stop. You can't do this. We're not killing him."

"You'll do whatever I tell you to."

The kid scrambled to his feet, looking more afraid than I was. "Or what? You'll kill me too?"

"If I have to."

I met the kid's gaze and shook my head slightly. I didn't want to die, but I also didn't want to see him go with me.

He looked away, then squared his shoulders. "Put the gun down, Remy. It's over."

Remy—Scott's old friend. Of course.

"Don't make me hurt you, too, Brian. I have people waiting for this soil sample. People who are willing to pay big money for it. If you're too much of a pussy to help—go home. Say nothing, and no one will ever know you were here."

"I can't do that," Brian said in a voice that cracked. "Don't do this; you don't have to do this. We'll find another way to make money."

"It's too late for that. Get out of here before you force me to do something I'll hate myself for."

"I'm not leaving. I won't let you do this. Think about Mom. She needs us. Both of us."

The sound of the slide of the gun being pulled back and a round being chambered made the hair on the back of my neck stand up. I'd have one chance to get this right. I peeked beneath my arm to see if his leg was within striking distance. It was.

Without hesitation, I threw my weight onto my front arms and rear kicked at his knees. It was enough to send him off balance. A shot went off, but I didn't pause to determine where it had hit. Rising from a crouch, I spun and gave him a dick punch with everything I had.

He hit the ground with a thud and a litany of swears. I grabbed the gun again and turned toward Brian.

"What are you going to do now?" Brian choked out.

"Call the police," I answered.

"This is going to break my mother." He started to cry. "She already can't pay the bills because she keeps bailing him out. I work after school to help pay our bills. She needs my income."

I believed him. "If you leave now—I never saw you."

Wiping blood from the side of his mouth, the kid backed up a few feet, then said, "Please don't hurt my brother. He wasn't always like this. We've just had some bad years since my dad left."

I looked him in the eye. "He would have killed you."

The kid sniffed and glared down at his brother. "Yeah, he's all yours." With that he turned and ran.

While Remy was still rolling around in pain, I called 911 and told the dispatcher my location. I said I'd found someone trespassing on my property. He had a gun and a shovel and was going to use both on me, but I'd incapacitated him. They said they'd send someone right over.

Just then I heard Crystal's voice. "Over there. I see him." At her side, in a sprint, was LJ.

Remy was sitting forward, still moaning. I kept the gun pointed at him.

When she was within a few feet, Crystal froze and her mouth rounded. "Oh my God, are you okay? We heard a gunshot."

"I'm fine." I nodded toward the man on the ground, then directed my comment to LJ. "I finally found Remy."

Shaking his head, LJ said, "I knew he was trouble."

"Fuck you, Scott," Remy said.

How close I'd come to being buried in the woods fueled a cold fury in me. I let him believe I was Scott and growled, "I'll help your family, but you—you'll have to help yourself from behind bars. I hope to God you get counseling, because I don't know if anyone can come back from where you are."

Crystal stepped closer to me. "Who is he?"

Her question hung in the air for a moment. An argument could've been made for returning to questioning everything she said. On the other hand, the woman I'd fallen in love with didn't have a devious bone in her body. She'd not only stayed to help me; she'd brought LJ. I lowered my voice. "He was a friend of Scott's until he decided betraying him could be more profitable."

Crystal said, "My uncle said someone contacted him last year and sold him some of Scott's seeds. They tried to reproduce Scott's crop and product but couldn't."

LJ said, "That's why he wants the soil. Your uncle must be trying to figure out what's different about it."

Crystal hugged her arms around herself. "He doesn't work for my uncle." Then she turned her attention to Remy. "Are you on someone's payroll?"

"I'm not fucking talking to anyone without a lawyer." Remy slowly moved to stand.

"Stay on the ground," I ordered. He glared at me and looked like he'd rise anyway until I growled, "Or I'll gladly beat your ass right back to where you are."

"That's assault." He sneered. "And there are witnesses."

I touched the back of my head, then held out blood-covered fingers. "They'd look away for the most painful ten seconds of your life."

He sat back, an ugly expression on his face.

In the distance a siren cut through the woods. I looked down at Remy and said, "I thought I saw you in the field but lost you. You hit me from behind with a shovel, then threatened me with a gun. We fought. You shot and missed. That's when I charged you and took the gun. That's the story we're going with."

"Why would I do anything you fucking tell me to do?"

"Because you care about your family. You wanted to help your mother and brother. Then you tasted easy money, and it took you down a bad road."

"No, that road started when I killed my father and buried him in the basement. He always did like it down there. That's where he used to drink and then take us to—"

"I get the idea." I cut him off.

"Over here," LJ called to the police. "Quickly, please."

Crystal was standing absolutely still, shaking visibly, but not saying anything.

I would have gone to her, but I wasn't taking my eyes off Remy until he was handcuffed and safely being taken away. I felt for him, but he was also the man who'd been willing to kill his brother a few minutes earlier and apparently had offed his father. "You know I need to tell them about your father. If you did it to protect your family, protect them now. Or don't. The choice is yours."

I lowered the gun as soon as the police came into view, then turned it in my hand to give it to them. I gave them my real name, then the modified tale I'd prepped Remy with. They turned to him and asked him if that was what had happened. He nodded, and they hauled him up to his feet and put him in handcuffs.

"There's one more thing," I said, waving a police officer over to the side. "You'll want to check the basement of his house."

CHAPTER THIRTY-THREE

CRYSTAL

I stood to the side as Jesse spoke to the police. LJ stayed with me.

He cleared his throat before speaking. "You were right to come get me."

I continued to hug my arms around myself. "I didn't know what else to do. And luckily you were outside."

"You really don't know if Remy is working with your uncle?"

If life were simple, I would have had an answer to that question that I could stomach. "I really don't know."

"If you did, it wouldn't have made sense to involve me. I believe you."

Losing patience, I snapped, "I don't care what you do or don't believe."

"Fair enough." He raised a placating hand. "We definitely started off on the wrong foot." After a moment, he added, "So you and Jesse seem to have hit it off."

"Please be quiet." I really couldn't discuss my relationship with Jesse when I felt so close to throwing up. He'd almost been killed. Killed and buried. I'd almost just lost another person I loved.

I wanted to run to Jesse, throw my arms around him, and sob into his arms while telling him how glad I was he was okay.

I wanted to grab him by the shoulders and shake him for being stupid enough to try to deal with Remy and whoever else had been with him on his own. Who had been with him? Why would Jesse want to protect anyone who had been involved in bashing him over the head with a shovel? It didn't make sense, but lately more and more was not making sense to me.

One of the officers announced he would be in touch with follow-up questions; then he and the other officer led a handcuffed Remy away. Jesse walked over and simply stood in front of me for a moment.

LJ said, "I'll give you a minute."

I didn't respond. Jesse nodded without looking away from me.

Neither of us said a word until, in unison, we said, "I'm sorry."

To get it off my chest, I rushed to say my part first. "I should have told you I'd spoken to my uncle. I would have if I'd thought it was a problem, but he promised he'd back off. I asked him to leave you and your family alone, and he swore he would."

Jesse's expression tightened. "I should have given you a chance to explain before losing my temper and telling you to go back to the farm. I don't want to go backward with you; I want to go forward."

My eyes filled with tears. "I'm so angry with you for almost getting killed."

He made a face. "I'm not really happy with myself regarding that. It was hotheaded and stupid. A shovel to the back of my head woke me up to that. Getting LJ was smart, although it might have gotten both of you killed as well. Don't risk your life for mine again."

I sniffed. "Don't go chasing armed people around the woods again, and I won't have to." I glanced around. "There was someone else here, wasn't there? Who was it?"

"Remy's little brother. He looks fourteen, maybe fifteen. That whole family needs help. I don't know what Remy said to him to get him here and holding a gun, but when things went south, Brian was willing to die rather than help his brother kill me."

A shudder rolled through me. "How did Remy think he would get away with something like that?"

"Remy isn't thinking much through lately. His father sounds like he was a real piece of work and abused his family. Remy snapped a few years ago, killed him, and buried him in their basement. No one is ever right again after something like that. Really, compared to that, this must not have been that hard. He was already lost."

"I guess."

"Brian isn't. I don't believe he knows about his father, though. Don't say anything to anyone, but I'm going to offer to pay for counseling for the family. They'll need support, or that mother will end up with two children in jail."

I searched his face. "That's an incredibly kind thing to do, considering what you just went through."

He raised and lowered his shoulders. "Or practical. You have to wonder if anyone knew about Remy's father and did nothing. I don't believe monsters are born—they're made. Maybe it's too late to help his family, but if they really are survivors of abuse, they deserve a second chance."

"Yes." In that moment I saw so much of what I loved about Jesse. He was strong and confident but caring as well. Due to their different upbringings, he might think he had little in common with Scott, but I didn't see it that way. Scott helped broken animals. Without fanfare, Jesse planned to help a broken family. Still in shock over what had almost happened, I asked, "How are you not freaking out?"

He gave me a sad smile. "Oh, I am—on the inside." He stepped closer and ran his hand through my hair. "I have even more to live for now."

I swayed and let out a shaky breath. Being with him was a wild roller-coaster ride but one I didn't want to get off. "Yes, try to remember that the next time you even consider doing something like this."

The look he gave me was hard to interpret. I wanted to hear a simple *I promise I'll never risk my life again,* but I had a feeling that, given the same situation, he'd still go into those woods. His loyalty to his family outweighed everything else.

He'd said he loved me. Would that loyalty extend to me? Could it be shaken if my uncle didn't keep his promise? "What do we do now?" I asked.

"We go to the farm. Jill and Ryan are waiting for us."

I swallowed hard. "And pretend this never happened?"

He touched the back of his head and winced. "That might be tough. Plus this is a small town. They'll hear that something happened. We might as well tell them the truth."

Panic began to rise within me. "I don't know what the truth is. I know what I want it to be." My throat constricted. "What if it isn't? I don't want to choose between two people I love."

"Hey." His hands cupped my face. "I won't put you in that position."

"It's not you I'm worried about."

He pulled me to him and hugged me to his chest. We stood like that for a long moment, and then he said, "My father has gone through his whole life expecting every woman to lie to him because his wife did. Not one of the women who came into his life was able to change his mind. Trust is a leap of faith he's never been willing to take."

I nodded against his chest, soaking in his strength. "I doubted my uncle when I heard why Remy was here, but I want to trust him. I love him. He wouldn't lie to me." I raised my head to look Jesse in the eye and told him how my uncle had explained his reasoning for wanting me to see Scott again. "I know how bad it all sounds, but I believe he really had good intentions. He was hoping Scott and I would hit it off and I wouldn't be alone."

Hugging me closer, Jesse said, "You're not alone anymore—you have me. And we'll figure this out."

"My uncle is a good man. He wouldn't do this."

Jesse's heart thudded loudly in his chest. "I have an idea. It might be a crazy one, but my gut tells me it's what we need to do."

Oh God. Okay. "I'm in."

He tipped my head back so he could look me in the eye and smiled. "You don't even know what I'm about to suggest."

"I don't have to."

He kissed me then, and it was everything I needed. Warm. Reassuring. Loving. When he raised his head, he said, "It's time we leap together."

I gave him a bemused smile. "What does that even mean?"

"We gather everyone together and talk this out—my family, your uncle—"

"Me," LJ said from a few feet away.

Jesse shot him a look. "We're having a private conversation."

He threw up his hands. "In the middle of the woods with me standing right here? What am I supposed to do? Pretend I can't hear?"

A groan rumbled in Jesse's chest. "You are one hell of a pain, but you're right. You're in this too."

LJ's chest puffed. "You'll like me a lot more once we've changed the course of history."

"We?" Jesse voiced his challenge.

"You'll see. The universe always has a plan, but most people are too afraid to embrace it. A farmer, a techie, a space station engineer, an oil mogul, and a genius chemist who just happens to be a flavorist. That was no accident. This was meant to be."

Meant to be. That was how it felt to be in Jesse's arms. The rest of it? Well, LJ's optimism was a much-needed balm on my frayed nerves. I winked at him. "I didn't like you when we first met, but you're winning me over." With a more serious expression, I looked up at Jesse and said, "My uncle told me that if I needed him, he would bring everything in his power to help me. If I call him, he'll come. When do you want to do this?"

"Today. We don't know how much Remy will share with the police. We need to get ahead of this."

I stepped out of Jesse's embrace, took out my phone, and sent a text to my uncle. I'm at Scott's farm. I need you. Could you come? Right now? His answer came in immediately. Are you safe?

Yes, but things have gotten complicated and I need you. Please come.

I'll be in the air in twenty. At the farm in little over an hour.

On impulse, I wrote: I love you. Thank you.

Love you, too. On my way.

Tears filling my eyes, I held my phone up so Jesse could see my conversation with my uncle. "He does love me."

Jesse pulled me to him again. "He sure does, and he's not the only one. When all this is over, let's go back to the house and get some sleep, because I brought more than one toy."

Heat flooded through me. "Yes, yes, I love the way you think."

"Still here," LJ said. "Wishing I weren't, but the two of you are my ride, and if you think I'm walking alone to Scott's house after what happened to you—you're crazy. So wrap it up, Jesse, call your family, and let's go."

Jesse started to laugh. I joined in. We laughed until we were both wiping tears from our cheeks, not because LJ's comment had been particularly funny. We laughed because we'd come so close to losing everything, had been shaken to the core, but somehow were still together—and still horny as hell.

We were going to be fine.

CHAPTER THIRTY-FOUR

JESSE

Crystal, LJ, and I were sitting in the farmhouse living room with Scott's parents. Crystal was at my side. Scott's parents were hovering around us. LJ sat across from us, sipping on lemonade Ryan had served. A plate of sandwiches sat untouched between us. I couldn't speak for anyone else, but I was still too amped up to eat.

Earlier, the introduction of Crystal to the Millvilles had gone from warm to strained as soon as Jill noticed blood on the back of my shirt. One question led to another until Scott's parents knew everything I did about the situation—well, almost as much. I didn't tell them about Brian, because his shot at not following in his brother's footsteps would be even harder with an arrest record. I also left out the amount of sex Crystal and I had already engaged in, as well as the plans I had for her as soon as I could get her alone. Not that it would have shocked Scott's parents—I'd seen his mother's "drawer."

Crystal and I were honest with them because it was time to be. Life was about to change for the Millvilles, whether they wanted it to or not, and they needed to understand why. Remy would only be the beginning of the trouble that might come if word got out about what Scott had discovered and they didn't have a plan in place to protect the farm.

After assuring us that they would do whatever Scott needed them to, Jill insisted on cleaning the wound on the back of my head. Thankfully it was a small one, but as I changed my shirt and saw the amount of blood on it, I understood why she'd been so concerned.

Ryan clapped his hand to his thigh. "I still can't believe all this fuss is about Scott's little plant hobby. I remember when he first started it, I made him use our spare field. No way were we going to replace our soybean fields with his special beans. Is there even a market for them?"

"Yes, and it's more than a hobby," LJ said.

Not all the secrets were ours. I shot LJ a look. "Do they know who you are?"

"Who he is?" Jill repeated with widening eyes.

LJ shrugged. "Thanks for the creepy vibe you put to that disclosure." He stood and went to stand with Scott's parents. "I'm the same man you welcomed into your home—just a tad bit more successful than I let on that I was."

"Tell them your real name," I said. Hell, we'd come clean about everything.

"Leo Jarcisco." LJ pocketed his hands and waited.

Jill and Ryan exchanged a look. Jill shrugged. Ryan grimaced and asked, "Are we supposed to know the name?"

LJ's mouth dropped open, and I barked out a laugh. Crystal politely covered her mouth in an attempt to conceal her own amusement. "In some circles," LJ said, "I'm kind of a big deal."

Jill touched his cheek in a sympathetic, supportive gesture. "You're a big deal here. You've become like family to us. We love the motor home you found for us."

Ryan added, "One of LJ's friends bought it, then couldn't sell it for tax reasons, so he gave it to us."

Jill gasped and dropped her hand. "LJ, you lied to us about where you got it, didn't you?"

It was truly entertaining to watch a man as important as Leo Jarcisco duck his head in response to Jill's accusation. "I knew you wouldn't accept it if I told you I'd purchased it for you."

"Lying never works out," Ryan said with a shake of his head.

Jill hugged her husband's side. "He meant well, Ryan." Then she wagged a finger at LJ. "Next time, though, be honest with us. With all that you do around here, you've already done more than we could ever repay you for."

Again LJ was humbled, and I found myself liking him for the first time. "I was angry with the world before I met your family. You taught me how not to be. I'm the one who can never fully repay you."

When Jill hugged LJ and Ryan wrapped his arms around both of them, Crystal's hand slid into mine. A quick glance at her confirmed that her eyes were tearing up, but she was smiling. "I love this family."

I kissed her temple and murmured, "Me too."

The sound of a car pulling up the gravel driveway had me on my feet and walking to the window. I recognized the man who stepped out of the back of the vehicle, but only because I'd seen photos of him on the internet. Steadman. "Crystal, your uncle is here."

She joined me at the window. Although her expression was composed, I could tell she was nervous. "He made good time. Your family is still en route?"

I sent a quick text to Thane, received a response, then said, "They should be here any minute."

She took a deep breath. "Let's go greet him."

Jill stepped forward. "Should we wait here? Come with?"

Crystal met my gaze. "We leap together, right?"

"Right," I answered and took her hand in mine. "Why don't you all come outside and meet him. He could probably use some of your calming Millville vibes."

Shaking visibly, Crystal added, "He's the only family I have. I really need this to work out."

I put my arm around her waist. "It will. We've got this. Now quit looking scared before he thinks we're the reason."

She forced a bright smile. "You're right. Okay, let's do this."

Art Steadman was already on the porch when Ryan opened the door. Ryan welcomed him, inviting him immediately inside. Steadman walked by Ryan with a nod and sought out Crystal. He was dressed in an immaculate business suit, as if he'd been summoned straight from a meeting. I recognized the brand—one of my father's favorites.

Crystal left my side to go to him. Her voice shook a little when she said, "Thank you for coming so quickly."

Her uncle frowned down at her, then gave the rest of us a once-over. "What happened?"

Crystal reached a hand back to me. I linked my hand with hers and took my place by her side. She said, "This is Jesse Rehoboth."

Her uncle didn't offer me a hand, and I told myself I likely would have done the same in his position. He had no idea why he was there or what the "situation" was.

"It's good to meet you, sir." The last part was a by-product of how my father had raised me. Steadman showed no sign of having heard me.

Crystal waved her hand toward the others in the room. "This is Jill and Ryan—they're Scott's parents. LJ, Leo Jarcisco, is here as a friend of the family."

With a closed expression, her uncle said, "What are *we* doing here?"

Her eyes flew to mine again. "Waiting for Scott, Jesse's brother Thane, and their father."

The sound of another car pulling up the driveway punctuated her response. I said, "That's probably them."

Crystal turned to her uncle. "You came into my life when I most needed someone. I am already so grateful for you. This whole situation is insane, but I know you're a good man." She paused to squeeze my hand. "And I know the quality of this man. That's why I'm confident that although things might get rocky in a few minutes, we'll come out of this all on the same side and with a plan that will work for all of us. I'm counting on you to bring one of your win-wins spins to this."

Steadman was a man of few words and calculated action. His only concession was one nearly imperceptible nod.

The door flew open, and Scott bounded in. "Mom. Dad. Everything okay?"

His parents took turns hugging him. His father said, "We're fine."

Scott's eyes rounded when he spotted Steadman off to the side. "What's he doing here?"

Jill said, "Jesse will explain it better than we could."

Before I had a chance to, my father entered the house, followed by Thane. They had a presence that brought the energy of any room up a notch. My father was a formidable opponent—unapologetically aggressive when it came to closing a deal. Thane was more reserved but didn't miss a thing. I hadn't told them more than Crystal had told her uncle. We'd decided it would be best to put everything out in the open at once.

I brought Crystal over to meet them. "Crystal, this is my father and my brother Thane." I called out to Scott. "Scott, get over here. I'm introducing Crystal to the family."

Scott trotted over, taking a spot on the other side of my father from Thane. "Crystal, it's amazing to finally meet you." She clung to my hand even as he pulled her in for a hug that lifted her off her feet.

When he released her, she said, "Well, hi. That was weird." When he frowned, she added, "Not bad. It's just—I thought because you look so much alike . . . but no." She went bright red, and he looked confused.

I stepped forward to save both of them and gave Scott a hearty pat on the back. "Wearing my most expensive suit, I see."

Scott laughed and scratched at the lapel. "You can't even see the little ketchup I dropped over here."

I shook my head and groaned. "Scott, Dad, Thane, this is Crystal Holmes. Crystal, this is my family."

My father looked her over without saying anything.

Thane offered his hand. "It's nice to meet the reason I'm doing most of the work on our latest contract."

Crystal shook his hand vigorously and said, "It's nice to be the reason."

A brief silence fell over the room. My father had issues with women, but I'd been hoping he'd give Crystal a warmer reception, if for no other reason than she was important to me. It was hard not to be disappointed.

Crystal looked from me to my father, then leaned closer to him and said, "Not today, because we already have so much to work through, but I *will* hug you. Most likely on a regular basis. It'll be awkward at first, especially if you try to run, but after a while you'll understand I can't help myself and just accept it. I love your son, and that means you already have a place in my heart."

From across the room, Jill said, "I hope Scott finds someone that wonderful." I didn't say a thing.

"She sounds like you," Ryan said, then gave his wife a brief kiss.

My father's expression didn't change at first; then a slight smile stretched his lips. "I've heard good things about you, Crystal."

Crystal smiled back. "Same. I also know you're an incredible father because your son turned out pretty damn wonderful."

My father's eyes sought mine. "He did. And thank you." With a dramatic sigh, he said, "I suppose I'll have to resign myself to being hugged."

"You'll survive," I said, a smile spreading across my face as well. He nodded slowly, and I felt a hundred pounds lighter.

Scott's father called to his son. "Hey, Scott. Thane says you've been making friends in the city. Any of them women?"

Scott's face flushed. "Maybe."

"What's her name?" Jill asked as her face lit with a pleased smile. "Why haven't we heard about her? And where is she?"

Scott loosened his tie—actually mine, but I let that go. "Could we talk about this later?"

As entertaining as it was to watch my twin squirm, Crystal and I had gathered everyone for a reason. "Scott, the time for secrets is done. You need to tell everyone everything."

"I have feelings for her, but we're still figuring things out. She—"

"Regarding your beans." I rolled my eyes skyward. "I don't care about your girlfriend." Crystal elbowed my ribs, and I corrected myself. "I care, but there's a more pressing subject we need to discuss. I caught your old friend Remy stealing soil from your property. He's currently in police custody for attacking me."

The mood in the room changed dramatically. Jill encouraged everyone to take a seat. Crystal and I remained standing. "So we're all on the same page, I'll start at the beginning." Although most of the people in the room knew some of the story, I began with meeting Scott and feeling he needed help saving his farm. I shared my impression of Scott's lab, then my struggle to protect his secret while getting to know Crystal. "I don't want to imagine my life without Crystal in it, which is why we gathered all of you. We want to fix this together. Crystal, they need to hear your side."

She took my hand. "Uncle Art, I want to tell them everything. Is that okay?"

He folded his arms over his chest. "I've done nothing I'm ashamed of."

Crystal started her story back with the death of her parents. She sure knew how to work a room, I thought with pride. By the time she was describing her uncle's involvement, he was all but forgiven because part of his plan had been to find a family for her. If Jill and Ryan could have snatched her then for Scott, I think they would have. I hoped he'd found a woman they'd like as much as Crystal—I didn't imagine that could be easy.

Scott was not as impressed. He waved a finger in Crystal's direction while looking at me. "So you chose the spy?"

I stiffened. "Crystal never spied on anyone for her uncle."

"Without her, though, my work might still be a secret."

"No," Steadman said with a dismissive wave of his hand. "Your plants and samples of your 'meat' are already out there being purchased by anyone who's willing to pay for them."

"Like you," Scott said with disgust.

"I didn't know it was stolen when I purchased it."

"But you did when you sent your niece here to manipulate her way into my lab." I understood Scott's anger, but if he crossed a line, I'd side with Crystal.

Crystal raised a hand in plea. "We can't go back and change the past. All that matters is how we move forward."

Steadman added, "If it makes a difference, I haven't had contact with Remy since I found out how he'd come into possession of the materials he sold me. He wasn't stealing a soil sample for me."

My father spoke up. "Scott, it's unrealistic to believe something like your discovery wouldn't be put up on the open market by someone like Remy. That was a poor decision on your part."

Scott's eyebrows came together in a frown. "Remy needed a second chance. He got in a bit of trouble, but he was sorting it out. It's not like I don't know him. We grew up together."

I inserted, "Did you know he killed and buried his father in his basement?"

Scott's mouth hung open, then snapped shut. "No."

"It's true."

"I don't believe you."

"Acknowledge that you didn't know him as well as you thought, and let's move on."

Scott rose to his feet. "Fuck you." His language seemed to surprise those around him, but no one addressed it.

I said, "Hey, it's not my fault your childhood friend is a sociopath."

"What the hell is your goal here?" Scott shook his head.

"I'm trying to wake you up to the fact that not everyone is trustworthy."

"What makes you think I'm not already painfully aware of that?"

I waved a hand in the air. "You gave Remy full access. That's all the proof I require."

Scott ran his hands through his hair. "Stop. I'm done talking about this with you."

I didn't like the truth any more than Scott did, but my family had always believed ripping a bandage off quickly was better than worrying if it would hurt. The pain in Scott's expression made me wish I'd found a better way to tell him. I sought a way to soften the blow. "Apparently he was being abused down there."

"I don't believe you. If Remy killed his father, I would know." Scott looked from me to his father. "If he'd been abused, we would have seen signs, right, Dad?"

Ryan came to stand beside Scott. "Remy has always been troubled. This would explain why."

LJ pushed out of his seat. "Let's not go down dark rabbit holes. We can't leave here without a plan."

"For what?" Scott looked irritated. We were trying to help him. It was frustrating that he couldn't see that.

Steadman stood. "For whoever is sent next. Your lab isn't safe here, and nor are any of you once word gets out about what you're hiding."

"Are you offering to protect us? That seems like a convenient and less expensive way to gain access to my land than your previous offers." Round one went to Scott. I couldn't fault him for pushing back. I would have.

My father rose to his feet as well. "Art, your potential personal gain is too great for anyone here to trust your motives."

Steadman laughed without humor. "And yours isn't? Let me see if I have the facts straight. Your sons get a contract to help design a space station. Pretty lucrative deal. But instead of getting right to work on that project, Jesse offers to watch over Scott's farm and just poke around. It's almost as if he knew what he might find. What would a space station pay for a renewable source of both food and fuel?" LJ opened his mouth to say something. Steadman barked, "Don't even get me started about *your* possible reasons for being here. When it comes to having a conflict of interest, I'd say you're all as guilty as I am."

No one spoke at first.

Crystal looked into my eyes, gave my hand a squeeze, and said, "You do all have good reasons not to trust each other—and me as well. Jesse and I have visited that feeling several times since we met. We finally decided trust is a leap of faith we are willing to take—together. That's why you're all here. We're asking you to leap with us. What if my uncle is a good man who wants to help Scott protect his work? What if LJ really does just want to save the world? I could be a flavorist who came simply to deliver a package but who fell in love and now also wants to help. What if we choose to see the good in each other and start there?"

I hugged her then, because I'd never been so proud of anyone. "We just might see we're better together than we ever were apart." I turned to Scott. "At the end of the day, it's your discovery. If you decide you want to go it alone, we have to respect that—but it'll be a dangerous path to choose. This won't stop with Remy. Someone else will find out, and we'll be in this place again."

Scott turned to his parents. "I do need to figure out what to do next. I never wanted my work to endanger either of you."

His father seemed overwhelmed. "This still feels so unreal."

His mother walked over to him and put a hand on his arm. "You'll figure it out; you always do."

Scott looked around the room, seeming to weigh each of us before moving on to the next. In the end he spoke to my father: "What would your next step be?"

My father straightened his shoulders. "I'd find a reputable lawyer and have everyone sign a contract, not because I don't trust them but because clarity is the key to working with family. If it's in writing, there's less room for misunderstandings."

Nodding, Scott turned to me. "And you?"

"I usually follow my father's advice." I looked down at Crystal. "However, recently I've found another voice I trust. What do you think?"

Crystal beamed a smile up at me. "I think trusting someone can be scary as hell, but you're only half-alive if you never allow yourself to. I'll gladly sign an NDA, as well as problem solve the taste issue if you'd like."

I smiled down at her. "I'll sign anything as well. Half-alive is exactly how I felt before I met you."

"So much for brainstorming for solutions," Scott joked.

LJ added, "It's not about us anymore, Scott. Give them a minute; they might remember we're here."

CHAPTER THIRTY-FIVE

JESSE

It took a bit, but the conversation eventually relaxed and flowed to topics mundane enough to allow Crystal and me to step outside alone. We made our way to one end of Molly's paddock.

"We did it," Crystal said, slipping beneath my arm to give me a tight hug.

I dipped down for a quick kiss before saying, "We did. There's a lot to work out, but at least everyone seems willing to work together."

She rested her head on my shoulder. "Scott's life is about to change. I hope he's ready for how much."

"He's not alone—that'll make the difference."

Crystal raised her head. "Speaking of not being alone, you think whoever he's seeing knows he's not you?"

I hadn't put much thought into that. "I sure hope so, because after today I intend to be myself again."

"Jesse," Scott called out from behind us.

We turned, and I asked, "Do they need us back in the house?"

"No," he said as he came to a stop in front of us. "But I need to talk to you privately about something."

Crystal shifted as if to leave us. I held her to me. "Whatever it is, you can say it in front of both of us."

He hesitated, then said, "I need a little more time as you."

"It's time to switch back, Scott. If this is about a woman, she'll understand."

Crystal tipped her head back and raised her eyebrows. "Really? Was it that simple with us?"

My face heated. "Okay, so it's not as easy as that. Still, the truth is the only door that leads to anything real. Who is this woman?"

"I don't really want to get into that."

"Sorry, when you're using my name and my life, you don't get the privilege of privacy."

"I guess you'll just have to trust me."

"Not when it comes to my whole life."

Scott snorted. "Oh, so trust is only a thing when pertaining to *my* name? *My* life? *My* work?"

Crystal wrinkled her nose. "He has a point, Jesse."

"Damn right I do," Scott said. "If you want me to trust you—trust *me*."

I groaned. "How long do you need?"

"A week. Maybe two."

I'd been working remotely. I could continue to. "I'll talk to Thane. If it's okay with him, you can continue to be me for a little while longer. But—and this is a big one—stay out of the office. And avoid anyone I know if you can."

He didn't say he would, but he'd heard me, and that was what mattered. Molly called out, and I turned to see she had her head poking out between the fence rails. I scratched at her head with a smile.

"She likes you," Scott said.

I smiled down at Molly. "We understand each other. We're both a little uptight."

"You're different here."

I kissed the side of Crystal's head and wrapped both of my arms around her. "Not just here."

Scott nodded. "I've found myself changing as well. It took a while to get into your head, but I do a decent impression of you now." He stood straighter, tensed his face, and growled, "I'm sorry—what was it in my expression that led you to believe I care?"

Crystal burst out laughing. "Nailed it."

I laughed along but gave her a playful shake. "I'm not that bad."

Crystal and Scott exchanged a look, then laughed more.

A car pulled up the driveway. "I don't recognize the car," Scott said. "It could be the police with more questions."

Crystal tensed against me. "Why wouldn't they come in a marked vehicle?"

"Could be a detective," I answered. As possibilities flooded my head, I looked down at Crystal and said, "You should go in the house."

She didn't budge. "Not going anywhere."

I glanced at Scott. "I hope your woman is less stubborn."

Crystal pinched my side. "No sexist remarks while I'm praying for all of our lives. You wouldn't want me to leave you off that list."

I would have assured her there was nothing to worry about, but the day hadn't exactly been uneventful. If a prayer was what was needed to get us through the rest of it, I wasn't about to suggest it wasn't necessary. "Right, saving sexist remarks for when we know we're safe."

She rolled her eyes, but my comment brought a smile to her face. Goal accomplished.

As soon as the doors of the vehicle opened and the passengers stepped out, all tension left my body. "It's the Romanos."

"The Romanos?" Scott asked.

Crystal relaxed against me. "They made a robotic leg for Alphonse." When we walked over to greet them, she blurted, "We totally forgot you were coming."

Mauricio Romano looked slightly offended, then smiled. "I'm not used to being forgotten."

His wife laughed as she shook Crystal's hand. "Don't mind Mauricio; we're still working on trimming down his ego."

It was a great icebreaker. We were all smiling. I introduced myself and said, "Sorry, it's been a crazy day."

Wren pointed from me to Scott. "Jesse and Scott. Do you own the farm together?"

Scott stepped forward. "No, I'm the farmer; Jesse is the businessman."

"Oookay." She cocked her head to one side in confusion. I glanced down and smiled. I was dressed in worn jeans and a T-shirt. Scott was in a suit.

Crystal chuckled. "It's complicated at first, but then you just go with it and enjoy the ride."

Mauricio opened his mouth to say something, seemed to change his mind, then said, "But there's only one Alphonse, right?"

As if on cue, Alphonse waddled out of the barn toward us, making enough noise it was comical. Crystal said, "It's like he knows you're here for him."

Wren bent to greet the duck. "Hello, little fellow. I brought you something special."

Mauricio returned to their car to retrieve a small bag.

Scott bent to pick up Alphonse, then held him while Wren removed his stiff prosthetic leg and replaced it with one that looked more like his real leg. She made a few adjustments to it, then set Alphonse down. The duck took a few slow steps, testing the new leg, then waddled off quacking.

"Off to show his friends," Mauricio joked. "He could have at least stuck around for a photo shoot."

"I'm sure he'll be back," Wren said with a smile.

"Would you like a tour?" Scott asked.

"We'd love one," she answered, and the three of them stepped away.

LJ appeared. "Hey, who invited the Romanos? Because that was genius. My vision for where this could lead is exploding." When neither of us answered him, he said, "Seriously? You expect me to believe it's purely a coincidence that Scott now has the country's leading robotics experts at his farm?"

Crystal tipped her head back and met my gaze. "Just because it seems unlikely doesn't make it less true."

I smiled. "Like us."

She wrapped her arms around my neck and went up onto her tiptoes to kiss me. That was all it took for the world to fade away. Never had I imagined I could find someone who would become so much a part of me. I'd never been one to put much stock in fate, but as we kissed, I thought about how many twists and turns our lives had needed to take for us to have even met each other. The realization of how easy it would have been for us to never have been brought a roughness to my caresses. I didn't want to imagine my life without her.

"And they're gone again. I'll see you both back in the house. Take your time."

LJ's comment wasn't enough to lessen the passion in our kiss for either of us. We'd beaten death, survived our families, and all I wanted was to retreat to the rental house with Crystal in my arms. I raised my head. "Do you think they'd miss us if we—"

"Not if we're quick."

I swung her around in my arms and growled, "And if we're *slow*?"

She laughed and writhed against my hard cock. "I'm sure they'd understand."

CHAPTER THIRTY-SIX

CRYSTAL

A couple of hours later, naked in Jesse's arms in the bed of our rental home, I smiled and sighed. "We should go back. I hope none of them are upset."

He gave me a long, deep kiss. "We could give them something to celebrate." His eyes were riveted to mine.

"Like?"

His hands ran up and down my back. "I don't have a ring to give you yet, but we can buy one you love as soon as you'd like. I should probably wait, plan something romantic, and ask you somewhere where I can drop to my knee, but I need to know you'll be mine. Marry me, Crystal."

My eyes misted up. "Are you sure?"

He ran a thumb gently down my cheek. "I've never been more sure about anything. We'll find a place with a few acres next to the city."

"A few acres?"

"For Molly and her donkey. She wants us to adopt her."

Joy filled my heart. "Does she now? I didn't know she spoke."

I was joking, but his answer was serious. "I didn't know, either, but it's all in her eyes. She trusts me to be there for her, and I want to be."

I needed to know if his idea of a life together was the same as how I wanted it to be. "Our kids will love her."

He smiled. "All six of them."

I laughed. "Six? Are you crazy?"

"Five?"

"We'll start with one and see how it goes."

"Deal."

We sealed it with a kiss. I bit my bottom lip. "We're going to be busy people."

"We'll make it work. We're unstoppable when we're together."

"We are." I took a moment to imagine life with him, and it might have been my imagination, but I felt my parents' approval. "I'm in."

He rolled on top of me and gave me a deep, passionate kiss that said he was as well. In the background my phone announced a message with a distinctive sound linked to Ellie. A second message came in a second later.

I groaned. "That's Ellie. I should check that to make sure everything is okay."

He rolled back, grabbed my phone from the nightstand, and handed it to me.

Ellie: Checking if you'll be back tonight. Jonathan wants to come over.

I read the message aloud, then answered her. I'm with Jesse. You'll have the place to yourself.

He's ready to give us a second chance. No more secrets. No more lies.

That's fantastic. And how things should be. We'll talk about it more when I get back, but we landed a huge new client.

Awesome. How is Jesse?

He's . . . amazing, loving, brave, perfect for me . . . wondering how long I'll be on the phone with you. Good luck with Jonathan.

I'll text you tomorrow.

Yes please.

I placed the phone between the pillows and turned my attention back to Jesse. "I hope they figure it out. He loves her. She's beginning to believe they're possible."

He gave me a quick kiss. "Believing is half the battle."

I cupped his face. "Without even realizing it, I'd stopped believing I could be this happy."

"And I'd never let myself begin to."

"Thank you for not getting killed today." I said it in a joking tone, but it wasn't a joke.

He hugged me closer. "Thank you for wearing that shirt on the first day we met." He chuckled and ran a hand down my bare ass.

I tried to give him a stern look. "It was a perfectly respectable shirt until the buttons let go."

"Sure it was." He sighed and gave my ass a swat. "I want to see you in it again. And again."

My cheeks flushed even as my thoughts went back to the first day we'd met and the reason why. "Did Scott ever tell you why Scott needs to still be you? Is it really all about a woman?"

Jesse slid his hand down my stomach to cup my sex. "Do you really want to talk about my brother right now?"

I moved my leg up onto his hip to give those talented fingers better access. "No, I don't." When he dipped a finger inside me, I gasped with pleasure. "I love you, Jesse."

Against my lips he murmured, "I know. Now just enjoy."

A woman didn't need to be told that twice.

CHAPTER THIRTY-SEVEN

SCOTT

Late that evening, I stood on the porch, breathing in the familiar aroma of home. Jesse and Crystal had slipped away together as soon as things calmed. Thane and everyone else left soon afterward. LJ lingered for a while and helped with the barn chores, but finally even he went home. I intended to return to Jesse's apartment that night, but I knew my parents had questions.

My father was the first to join me. "I figured you'd be out here," he said.

I nodded without turning away from the view of the barn. "It's as strange to be back as it was to be away for so long."

"You look good in a suit," he said. "It takes getting used to, but you'll probably be wearing one a lot from now on."

I made a noncommittal sound. "I'm not going anywhere, Dad. This is my home."

"Jesse said you asked to continue the switch for a few more weeks. Is that because of the woman you're not comfortable sharing the name of?"

My father was too good of a man for me to ever lie to. "Yes and no. More yes than no."

"You've never been secretive about a woman before. She's not married, is she?"

"No, she's not married."

"You know we'll accept anyone you choose as a partner. All we care about is your happiness."

"I know, Dad. And I'm grateful for that."

"But?"

"But it's complicated. Her father is one of Jesse's clients." I cleared my throat. "And she still believes I'm Jesse."

I stole a look at my father. He looked just as concerned as I'd known he would. "Oh, Scott, do you really think that's a good idea?"

"I'm sure it's not, but that doesn't change how I feel."

"And how is that?"

"She could be the one, Dad."

He brought a hand up to rub his chin. "She might not feel that way once she realizes you've been lying to her."

My shoulders slumped a little. "I can't do much about that until I resolve a couple of separate issues."

He put his hand on my back. "Whatever you're worried about, whatever you've done, you're not alone. Tell me what you need."

No one could have asked for a better father. It was time to come clean on a couple of fronts. I straightened and turned to face him. "When I stepped into Jesse's life, I thought it would be for a day. I love my life here, but there's always been a side of me that didn't quite fit."

"I'm not sure what you're trying to tell me."

"I've been thinking about what Jesse said about Remy. Remy buried his father in his basement? I couldn't wrap my head around that at first. How could there have been so much I didn't know about him? Then I realized I've kept a good portion of myself a secret even from you and Mom."

My father's expression turned sympathetic. "I've seen your lab, Scott. I thought you were tinkering down there with plants, but what you're working on could change the world. You're so lucky LJ and Jesse were here to help you protect it."

"Lucky? I wish it were that simple. LJ has been trying to re-create growing the beans elsewhere. Jesse brought not only Steadman's niece but Steadman himself to the farm. I'd like to believe that the Romanos built a prosthetic leg for Alphonse because they care about ducks, but that also gave them access to the farm. It's all a little too convenient to be believable."

"You think your brother would try to steal your discovery?"

"I haven't known him long enough to know if he would or wouldn't."

My father sighed. "Either way, you'll need someone on your side. If Remy put your beans out there for people to buy, someone else will come for a soil sample. You can't hide anymore."

"They can test the soil all they want. The 'secret ingredient' is a viral vector. It's essentially how I deliver genetic instructions to the plant's cells. I inject it into each plant as a seedling. It has to be timed just right. Too soon, and there are off-target genome effects. Too late, and the transduction fails. Once the plants' cells begin to replicate with the modified DNA, they decay in alternating layers. That layer of decay is what allows the substance to receive nutrients so easily—like a soil would. I came up with the idea after watching a special on how when surface fires ignite ground fires, the organic soil horizons can smolder for years. I started thinking about how every layer of something has a different purpose. A few more tweaks, and I had a bean that could be harvested in weeks rather than months, could be made into an edible, biodegradable substance that also burns long and hot enough to be an alternative fuel."

"I'm not sure I understand everything you just said, but couldn't your vector or whatever be stolen as well?"

"Not easily. I cultivate a small batch for every crop, and I've been careful to not record enough about it that anyone could replicate it. For now, I'm the only one who can make more."

"This is crazy. You didn't even go to college."

"Not all learning happens in a classroom. I read—a lot. And the internet has allowed me to take whatever classes I wanted to. You'd be surprised what you learn if you put in the time."

My father shook his head back and forth. "I had no idea. I thought you wanted to be a farmer."

I turned so I was leaning back against the railing. "I do. Nothing has changed, Dad. I love being here, being your son, giving misfit animals a soft place to land."

"Being my son? Why do you say that like you've thought not? You're our miracle, Scott."

"And you and Mom are mine. I've never wondered who my birth parents were until I met Jesse and stepped into his life."

My father swallowed visibly. "Did you find them?"

"No, but I have some leads. I wanted to see where they led as Jesse. I didn't want anyone coming here and upsetting Mom."

"We never hid that you were adopted. We always wanted you to know, and Mom and I always knew that one day you would have questions. We kept a file of paperwork for you for when you did. I'll give it to you before you leave."

"Thanks, Dad."

My father took a seat on a sliding chair. "I'll need time to process all this, but there's still a lot I don't understand. Why didn't you ever tell us what you were studying? Why the secret lab?"

That was complicated as well. And the reason wasn't something I was proud of. He was my father, would always be my father, but there was a small part of me that always felt the sting of being unwanted by my biological parents. I didn't talk about it, but a part of me would always wonder why they hadn't kept me, would always wonder how similar I was to the son Ryan and Jill might have had. "I tried to tell you about my beans in the beginning, but you thought I was wasting my time, and I—I wanted to be the son you would've had if you'd had your own."

"Now stop right there. You are the son I had. You are my own. I don't ask myself if you would have been any different had you come to us in another way. You did come to us, and that's all that's ever mattered."

The door to the porch opened, and my mother came out to sit beside my father. "What did I miss? If it's about your lady friend, I hope that's not the reason you look so glum. What's her name?"

They deserved the truth—all of it. "Monica Bellerwood."

"Bellerwood?" My father scratched at the back of his neck. "Why does that name sound so familiar?"

I pocketed my hands. "Monica's father is Walt Bellerwood. His company contracted Jesse's to build the air system for his space station project."

"How exciting," my mother said.

"Jesse's biggest client." My father's mouth rounded. "And she still thinks Scott is Jesse."

My mother's eyes widened. "Oh, that's not good."

"Sounds like he got himself in a real pickle of a situation." My father put his arm around my mother's shoulders. "Do you want to talk about it?"

I did and I didn't. In all the world, though, there wasn't anyone I trusted more than my parents. "I don't know where to start."

My mother gave my father's leg a pat. "Start at the beginning. I want to know all about this woman. I have a feeling we'll be meeting her real soon."

ABOUT THE AUTHOR

Ruth Cardello's addictive, escapist romances about rich alpha men and the strong women who tame them have made her a *New York Times* and *USA Today* bestselling author. The Legacy Collection, the Barrington Billionaires, and the Corisi Billionaires are just a few of the many sizzling series she's written.

Ruth was born the youngest of eleven children in a small city in northern Rhode Island. She was an educator for two decades—including eleven years as a kindergarten teacher—before she decided to see if she could turn her dream of writing into a career. She's lived in Boston, Paris, Orlando, New York, and Rhode Island again before moving to Massachusetts, where she now lives with her husband and three children.